# FORGIVENESS

## NOMAD BIKER ROMANCE SERIES

### CHIAH WILDER

Copyright © 2019 by Chiah Wilder
Print Edition

Editing by Lisa Cullinan
Cover design by Cheeky Covers

All rights reserved. This book or any portion thereof may not be reproduced or used in any manner whatsoever without the express written permission of the author except for the use of brief quotations in a book review. Please purchase only authorized additions, and do not participate in or encourage piracy of copyrighted materials.

Your support of the author's rights is appreciated.

**Disclaimer:** This is a work of fiction. Names, characters, businesses, places, events and incidents are either the products of the author's imagination or used in a fictitious manner. Any resemblance to actual persons, living or dead, or actual events is purely coincidental.

I love hearing from my readers. You can email me at chiahwilder@gmail.com.

Make sure you sign up for my newsletter so you can keep up with my new releases, special sales, free short stories, and other treats only available to newsletter readers. When you sign up, you will receive a FREE hot and steamy novella. Sign up at: http://eepurl.com/bACCL1.

Visit me on facebook at https://www.facebook.com/AuthorChiahWilder/

## Insurgent MC Series:

Hawk's Property
Jax's Dilemma
Chas's Fervor
Axe's Fall
Banger's Ride
Jerry's Passion
Throttle's Seduction
Rock's Redemption
An Insurgent's Wedding
Outlaw Xmas
Wheelie's Challenge
Christmas Wish
Insurgents MC Romance Series: Insurgents Motorcycle Club Box Set (Books 1 – 4)
Insurgents MC Romance Series: Insurgents Motorcycle Club Box Set (Books 5 – 8)

## Night Rebels MC Series:

STEEL
MUERTO
DIABLO
GOLDIE
PACO
SANGRE
ARMY

## Steamy Contemporary Romance:

My Sexy Boss

## CHAPTER ONE

# FLUX

"Hey, Flux. I guess I'll see you tonight at the Alamo Ale House around the usual time?"

Jared "Flux" Hughes glanced up from his phone as he leaned against the open doorjamb of his motel room. Flicking the ash off his joint, he stared at the hulking dude who was passing by his room with a sweet piece hooked under his arm. The pretty redhead could barely walk straight and giggled while she threw Flux an appraising look. Even though he didn't know who the hell the guy was, he grunted at him and a large grin spread over the bastard's face like he'd just won the damn lottery.

"Gonna have me a good night." The guy winked and planted a kiss on the redhead as they threaded their way into a motel room a couple doors down from Flux's. "See you over at the bar, okay, buddy?"

"Sure, *buddy*." Flux threw his joint down and stubbed it with the toe of his boot, lit up another one, then rested his head against the doorframe. The shallow solidarity and the haze of weed numbed him as he slightly closed his eyes.

Flux inhaled and took a sharp hit of the hot-as-fuck air that made rivulets of sweat crisscross his chest. Though the AC unit clunked on in the background, he preferred the heat. At the very least, it made him feel *something*. He winced on another thick drag as the smoke curled around him. *Tucson, Arizona, is nothing but fuckin' cacti and sand.* The thought ran through his mind over and over while he watched the sky go up in flames as the sun hit the horizon. Most people would have thought it was beautiful or some shit. Flux just wanted a beer and an excuse to crash.

"Another fuckin' day over … and how the hell many more are there gonna be?" he muttered under his breath as he scanned the parking lot in front of him.

He was always aware of what was happening around him—an old habit from his time with the Insurgents MC, and it stayed with him despite his nomad status. If anything, his lack of backup was reason enough to pay extra special attention to his surroundings, which meant fight or flight was a hardcore green light. Plus, it kept him spry and quick on his feet in the rodeo ring when it was only him against a 1,500-pound confused and manipulated bull looking to take out its frustrations on a guy scrambling across the dirt who had just been thrown on his back.

Flux flicked the joint onto the ground and rubbed it out with his heel. He groaned and massaged the back of his neck. His eyes slid closed for a few seconds, then he forced them back open and swallowed hard, refocusing on the parking lot, which was starting to fill up for the night with the day's rodeo crowd who didn't feel like driving home.

Envy overtook him as he watched them; their night was as good as gone. Pressing the palm of his hands against his eyelids, his jaw clenched. Flux's night was just getting started—insomnia was a real big bitch, and it had some nasty talons stuck into him. He could tell that it was going to be another long one by the way the weed sat through his system. *Time to get a new dealer … again.* Damn body absorbed pain and took on immunities like a fucking champ. Only this time? He didn't feel much like cheering. For fuck's sake, he didn't feel much of anything and that's the way he preferred it.

The only thing about the night that would be different than any other was the pretty face Flux may or may not bring back to his bed. Otherwise, it was a never-ending line: same time, same place, same shit.

He cracked his knuckles and watched a few kids hop out of a minivan while their parents struggled to get all their gear from the hatchback.

"April, Billy! Get over here. Your mother needs help," the cookie-cutter father with a cowboy hat called out.

The two pre-teens grumbled as they walked slowly to the back of the van.

"Take chances to be kind when you see them," their father said as he picked up a couple of suitcases.

A small girl of about four rushed over, her dark hair blowing in the hot breeze. "Gimme, Mommy." The small voice was as bright as a sunbeam.

Flux stared at the girl as another voice from long ago filled his ears. He clenched his hands into fists until his nails dug into his sweaty palms. The child took the small bag from her mother and followed her father across the parking lot. As if sensing Flux's gaze, she turned her head toward him and a shy smile tugged at her lips before she rushed into the room.

Flux stared at the empty spot she'd just occupied and a rush of memories flooded his mind. *Fuck no! No!* Welcoming the pain, he pounded his fists against his head, hard and steady, as he shoved the recollections that threatened to resurface back into the padlocked box that lingered in the dark corners of his mind. For several seconds, he stood there gulping air until the shadows were gone while he crossed his arms over his chest and slowly relaxed.

The screech of rubber caught his attention, and he side-eyed over to the commotion as a cherry-red pickup truck pulled into a spot, spitting gravel in the process. The ignition jerked off with an audible hitch that bounced across the parking lot, and Flux weighed the idea of heading out to the bar now. The truth was, he wanted to get back on his Harley—even the smallest ride cleared out his skull for a couple seconds. His fingertips were already itching to clutch the vibrating handlebars as he sat there turning it over in his brain.

His attention got shot to shit when a curvy blonde hit the pavement from the pickup's driver's seat and slammed the door. Flux homed in on the lucky SOB who got to stare at the chick's tight ass in those jeans when he came out of the other side of the truck. The man, who was wearing cowboy boots and a hat, hissed something barely audible—a faint echo across the air. But whatever he said must've had something to do with Blondie because she squared her shoulders and threw the cowboy a death stare. After a few seconds, the chick sashayed around the car in sky-high heels, which made her wavy hair sway back and forth across her back.

A low growl came from the back of Flux's throat. *Come on, baby. Turn around so I can see the rest of you.* The woman pointed a finger at the man, and even though Flux couldn't hear their argument, there was no doubt it was heated. Blondie was right up in the dude's face, and she was giving it as good as he was—which was impressive considering Cowboy had a good foot on Blondie. When the dude raised his arm with his hand clenched into a fist, Flux straightened up as a shot of adrenaline surged through him. If this jerk had any idea of hitting this chick, Flux would make sure the asshole would spend the rest of the night in the emergency room. No matter what the situation, Flux never tolerated that shit, and he wasn't about to make an exception now.

"You cold bitch!" the man screamed.

"And you're an asshole!" she yelled back.

The guy threw his hands up, fists flexing in the air before he shoved off the passenger side of the truck. "You're a fucking waste of time." He gave her the middle finger and stalked away toward the motel rooms at the far side of the lot.

Flux relaxed and chuckled as he watched Blondie fluff her hair as if she didn't give a damn that Cowboy had just stormed off. *Look my way, baby.* If she looked half as good as her backside and profile, he may have to approach her and strike up a conversation. At least there was *something* different going on at the motel, because for the past several days, the highlight of his nights had been watching the local hookers pedal in the parking lot while unsuspecting tourists gasped and averted their eyes.

When Blondie turned to watch the asshole stomp away, Flux jerked backward, nearly tripping over himself and back into the motel room. He sucked in a sharp breath. *Damn!* It wasn't just a sweet ass she was rocking, she was fucking gorgeous. And those lips... He groaned inwardly.

Even in the fading light, Flux could see the pink tint of sunburn painted across her nose and cheeks. Her golden hair danced around her shoulders in a mass of waves his fingers itched to touch. An inch of skin peeked out between the bottom of her tight tank top and the top of her even tighter jeans—a tempting sliver of flesh that he had a sudden, overwhelming desire to explore... with his tongue. His gaze moved upward and landed on a pair of rounded tits that he guessed would fit just right in his large hands. He skimmed the bottom of his lip with his front teeth. *Fuck.*

Flux's Levi's grew tight in the crotch, and he shifted as he tried to relieve some of the discomfort. *What the fuck? One look at this hot chick and my dick acts like I'm in high school?* The glaring fantasy that shot through his mind of her plump lips locked around him and his hand tangled in her hair while she stared up at him up? Yeah, that wasn't helping to calm him down. *Fuck.* Flux stood stock-still as he watched Blondie pull down that damn form-fitting top, then strut her fine behind in the opposite direction while she tossed her car keys up and down into her open palm. He blew out a long breath then closed the door to his room. After that tease, he needed to get his ass to the bar and lose himself in a few beers and shots of whiskey. Flux strode over to his motorcycle, looked one last time at the hot chick as she entered her room, revved up the engine, and sped away.

The country-themed dive bar wasn't packed to the studs with locals yet, but Flux knew it was only a matter of time before they started to pour in. Since the rodeo had been in town, the Alamo Ale House had been his go-to watering hole. The beer was cold, the food was edible, and it didn't cost him an arm or a leg when he got the tab. But if truth be told, it was like any other dive he'd frequented on his constant travels while his life swirled further down into the depths of hellish darkness—one fucking second at a time.

"Whatcha want, honey? Jack or Budweiser?" the waitress asked.

"One of each, Cassie." The cute brunette had become one of his favorite barmaids—she remembered what he drank and she left him the hell alone. All the other waitresses tried chatting him up, batting their lashes and hinting for rides on his bike and on his dick. He didn't go for that shit. No woman had ridden on the back of his bike except for … Alicia. *No fuckin' way I'm going* there.

"Here you go, honey. Just call me over when you're ready for another round." Cassie turned around and headed toward a table of men.

Flux recognized the bull riders at the table. He'd worked with all of them at one time or another. He was the one responsible to keep these guys safe once the bulls threw their asses off of them. Flux had only been seventeen the first time he'd faced a half-ton bull in the rodeo arena. As a bullfighter, his job had been to distract the animal once the bull rider was on the ground. He'd loved the rush of adrenaline and had decided that would be his career until one hot and humid day when he was nineteen years old, he met Hawk, Banger, Throttle, Hubcap, and Tank at a biker rally in Elgin, Texas. The town was just south of Johnson City, his hometown, and he'd never seen so much chrome, tattoos, and badass motorcycles as he did that weekend. After that, Flux had traded in his horse for a Harley-Davidson, and he made his way to Pinewood Springs, Colorado, to prospect for the Insurgents MC.

Flux shook his head. *Damn … that seems like a lifetime ago.* When his world had flipped upside down in such a horrific and unspeakable way, he couldn't get his head on straight. He couldn't stay still—he was restless and had to get away and keep one step ahead of the memories. He'd gone to Banger, the president, and told him he was too fucked up to be any good to the brothers. Flux wanted to go nomad, and after a unanimous vote from the brotherhood, his bottom rocker was replaced by the word *Nomad*. That had been six years ago, and he'd crisscrossed the country more times than he could count, but the fucking memories never went away—they were constant reminders of the guilt that ate at him all the time.

"Come on, honeycakes. Let me give you a kiss," Chet Teel said, his Arkansas drawl irritating the hell out of Flux, but then, *anything* Chet did irked the fuck out of him. The bull rider and the bullfighter didn't care too much for each other.

"You got enough women clamoring to give you a kiss—you don't need one from me," Cassie said as she placed a bunch of beer bottles in front of the men.

"But you're the one I want, honeycakes." Chet wrapped his arm around the brunette's waist, but she spun out of it and rushed away. "I didn't want that bitch anyway." Chet picked up his beer and brought it to his lips.

"That's right—you're still trying to get lucky with Maggie," Louie said. The other men guffawed.

"Damn right," Chet replied, glaring at them.

Flux caught Cassie's eye and lifted his chin. She ambled over.

"Another round?" Her gaze went to his full glass of whiskey.

"Might as well." He jerked his head toward Chet. "If that asshole proves to be more than you can handle, let me know. I'll take care of him."

A soft smile turned up her lips. "Thanks, Flux, I'll keep that in mind. I'll be back in a few with your drinks."

Flux watched her disappear into the burgeoning crowd and took a long drink from the neck of his beer. He was positioned in the corner of the bar and it gave him full view of the door. It was a perfect angle to watch for any signs of trouble or any hot chicks who might pique his interest.

Soon a good-looking redhead was on his radar as she made a beeline for his loner corner like a homing missile. *Fuckin' great.* Flux ran a finger through the condensation along the side of his beer bottle, then put it down in front of him. The only woman he wanted to approach him was Blondie, not this pumped-up woman who looked like a typical biker groupie: too much makeup, too-small clothes, and desperation oozing out of every pore. He made sharp eye contact, shook his head no, and abruptly looked away. "Take the fuckin' hint, *sweetheart*," he muttered, refusing to look and see if she was still charging forward on her misguided quest to get her fingers wrapped around his dick.

The front door pushed open, and the small hairs on the back of his neck sprang up when he saw Blondie walk in and sway her way across the room until she stopped in front of a vintage jukebox. Her curvy hip rested against the machine while she stared at the contents. In the five nights that Flux had spent at the bar, he couldn't remember anyone getting near the jukebox that was stocked with forty-fives. Maybe he'd just go on over and help the sexy lady make a good selection. Blondie would be an improvement to the women he'd brought back to his room the past few nights, and he had to admit that he'd love to have a few rounds with her between his sheets. If she was even ten percent as good in bed as she was sexy, he'd have hit a home run. He might even break his damn rule and invite her for another night in his bed. His one-night-only rule kept him sated—no emotions, just carnal lust. That was just the way he needed it.

All of a sudden, his radar pinged loud in the back of his head. He swung around in time to see the redhead with the fake tits sliding into his booth with a sly grin on her gloss-covered lips. Great, the Instagram queen hadn't taken the hint. He bristled inwardly and scooted away so she wouldn't have any doubts about his level of interest.

"Wow, nice leather." Painted fingertips reached out and stroked his cut. "I bet that badass Harley is yours in the parking lot. Am I right?" She cocked her head to the side. "Who's your gang?"

Irritation pricked his skin. She acted like she had him all figured out and was ready to sign up to be his old lady or some shit. *Not tonight, not any night.* Flux wasn't having it.

He caught her wrist with one hand and cleared his throat. "MCs are clubs—not gangs. You're wasting your time. Move on and find someone else."

Their eyes met, and then she blinked back at him as that high-glossed mouth opened and closed a few times before he let her wrist go, leaving her hand suspended in the air until it fluttered back down into her lap.

"Come on, baby," she said, sliding closer to him. "Do you want me to play hard-to-get, is that it? I know what bikers like." She arched her back, thrusting her tits out even further. "Don't you like what you see?" She giggled, the sound cutting through him like broken glass.

*Fuck ... she's a trashy redheaded Barbie.*

"Buy me a drink and you can tell me about your *club*."

Flux hailed Cassie over to the table with a sharp wave.

"A shot of Jack."

The waitress shifted from foot to foot and looked at the grinning biker groupie who wanted to take a walk on the wild side that night. Cassie threw Flux a questioning look.

"She's leaving." He drained the last of his beer and handed it to her. "Bring me another one of those too."

"Will do." Cassie walked away.

The redhead huffed. "I can't believe you! There's not one man in here who wouldn't kill to be with me." She slid out of the booth.

"Yeah there is, *sweetheart*—me. Why don't you peddle your wares at that table?" He pointed to Chet and the other bull riders.

"You're a jerk—a real asshole."

Flux stared straight ahead. "Tell me something I don't know."

The woman shoved the table at him and stalked away then headed straight for Chet's.

Flux snorted and banged down the shot of whiskey.

## CHAPTER TWO

# FLUX

FLUX IGNORED THE dagger-like stares the redhead kept throwing at him. Being rude wasn't his go-to method with chicks unless they didn't catch-the-fuck-on that he wasn't interested. He'd told the groupie he wasn't, so it *wasn't* his damn problem if she thought he was simply talking out of his ass.

He shifted his gaze back over to the jukebox and saw that Blondie was still standing there, moving her hips in rhythm to some country song. He'd have preferred some hard-hitting music from Five Finger Death Punch, but having grown up in a house where country music was the norm, he loved the music from Alan Jackson, Brad Paisley, and a number of other country-western singers.

At that moment, all his attention was hyper-focused on Blondie's swaying body. The song ended, then a country ballad came over the speakers and swallowed up all the other sounds in the joint. Flux recognized it but couldn't remember who the hell sang the song. He slid out of the booth and made his way over to her when another guy swooped in and tipped his cowboy hat at her, which made Flux bristle and scowl. There was no way in hell he was going to let this guy near Blondie—at least for that night. She took a couple of small steps backward, and Flux saw his opening, so he didn't hesitate.

"You wanna take a spin?" he asked, coming between the frowning dude and the woman who'd been teasing his dick since he'd first seen her earlier that night. Flux tipped his head toward the small scuffed-up dance floor that was packed with couples. "Looks like we'll have to compete for space."

While the guy walked away, Flux couldn't take his gaze off the woman in front of him, who was boldly eyeing him up and down while rubbing a finger across her chin as if she was considering it.

"Sure, why not?" She laughed, a sound so big and bold that it made him grin, which was something he rarely did in earnest.

Up close and under the soft overhead lights, she was a knockout, and Flux stood still and took in her beauty.

"So are you just going to stare at me, or are we gonna dance? You did ask me, right?"

Her sauciness caught him off guard; at the same time, her boldness turned him way the hell on. Now, here was a chick with some balls.

Without answering her, Flux took her hand and led them to the dance floor. The second their fingertips brushed, a tugging line of awareness pulled taut along every inch of his body. *It must be the booze and the weed.* He ignored the other option that it might have been *her* altogether and wrapped his arms around her tiny waist and stared down into her eyes as his pulse quickened. Even through the haze of the damn fog machine, her eyes were stellar. They were grayish blue and sparkled like storm clouds right before lightning hit. Her features were delicate, regal even: high cheekbones, small nose, short and narrow jaw, clear and smooth skin. And her lips were so full and pink. *Fuck ...*

"What's your name, Duchess?"

She laughed and shook her head, then rolled her eyes.

"If you can mock me, you can at least have the guts to admit who's doing the ball busting."

She grinned up at him like the cat that ate the canary. When her hands tightened along the back of Flux's neck and she leaned slightly closer to him, he did his best to keep the smirk off his face. She wasn't in the bag yet, and something told him she wouldn't be his typical catch and release. She held herself poised in his arms as her soft scent wrapped around him. It smelled like a cotton shirt that was fresh from the dryer, and it was playing havoc with his cock.

"'Duchess works just fine," she said with her lips pressed close to his ear. Her warm breath only added to the strain behind his zipper. "What else do you have for me, smooth talker?"

Flux pulled back a bit and let all the depraved things he wanted to do to her fill his eyes while they locked gazes, and a slow, lazy smile tilted up one side of his mouth.

"Duchess, you ain't seen nothing yet."

"I bet I haven't." She ran the tip of her fingernail down the side of his face while she pressed closer against him. "I bet you're a real regular with the ladies, aren't you, Casanova? A little rough around the edges and that bad boy vibe makes all the women swoon and want to drop their panties for you. Am I right?"

Flux cocked his head. "Why do you assume I think every woman wears panties?" He stroked his finger across her lower back. "Although, if we're going to go there, it would be better to get your name first, so I can write you a thank you note in the morning."

Duchess laughed again, throwing her head back so her neck arched in a line that led his attention right to her perfect tits, where her cleavage showed through the neck of her baby blue tank top. His jaw clenched as a ripple of arousal shot right to his crotch and threw him so hard and so damn sharp, he nearly lost his footing. Fuck—this woman kept him on his toes.

The song wound down, but neither of them pulled apart from each other. Flux kept his fingers gently grazing her flesh through her tank top while she stared up at him as if she was trying to get a read on him. He wished her luck on that one; she would see only what he wanted her to see and nothing more.

"Buy me a drink, big guy." She unhooked her arms from around his neck and crooked her finger at him as she cut through the gathering crowd and headed to the bar.

Normally, Flux didn't take orders from chicks, but there was something intriguing about this woman. She sparked something in him that was pushed deep down inside. No one had ever done that in the past six years. He followed her delicious, wiggling ass until he was pressed next to her with one of his elbows on the bar, the other against hers—skin to skin.

"Two Irish Car Bombs," she said to the bartender, then turned to Flux and put her hand out for payment.

His eyebrows popped up and a deep chuckle rumbled from his chest. "Put it on my tab," he shouted at the bartender above the noise. "Certainly think you're entitled, don't you, Duchess?"

She pivoted and leaned in close, so her tits pressed against his side and her lips brushed against his ear. "The secret is to go for what you know you can get. Everything after that ... it's cake," she whispered.

The intimate contact nearly made him pull her hair back and claim her mouth as he ground against her. Her warmth seeped into his bones, and he kept his gaze locked on those plump lips.

"Oh, yeah?" Flux ran his hand up her back, and satisfaction coursed through him when he felt her shiver under his touch.

For a long pause they held each other's gaze, then she drew back and reached for her drink. "You want to race?"

Her eyes shined with playfulness, and he found himself nodding as they downed and chugged their drinks like he was back, prospecting in the clubhouse. With a wince, he slammed his glass down on the bar. Her smile only grew brighter as she wiped her mouth with the back of her hand.

"I think that was a tie," she said, right before a hiccup slid out of her mouth and she covered it with her hand. A deep red flush shot up from her chest and into her cheeks as she removed her hand, bit her lip, and trailed a finger on the bar in idle circles while she looked away from him. Duchess was clearly embarrassed, and it was fucking cute. Flux shook his head. *When's the last time I thought anything was* cute? Then a memory slipped past his barriers and stabbed his brain, and he quickly motioned the bartender over and ordered another round of beers without asking.

"Are you trying to get me drunk?" she asked as she looked up at him through her thick lashes.

"Nah … I'm trying to get myself plastered."

Laughing, she moved away from him slightly, and he wanted to yank her back and relish the feel of her soft skin against his again. He'd bet all her curves were soft and supple, and his dick punched against his zipper again. *Dammit!* This woman intrigued the hell out of him. One minute she was bossing him around like she owned the place, the next, she was as charming as a southern belle with manners. The switch made his head spin in three-sixties. There was no doubt about it—she was definitely different than his normal catch, and he enjoyed the contrast a little bit too much.

She clinked her beer bottle to his, took a long gulp, then leaned into him again to rest her head on his shoulder; that was when he decided it was time to seal the fucking deal.

"It's too damn noisy in here. Let's go back to my place, Duchess. I'm staying at the Longhorn Motel."

There was no point in being subtle since they'd both been flirting up a storm for the last couple of hours. They both knew the score, and she'd definitely given him the signals that she wouldn't be adverse to having some fun behind closed doors.

"The Longhorn? What a coincidence … I'm staying there too. I just got into town today."

"That's great. So what do you say?"

"I had fun tonight."

"Me too." Flux put the empty bottle on the bar. "But tonight isn't over yet."

She smiled up at him as if she didn't have a care in the world, polished off the beer that sat in front of her, then slid the bottle across the bar. "Thanks for the drinks and the dance, but I'm going to pass." Then she gathered up her purse and walked away, her sweet hips swaying, without even a glance backward. *What the hell?* He watched her gorgeous ass and killer heels trot right out of the bar and out of his life. The rarity of the moment left him speechless.

This never happened to him ... like *never*. Flux coughed into his fist. Shaking his head, he slammed his hand on the bar. Fuck him for wasting his time with Duchess. Flux looked around to see who he could score with, but all the faces were a blur. He blinked several times, yet everything was still fuzzy. There was no way that should've ended like that, their chemistry was insane. The idea that it might be one-sided went right out of his head the second he thought it. He wasn't an idiot when it came to women, and Duchess had been giving him straight-shooting signals all night.

"Hey, baby. I saw your luck ran out with the stuck-up blonde. You wanna try again with a winner? Come back to my place for another drink?" The redheaded groupie's voice slurred against the back of his neck.

There was no doubt that this chick was a sure bet, but he didn't want her or any other woman—he wanted Duchess, plain and simple. Flux scrubbed his face as he tried to figure out why the hell they weren't already fucking in his bed.

"So what do you say?" Black streaks sat under her eyes.

Flux clasped her shoulder. "Not tonight, but thanks for asking." Her face fell, and for a split second he felt sorry for her, but he wasn't the type of guy to give mercy fucks. "Good luck in here though," he said over his shoulder while he paid his tab.

"You sure 'bout that? You're missing out on a good time." The woman swayed toward him and he stepped away.

"I'm sure." Anywhere a biker went, cut chasers were a dime a dozen, but the idea of boning anyone other than Duchess right now didn't appeal to him.

Redheaded Barbie stared daggers at him and he pretended not to notice. It wouldn't be the first or the last time a chick had gotten pissed at him for not wanting to fuck her. It was the way it went. Hell, it had just happened to him with Duchess, and he wasn't going to worry about it. The way he looked at it, it was *her* loss—he knew how to please a woman. *She's probably never had a real good fucking in her life.* He tipped his head at Cassie, then slipped on his leather jacket and headed out into the dark desert night.

When he parked back at the motel, Duchess's pickup was parked in the lot. He hated the fact that he had looked for it. *Stupid, rookie move.* He wondered if she was banging the asshole she'd been fighting with in the parking lot earlier that night. That thought made every muscle in his body tense, and he had the urge to break down her door and give the bastard a severe beatdown. *What the hell's the matter with me? She's just a piece of ass and nothing more. I don't give a damn what she does.* Flux ran a hand through his hair, breathing out a raspy exhale as he mentally gave himself shit for thinking too much about a woman he didn't even know and who probably had a jerk boyfriend, which was most certainly the reason she'd blown Flux off. *Get your fuckin' head screwed on straight, man.* Flux slammed open the door to his room and rifled through the leaflets on the desk for a list of pizza joints in the area.

He snapped on the television then placed his order and leaned back against the headboard. While he stared at the screen's images, golden hair and stormy blue eyes clouded his mind.

It was going to be a long night.

## CHAPTER THREE

# FLUX

FLUX SCRUBBED A hand down his face and took another sip of water from his bottle. The late afternoon sun beat at his back, and the idea of hiding out somewhere to take a nap seemed damn appealing, but then it wasn't as if he ever slept anymore. Not with the nightmares—they were always there waiting to haunt him.

A shiver licked down his spine and his breathing hitched. Vague images pushed their way through the back of his brain and played across his memory like an old VCR tape. All of his muscles tightened on instinct, and reality wavered around him for a second.

*No. Fuck, no.* He was locking that shit down. Not here. Not now.

The memories threatened to swamp him as he screwed his eyes shut and tried to focus on his breathing. A steady rhythm of in and out—it was some meditative BS he'd picked up in passing, and sometimes it threw the deadbolt back on the stuff that haunted him second to second, heartbeat to heartbeat. His jaw clenched as he vaguely heard the water bottle crunch beneath his fingers.

*The goddamn blood.*

*There was so much red smeared across the countertops and on the hardwood floor. Pancakes were still sitting out. The griddle was smoking. He remembered thinking that the pancakes must be hard as bricks by now. A weird, detached fragment of a thought. More than a few of them were burned, which was typical for Alicia.*

*Emily's toys were still scattered across the living room carpet.*

*She wasn't in the room with her mother.*

*There was only one body lying naked and unseeing on the floor in the kitchen.*

Flux grimaced and shook his head. Nothing cleared out the horror scrolling through his brain. Reality ripped into two pieces. He was somewhat aware that someone was speaking to him, but he couldn't respond. As if he were someone else, he sensed his body lean against the rails of one of the animal pens, head down, while the reality of terror and agony from that day continued to play out before he could rub it away again.

*Her limbs were bent at odd angles, her mouth open in a silent scream. One of her hands was formed into a claw, and he swallowed past the horror that prickled across his skin.*

*Someone's hand landed on his shoulder, dragging him backward from the kitchen.*

*He flung himself at them, fighting to stay near Alicia. There were words, soothing at first, and then pissed, but he didn't hear any of it as his brain snapped and he fired off words of rage and self-hatred. He became a tornado of hate, singularly focused on staying with his wife and their—*

"Yo, Flux. You okay?"

The voice shot through him and he struggled to stand up straight and pay attention while the painful memories of his past still clung to him like cobwebs.

"Yeah. I'm ... uh, solid," he rasped out, stumbling as he blinked against the suddenly overwhelming glare of the sun. Bit by bit he clawed back to himself as memories faded into the background where they belonged, and he shoved the lock back on the evils of his past.

"You look a little pale. Do you want me to get you some juice or something?"

Flux blinked and focused on his bullfighting co-worker, Pete, as the guy took a step further into his personal space and sized him up. They worked together hand in hand in the ring, and lives counted on them being in sync, but Flux didn't consider Pete a friend. Since Flux had gone nomad, he lived a solitary life, and on the road, his only friends were bitterness and recriminations. Once in a while, he'd return to Pinewood Springs and meet up with his brothers. He'd crash at the clubhouse and lose himself in booze and club girls—anything to stop the memories and numb the pain. His brothers saw the hollowness in his eyes, they'd pointed it out to him, but he didn't need the brothers to tell him he was a shell of his former self. That was what guilt, self-loathing, and loss did to a person—it made them not give a shit about anything.

"You still with me, dude?" Pete flicked his Stetson up onto his head.

"Uh … yeah. Just didn't sleep much last night."

A grin cracked his face. "Did you get lucky?"

Flux shook his head. "No, nothing like that. It's just so fuckin' hot around here."

"Isn't your AC workin' in your room?" Pete's eyes narrowed as he leaned in closer, his gaze running over Flux's face.

"It is." Flux stepped back.

"Jesus, you look like you just upended three pounds of raw hamburger meat into your system." Pete sniffed and grimaced. "And you smell like a fucking bar. What's going on with you, man?"

"I'm good … just didn't get much sleep, like I said." Flux pulled off his bandana, wiped the cold sweat prickling across his face, and retied it back on his head. "I'll be cool. Don't fuckin' fuss about me, dude." He knew he'd overdone the boozing and the smoking the night before, especially since he had to be on his game in the arena—the bull riders' lives depended on it. But deep down, Flux knew that after the rodeo closed up for the night, he'd pull a repeat of the night before and the one before that … and all the other nights. They were all the same except the chick never got away. Duchess was a first for him.

Flux kicked at the dirt, coughing when dust invaded his nostrils. He was still pissed that the sweet chick hadn't come back to his room the night before. *What the hell went wrong?* All the cards in his hand had been laid out perfectly, and she should've been his in a heartbeat. He'd be damned if he admitted that taking her back to his place would've meant more to him than just hooking up with the average biker groupie.

"Sure," Pete said, still eyeing him up.

The sound of Pete's voice brought him out of his musings. "Sure, what?"

"Where the fuck are you today, man? I was saying that if you're sure that you're solid, we need you behind the stalls. Charlie wants us to practice some new dodges, and Eddie wants to show us the beauty he bought at auction yesterday."

Charlie was a rodeo promoter and Eddie was a long-time bull owner.

Flux nodded and fell in behind Pete while his thoughts kept ping-ponging back and forth from his past to the sexy blonde who'd cock-blocked him. Since the past was a painful mess, he'd preferred to focus on his strike out. *Maybe she'll be at the bar tonight.* He rubbed the back of his neck. What the hell was he thinking, wanting to see her again? For Flux, there were no repeats. No exceptions. His bed was a revolving door and that's how he liked it. He didn't want to get involved.

Flux cleared his throat and walked the path along the grounds to the bull pens, where they kept the animals when they weren't being ridden. The stench of manure mingled with the scent of sweet hay as he passed by the arena and saw some of the steer wrestlers practicing their roping techniques and—

"Shit," Flux whispered under his breath as he spotted a rider leading her horse through barrel drills at the other end of the ring. Long golden hair gleamed in the sunlight as she worked the horse like a champ. Flux stopped and leaned against the steel bar and watched Duchess's gorgeous ass that was glued to the saddle as she maneuvered the brown stallion through its paces. From her expression, Flux could see she was completely focused and he almost called out to her, but he knew that could spook her or the horse, so he just stayed and watched her as a rush of excitement spread through him.

Pete circled back to him, lines creased across his forehead. "What the hell, man? Charlie's gonna be pissed if we don't get over there." He followed Flux's attention then chuckled. "I don't blame you for stopping. The way she rides her horse is a thing of beauty, and her ass isn't too shabby either."

Flux gave Pete a sideways look. "Who is she?"

"Maggie Haves. Haven't you ever seen her perform? She's one of the best barrel racers in the amateur circuit. Talk is that she'll be going pro in no time. The rumor is that Tara's knocked up and Tanner's the one who done it, so when Charlie found out, he benched her and called up Maggie to see if she could step in. She and Charlie go back since she started racing when she was a kid. It seems like she can never say no to him." Pete paused from his rambling for a minute to watch her, then went on, "Anyway, she got in yesterday afternoon. How's it that you haven't seen her at any of the rodeos you've worked?"

Clouds of dust blurred the stallion's legs as Duchess guided him expertly around the three barrels at a speed that made Flux wonder how she stayed in the saddle. *I bet her thigh muscles are real tight.* Visions of her legs wrapped around his waist as she pulled him deeper to her flashed through his mind.

"Maybe you worked the same rodeos as her but didn't pay any attention." Pete lit up a cigarette.

"There's no fuckin' way I wouldn't have noticed her. I'm not on the rodeo circuit the way you and the other guys are. I pick up work here and there when I need the cash."

"That's right—you just ride your motorcycle around the country. Doesn't that ever get old?"

Flux turned and looked at his colleague. "I'm guessing you've never been on a bike 'cause if you had, you'd never be asking me a shit question like that. Riding with the wind at your back is freedom. How the fuck can that get old?"

Pete held up his hands. "Didn't mean to knock your lifestyle, man.

It's just that I'm a rodeo cowboy through and through."

Flux focused his attention back to Maggie. *She's in the rodeo. Well, I'll be damned.*

"I gotta say that she's one of the best damn riders, and the prettiest." A cloud of smoke enveloped them. Pete's hand landed on Flux's shoulder with a thump and he bristled against the touch. "Too bad she's a rodeo girl, and we don't shit where we eat, you know?"

Flux grunted and cracked his neck. "That hasn't stopped the chicks from trying …" Flux crossed his arms and stared as Maggie reined the horse to a standstill and petted its neck while whispering into its ear. "I've had more than a few throw themselves at me, but that's not the way I roll. Kind of breaks my oath of a one and done. Anyway, fucking someone you work with is always complicated, and I'm into simple, you know?"

"I hear you." Pete took another puff of his cigarette. "Still doesn't mean the rest of us have to live that way. I don't seem to get lucky that much." He elbowed Flux lightly. "Not all of us have a bright and shiny motorcycle that makes the girls spread their legs."

Flux snorted and stared at Maggie as she hopped off her horse and led it to the gate of the pen. "Yeah, if life were that easy," he muttered and pushed off the fence, his gaze still fixed on her. *Damn … that ass.*

There was no way to suppress his immediate attraction to her body, let alone her mind. She didn't take shit and she gave as good as she got—which wasn't what he was used to. The majority of women he'd come across just placated him and gave him what they thought he wanted to hear so they could spend a night with an outlaw biker.

At the rodeos Flux worked, he had his pick of women competitors and employees who worked behind the scenes trying to get his cock in their pussies, but he didn't want to see the same woman twice after spending the night with her. Working together kind of blew that rule to hell. But there was something about Maggie that was different and made him want to forget about his damn rules, and hell if he didn't hate *that* something fierce.

Maggie straightened up and paused, and Flux was positive she looked at him from the corner of her eye, but her expression didn't change one iota. *You got a real good poker face, Duchess.* She pushed up her fawn-colored cowboy hat, tossed her head, and disappeared around the corner of the stalls.

Flux stared at the empty space Maggie had once occupied, and his lips turned up into a smirk. First, she hadn't hopped into his bed when she had the chance, and now, she hadn't given him the time of day. *Yep ... I'm definitely interested.*

"We better get our asses to the bull pens. Charlie's probably having a coronary." Pete tossed his cigarette butt to the ground and stubbed it out with the heel of his cowboy boot.

Flux nodded, and while the two men headed back to the pens, he tuned out Pete's jabbering. Flux had only one thing on his mind—the sassy, curvy barrel racer.

Yeah, he was definitely going back to the watering hole that night, and he knew *she'd* be there.

*Game on, Duchess.*

## CHAPTER FOUR

# MAGGIE

"COME ON, MAN, women can't rodeo any more than men can have babies, and it's damn stupid to try their hand at a sport that will more than likely get them seriously injured or killed. A woman's much better off in the kitchen looking after her man and making him happy."

Maggie bristled as she caught the tail end of a loud conversation near the bar at Alamo's while she nursed her beer. When she turned around to assess the supposed voice of reason, nothing shocked her more than when she saw Chet at the head of his little gang of bull riders taking the helm. God, the asshole set the women's movement back decades simply by breathing.

*How the hell did I ever date him? Biggest mistake of my life.* Granted, she hadn't known then what she knew now. And what she knew now made her slide off her barstool and stalk over to their boisterous table. When she stood in front of it, the talk died down real fast. Chet's gaze swung from his cronies and up at her before his smile lit up his whole face.

Ugh, he needed to spare her the charming cowboy act. Everyone knew it was a ruse. She did, better than anyone at that point, and waving his good ol' boy southern schtick in her face was like taunting a bull with a moving piece of cloth. Just about now, she planned on goring the jerk with her verbal horns.

"Honeycakes, what can I do for you tonight?" Chet put down his beer and stood up. "Did you have a change of heart about us?"

"Hardly," Maggie breathed out, not bothering to disguise her disgust at his suggestion. "I couldn't help overhearing your loud and ridiculous opinions, and I thought you could benefit from a third party throwing her hat into the ring."

Chet grinned wider and looked down at his cronies before he looked back at her and winked. He never was one to pick up on a hint. She crossed her arms and took a deep breath then narrowed her eyes.

"You do know we live in the century where women are highly competent and capable to do damn near anything they want in this world without a problem. Merely because we don't line up with your outdated ideas on men being the stronger sex doesn't make you're better than us. In fact, I've seen you flounder on that bull more times than I can count, Chet, and I've fallen off... hmm, how many times now?"

The idle chatter at their table went quiet, and Chet's easygoing demeanor took a backseat to his scowl. *There he is. The real man behind the mask.* Maggie straightened her shoulders and cocked her head as her hair fell across her shoulders.

"Men think because I look like I do that I don't have a brain in my head. Well, I do, and I'm sure as hell better in the ring than any of you. So next time you start assessing women based on outdated gender norms, maybe you should look at your scores in the ring and get back to me, okay?"

"Babe, we didn't mean—" Chet started in again as his hands flew up trying to smooth over the situation.

"Yeah, you did mean it. You meant every damn word." She whirled around and walked back to her stool. Without a doubt, they would bring up the subject again. Men like that never caught onto progressive ideas even when it was spoon fed to them, so they would go back to judging her gender and demeaning her purely because it was all they knew how to do—but at least she had said her piece about it. That was more than she had gotten to do in the past, when Chet revealed his true colors after several dates.

"Nice one, kiddo." Sadie, the bartender and owner of Alamo's winked at Maggie. "Next one is on the house. If they didn't buy a hefty tab's worth of alcohol here, I'd kick 'em out on their asses … but money is money."

"I get it." Maggie sighed and took another long drink, ignoring the sputtering of laughter coming from the table she'd just left. Chet's guffaws were the loudest, and they made her nerves snap in anger. *He's such an asshole.*

"Man thinks he's a god just because he rides bulls, but that doesn't give him a license to treat everyone with disrespect. One of these days, something big will happen to make him understand that fact." Sadie slid another beer bottle across the bar and patted Maggie's hand. "Don't let him get to you too much, okay?"

"He barely makes a dent on my radar." Maggie brought the bottle to her lips.

"Not like the one I saw you dancing real close with last night, right, sugar?" Sadie laughed and went to help another customer, but that didn't stop her from catching Maggie's eye with a less than subtle wink.

At the mention of *him*, a twinge went through her body and she stiffened as she tried to suppress it. A distraction was the last thing she needed on her agenda, but she couldn't deny how incredibly attracted she was to him. What woman wouldn't be? Tall, well-built, intensely blue eyes, which contrasted with his almost black hair, a sexy five o'clock shadow, and a strong jaw that had her wanting to run her tongue along it. The ink on his arms frightened and fascinated her.

Maggie took another gulp of beer and looked over her shoulder—he wasn't there. *Probably for the best.* She doubted such a strong and confident guy would come back in the bar looking for her after she'd shot him down the night before. She had to—he exuded danger and sexiness to the fucking max. It'd surprised her how attracted she was to him the moment she laid eyes on him. He wasn't the normal type of guy she went after. There was nothing clean cut or cowboy about him.

No ... the man was all muscle and sharp edges, and his brooding eyes hinted at more if only she would get to know him. And that was where the good-time train took a turn, and Maggie knew she had to get off the ride or risk getting too involved with him. He was the type of man that a woman would fall hard for, and she had no time for that.

At first, Maggie had regretted not throwing caution to the wind and ignoring her common sense, but when she'd seen him at the arena staring at her, she about fell off her horse. Of course, she acted like she didn't notice him, but her heart was pounding and the blood was rushing through her veins and it wasn't because of her practice session. *He* was the cause of it, and she couldn't have any of that, right?

Another too-loud laugh from Chet was followed by whistles and claps. *Look what a mess it's been since I dated someone in the circuit. No way I'm repeating my mistake with Flux.* Maggie shook her head slightly. *What the hell kind of name is Flux anyway?*

Sadie plopped another beer in front of her. "Compliments from the loudest guy in the bar." She tipped her head in Chet's direction.

Maggie groaned. "I don't want it. Give it to someone else." She glanced around and spotted a big burly guy with arms like ham and covered in tattoos. He wore a denim vest covered in metal and rock-band patches. "Give it to him."

"Oh, you're bad," Sadie said as she picked up the beer and walked away.

That was what Maggie didn't want—to be put into another situation similar to Chet. As it was, the man followed her around like he had her on a pin to his Google maps, and though she'd like to think it was only a coincidence, since they knew the same people and worked together, Chet's pseudo-stalking was becoming quite alarming. It seemed that every damn rodeo she signed up for, he was there too. That had to be more than a coincidence.

And now Flux worked for the rodeo as a bullfighter—one of the most dangerous jobs of all. Maggie had to admit that she'd never have guessed he'd work at a rodeo. From his baritone drawl, she figured he was from Texas, but him in a rodeo? No way.

She stretched out her back. *I really need to stop thinking of him so much. This is more than nuts.* But she really had a good time with him the previous night. She'd loved flirting with him, and the second they got out on that dance floor together, it felt so right. "Silly," she mumbled under her breath.

No matter what, she'd have to take a hard pass and stick to keeping the other side of her bed as cold as a grave. Too bad her body hadn't gotten that logical memo. She swiveled around on the stool, and her eyes couldn't help but scope out the crowded bar scene for Flux, even with her newest resolution. *What's the harm in just hanging out together? I won't go to his room tonight, but we did have a good time talking and dancing.* Their banter had been refreshing, and it was nice to be with someone who could keep up with her. Flux also didn't seem to have an issue with her less-than-southern-belle attitude; where her sass had gotten her into trouble before with other men, Flux seemed to enjoy a challenge.

Sadie came back over to stand in front of Maggie and leaned her elbows on the bar as something captured her attention over Maggie's left shoulder.

"What?"

"Man of the hour, six o'clock, and heading in your direction. Play nice." Sadie grinned, grabbed her bar towel, and moseyed on out of there as if her butt were on fire.

"Be careful what you wish for," Maggie muttered and brushed her hair away from her face.

With a less than subtle turn on her barstool, she swiveled to face the man head on and plastered a fake grin on her face.

"You weren't supposed to be here again," she said as soon as he was within earshot.

"Funny, last time I checked, you didn't own the bar." Flux stalked forward nearly getting into her personal space. "I also don't recall you giving me a name last night. Care to rectify that mistake?"

Maggie took a long sip from her beer then crossed her arms as she sized up the hunk whose body heat tingled along her skin. Every inch of her became intimately aware of Flux, but she was above her hormones. She wasn't a teenager, and she definitely wasn't looking for an easy lay—just a little bit of fun. Besides Maggie was positive he already knew her name. She saw him talking with Pete while she was in the ring. *Okay, Flux, I'll play along.*

"I don't care to rectify anything, and it wasn't a mistake." She looked up at him and gave him one of her saccharin-sweet smiles that drove men crazy.

"I suppose ignoring me earlier this afternoon was also a part of your plan too, huh?"

"This afternoon?" She cocked her head upward as if she were trying to jab her memory.

He snorted. "Is that the game we're playing, Duchess?"

A slight shrug and another winning smile. "I don't know, is it?"

"I bet that smile of yours gets all the men to clamor after you."

"The same way your leather jacket and bad boy vibe work for you."

Maggie noticed that with every word, Flux crept closer to her, his voice growling low with intensity. Somehow, he had wound up in between her parted knees, and she was looking up at him, barely breathing, but dragging the scent of leather and sandalwood into her lungs with every shallow inhale. Her fingers latched onto either side of the barstool's peeling vinyl.

"It's good that we understand each other."

She scooted back a bit on the stool.

"Am I invading the Duchess's personal space? Do you need to call your *bodyguards?*" he drawled.

His low, gravelly voice took her breath away and wrapped itself around her like a physical touch. The threads of desire that she'd been steadfastly ignoring ever since he'd come over wove around her insides and made the spot between her legs hum.

"I can handle myself."

Their eyes locked. His hands stayed at his sides, but a flash of intensity whipped through his cornflower blue eyes, and she watched a gulp bob deep in his throat.

"I don't doubt that." He shifted from one foot to the other and his small movement brushed his outer leg against her inner thigh.

The delicate touch left them both suspended as neither of them moved for at least the span of a heartbeat. *God, he's gorgeous.* And so very off limits. The heat in his eyes made shivers run up and down her spine. Flux wasn't grabbing at her or doing anything overtly sexual, and yet her body was responding as if he had slipped his hands under her skirt and buried his fingers into her sex. Her nipples peaked hard and tight against her bra as arousal flooded her whole body. She darted her eyes away from that dangerous heat in his.

"What's wrong, Duchess?" Flux said, the lilt of his accent driving her stupidly crazy.

Maggie's gaze switched back to him and his mouth turned up at the corners, but she wouldn't call it a smile. He looked at her as if she were a delicious meal he couldn't wait to devour. Their chemistry throbbed, crackling through the air between them.

"It's kind of stuffy in here," Maggie said, dragging her gaze away from his. *Really? That's the best you could come up with? How fucking lame.*

A deep chuckle rumbled in his chest. "You're certainly different from the women I'm used to. I'll give you that, darlin'."

Flux skimmed his thumb against her lower lip, and she couldn't stop herself from lightly tasting his skin. A crooked smile tugged at the edges of his mouth when he bent his head down, and goosebumps scattered across her arms. Then his lips brushed against hers. She closed her eyes but her voice of reason yelled at her. Immediately, she jerked her head back.

"What's wrong?" he asked, his face inches from hers.

"I just remembered, I have something to do." Not the greatest answer in the world, but she couldn't think straight since her mind was in a sexual fog. What was it about Flux that made her body respond to him like that? She had to nip it in the bud—whatever this *thing* was between them. Besides, Chet was burning a hole into both of them, and she didn't need to deal with the two of them swinging at each other.

Then a thought crossed her mind and a slow smile spread across her just-kissed lips. Maggie had the perfect way to rein in their out-of-control hormones. *This will be perfect, and afterwards, he'll stay far away from me.*

She laughed and looked him in the eyes.

## CHAPTER FIVE

# MAGGIE

"DO YOU WANT to go somewhere else?" Maggie licked her lips, unable to draw her attention away from Flux, but all too aware of Chet behind his shoulder. "I think I've had enough of this place for the night."

The last thing she needed was the gossip or anymore alcohol in her system, and if they stayed any longer, she might do something she'd regret.

"Yeah, sure. Whatever makes you comfortable, Duchess." A slow grin lit up Flux's face as if he was sure he was going to get lucky.

"It's Maggie, by the way." She slapped her hand on the bar behind her back to signal to Sadie that she was heading out for the night and needed her check. "I have just the place in mind. We'll take my truck."

"Well then, I guess you're in charge, *Duchess*." Flux's hand pressed into her lower back and nearly took her breath away.

She moved to the side and he dropped it. "Why do you keep calling me that?" It wasn't as if she hated the moniker or anything, and it wasn't the worst thing she'd ever been called, "Duchess" was actually kind of cute—it was only alarming when *he* said it, because the single word held so much more intimacy than her real name.

"It's the way you carry yourself. You're regal and you don't take shit from anyone."

Maggie bit her lower lip and watched as Flux's chest expanded the smallest bit.

"You ready to cash out? It's an early night for you," Sadie said behind her.

Maggie tried to swivel around to pay the tab. "Uh … I think you have to move …" Her eyes flicked down to her legs and up at Flux who was between them. "Do you mind?"

"What's the magic word, Duchess? Come on, don't act like you weren't raised with manners." His eyes gleamed.

Maggie blushed crimson and inwardly cursed herself for it. She never liked being so transparent and vulnerable when she was embarrassed, and the way Flux dragged those emotions out of her without doing much at all didn't make handling her reactions any easier.

"Well, one of you has to move or, at the very least, slide a piece of plastic my way," Sadie said.

"*Please*, Flux." Maggie noticed the way his eyes lit up and then smoldered when she spoke his name. "I need you to work with me here, otherwise consider my offer rescinded."

He took two slow, deliberate steps backward. The breathing room was immediate, though she hadn't noticed how cold it was in the bar until his warmth was gone.

With his gaze still locked on hers Flux took out his wallet, but Maggie pushed his hand away. "You don't need to pay my tab."

"I know that, but I want to." He waved the bills at Sadie. The bartender looked from Maggie to Flux then back to Maggie.

"I don't feel comfortable with you paying my tab." Maggie took out a credit card and slid it toward Sadie.

Flux reached out and snagged it. "It's just a fuckin' tab, Duchess. It doesn't mean we'll be joined at the hip."

The dark look he threw at Maggie took all the argument out of her. "Fine," she muttered as she slipped the credit card back into her wallet. She slid off the stool, making sure to keep her attention on Flux and the door rather than Chet and the jackasses behind her, who were making a bunch of rowdy noise again.

Before she could take a step, Flux's warm palm rested against her lower back, where her top was riding up, as he steered them both toward the door. His touch pulsed along her nerve endings and sent the butterflies in her stomach reeling. When they were halfway to the door, he leaned down as they walked and his lips lightly brushed her earlobe. His warm breath tickling across her flesh nearly made Maggie lose her footing.

"I didn't tell you yet how pretty you look. I like the way your clothes hug your curves."

"Thanks?"

He chuckled. "And thank you for not making a scene at the bar when I paid. You played nice, Duchess. I can't wait to reward you."

"What? Like a Border collie?" She stopped right before the entrance and squared off with him.

"No ... that's not exactly what I had in mind." Flux played it cool, although she noted the small bit of hesitation as he looked to the double doors and back again. "If I make you uncomfortable, you can go at any time. We're taking your transportation, remember?"

With her nerves settling down a bit, Maggie nodded. Flux was right. If anything happened that she didn't like, all she had to do was kick him out on his ass, put her foot to the gas and floor it out of there. *He's not like Chet.*

Her eyes darted around, then landed on his. "Just so we're clear, what are your expectations?"

"You really want to have this conversation *here*, Duchess? It can't wait until we're outside?" Flux's gaze jumped around the crowded bar as if he was assessing possible threats.

The energy in the bar had all but ground to a halt, and a bunch of eyes were trained on them. *Shit, he's right.* Despite herself, she glanced in Chet's direction. He looked like he was going to implode as his mouth twisted with rage.

That was the clincher.

"Let's get going, darlin'." Flux grabbed her hand and she didn't resist. "You can continue your inquisition once we're in the truck."

The hot desert air wrapped around them as Maggie slid behind the wheel of the pickup and let her forehead rest on the steering wheel for the briefest second while she caught her bearings. Flux pulled open the door on the passenger side and slipped into the seat.

"Do you want me to drive?"

His low question dragged Maggie out of her head and she startled in the seat. She put the key into the ignition and turned over the engine. "I got it," she reassured him and carefully navigated out of the packed parking lot.

They were both quiet. Although Maggie didn't know the reason for Flux's silence, her head still spun and her lower back tingled with warmth from his touch that was no longer there. Why did he unnerve her so deeply? She mentally shook off the distraction and pressed her lips together, driving by memory more than anything else.

"What are we doing here?" she asked again.

"We're driving," he quipped, and she watched him stretch out his legs from the corner of her eye.

"That's not what I meant—"

Flux cleared his throat. "I know, I know."

There was another beat of silence between them. She got the feeling he wasn't used to having these kinds of conversations.

He bent over to search for something underneath the seat. "How the fuck do I push this back?"

"The switch is on the side of the seat. Just move the knob back." After he settled down, she threw him a sidelong glance. "So?"

An audible sigh, and then he turned sideways so he was facing her. "I'm not looking for anything serious. Fuck, even being in this truck with you goes against every rule I have, but I'm here, so let's just leave it at that."

"You have rules? Are they written down?" She chortled.

"Smartass." Flux jerked his head back as he stared out the front windshield. "We're going back to the rodeo? Is this a fuckin' joke?"

"Look and see, before you judge," she said offhandedly, as she turned into an employee parking lot, shut off the engine, and pocketed her keys. Maggie turned to face him and made sure to keep her hands to herself. "I'm going to give it to you straight up."

"Good. I like that." Flux laughed. "Fuck, it's been a long time since I've laughed so much in one damn night."

Maggie quirked her lips. "Why's that?"

"One thing at a time." Flux stretched, rubbing his hands down his black jeans without answering her question.

"Fine," she breathed out. "Anyway, I'm not looking for anything earth shattering either, but if you want a one and done, I'm definitely not your girl. I don't jump into bed with anyone who takes a liking to me, and if you're not okay with getting to know me as a person before you get access to my body, there's the door." Maggie motioned to the passenger side door and sat back in her seat with a small huff. "What's your choice?"

Flux popped open the door and her whole body deflated in defeat. *Really? Shit.* She'd hoped he was better than that, but clearly she'd given him too much credit. Now, she was left pretending that the easy rejection didn't sting like hell. Of course, it made all the sense in the world that a badass biker turned rodeo bullfighter would want easy, simple, wham-bam-thank-you-ma'am fun.

He bent down and looked inside the truck. "Why the hell are you still sitting there, Duchess? You're the one who brought me here, although I can't figure out why."

His words were like a bucket of cold water poured over her head as she digested his rejection, which evidently wasn't one at all. Before either of them changed their minds, she scooted out of the seat and slammed the truck door, leaving all of her worries behind.

With Flux's quick stride and her nerves leading the way, it didn't take them long to make it to the stables where the rodeo housed all of the horses for the circuit. Maggie was pretty positive Flux didn't spend much time around there, given the fact that most rodeo employees tended to stick with their own kind—bull riders to bull riders, bullfighters to bullfighters, and so forth.

"Welcome to my home away from home." Maggie slapped the side of the barn on her way into the musty, manure-smelling passage, and a horse neighed in greeting. "If you want to get to know me then this is the place to do it."

She took a deep breath, cherishing the varied smells of leather and horse that most people couldn't stand unless they lived in this world.

"Grab a shovel, big guy." She stretched her arms out and didn't wait for Flux to get with the program.

"So, you're going to get our hands dirty—"

"So, we don't get our hands dirty. That's right. You're quick on the uptake." Maggie teased and looked back at the badass biker whose eyes were narrowed with both respect and something heavier, which she told herself not to look at too closely.

"We'll start by mucking everything out and then we'll replace the hay. Think you can handle it?"

"I can handle anything you throw my way, Duchess," he said as he picked up the shovel.

Maggie watched the muscles in his arms bulge as he began working, and she quickly turned away.

It occurred to her that this may not have been such a hot idea after all.

## CHAPTER SIX

# FLUX

DUCHESS WAS FUCKING clever as hell, Flux would give her that, but nothing about the exhausting, sweaty plan made a dent in his attraction toward her. He watched the way a bead of sweat ever so slowly disappeared down her T-shirt and wished he could follow it with his tongue. He licked his lips and jerked himself out of fantasyland. This woman was dangerous: He had to get his head on straight with her. A whiplash of frustration made him dig deeper into the pile of hay, sending chunks of the large bale in the wheelbarrow flying out and over them like snow.

"Shit!" Flux looked up and his gaze fell on her perfectly shaped tits. "Fuck!"

"Is this too much for you?" Maggie laughed and walked over to him and picked a piece of straw out of his hair.

The small bit of contact set his whole body on fire. While she showed him the offending piece, it took every ounce of self-control not to throw her onto the fresh pile of hay behind them and let his hands do the talking for both of them. He must have made a face or something because she dropped the straw and backed away, and her delighted, cocky smile became more guarded.

"How does a guy like you end up fighting bulls in a rodeo?" she asked, almost too brightly, as she turned back to the pile they were shoveling and dug in for another round.

Fuck, he shouldn't even be there, it went against his own rules. He was a damn mess. It was like as soon as he saw her at the bar, all his rules went to shit, and he didn't understand it. *She's just a sweet piece. Nothing more.* But then why did it feel like so much more?

"Are you going to share your story?" Her voice broke through his thoughts.

"Pass." His fingers tightened around the shovel handle and he put his back into the work, this time being careful not to channel his annoyance with himself into the helpless hay.

"I didn't know passing was an option."

"This isn't a date, Duchess."

"Fair enough," Maggie replied as she straightened out. She dropped the shovel and pulled her hair back with some kind of elastic band that women carried with them around their wrists.

Flux wanted to wrap her hair around his hands so bad. Nothing like a good tug on a chick's hair while he pounded the hell out of her pussy.

"You have a funny look on your face. Haven't you ever seen a woman pull her hair up in a ponytail?" Maggie stared at him.

He tipped his head her way. "Nice ink job." When she'd swept her hair up, he'd noticed a delicate black and white horse shoe on the nape of her neck with a ring of purple flowers circled around it. He couldn't guess the significance, outside of the typical good luck BS, but he had the strongest urge to kiss her right in that spot and run his hands down over that fine ass while he breathed in her sexy scent. Just thinking about all that made his dick rock hard in less than two seconds flat.

Flux cursed under his breath and turned back to his hay pile, hoping she didn't notice while he did some adjusting. Something about this woman turned him into a horny teenager and it was infuriating. It was like his sex drive didn't have an off switch. Wouldn't it be great if he could attribute it to playing a cat and mouse game—that she was the one who got away from his bed where no one had ever turned him down before—but it wasn't that simple. It seemed that nothing was easy when it came to Maggie. *Keep it simple at all times—yeah, right.* Another one of his rules thrown in the crapper.

"You've got some pretty serious ink on your arms. I bet there was a lot of time and money that went into their creations."

"You'd win that bet. You got any more tats in places that I'd like to explore?"

"No," she said quickly as she hoisted another shovel full of hay and spread it around the stall. "Horses have always been my thing. I've been riding them since I could walk. Combine that with my whole family being obsessed with the rodeo, and well, here I am."

"Simple as that?" Flux cracked his knuckles and leaned against the shovel. "Girl meets rodeo, girl falls in love?"

There was that cute as hell smile that made her cheeks dimple and a blush spread across her face before she moved to hide it. He loved catching her off guard. The way she scrambled to act all tough made him feel oddly protective, and he enjoyed the fact that he could push her off her cocky pedestal without being an asshole about it.

"You want my resume now?" She laughed, then threw a handful of hay in his direction as he dodged it, covering his head.

"Don't start something you can't finish, Duchess," he warned, unable to conceal the burst of playful possessiveness that had risen to the surface. When was the last time he'd felt that? *Six years ago before... don't fuckin' go there.*

Maggie's small tongue flicked out, taunting him.

*Damn, she's sexy.* He couldn't very well let that score go unsettled, now could he?

Before he knew exactly what he was doing, Flux let the shovel fall to the ground and was suddenly less than a step away from scooping her luscious body up in his arms. He remembered the feel of her beneath his palms when they were dancing. Maggie's curves had molded to him in the best way possible as they swayed together. Flux didn't hesitate as he grabbed her around the waist and fused their bodies together.

She gasped and her eyes grew wide.

"I warned you, darlin'," he said before his other hand threaded through her soft blonde locks. "You wanted to make this a game, but I forgot to tell you that I don't play fair."

Her lips parted and nothing came out; all her comebacks seemed to be at a standstill. Their flirtation had taken a dangerous turn and he knew, for better or worse, this was a breaking point.

"What do you say?" He ran his fingers over the tat on her neck. Her skin was like satin. *Fuck.*

Her blue orbs locked on his, and she tilted her head back slightly. "Do it," she breathed out, a delicate sound close to a whisper.

But to him, she might as well have shouted the words. Flux didn't dare breathe and desire rocked through his body as he growled and tugged her back to angle her head at the very second he took her sweet lips. The moment their mouths fused together, Flux couldn't get enough. Every part of him pressed closer against Maggie with his grip tightening possessively around her waist as she moaned into his mouth.

Flux slipped his tongue between her lips and explored her sweet mouth, possessing her completely with every sharp breath. She made a delicate little sound that went straight to his hard-as-hell cock. Fuck, she felt amazing, just like everything she'd promised without words when they had been dancing together. His hand glided down and grabbed her ass, squeezing it gently at first, then harder while she made little noises and bit his lower lip.

Maggie's fingers gripped his shirt before easing it up behind his neck. He ground against her as he kneaded the ass that had been on his mind since the first time he'd seen it, and she rubbed her soft tits against his chest. They were entangled in the throes of passion that left them panting. He couldn't recall the last time he had felt so much of... *anything.*

"Goddamn, darlin', you're ... Fuck," he growled. He was lost. Gone in the touch and taste of her, a little like beer and cherries. Her lower lip popped out of his mouth and she dragged him down with the same dominating force that was working through him. With their lips still fused together, they both maneuvered toward the bed of hay that they'd been working so hard to lay out for the past hour. Maggie sank down into it as if she belonged there and he lay over the top of her, in between her legs so that every inch of him pressed against her—there was no way she could doubt the effect she had on him.

There was also no question that the vixen gave as good as she got, and every time Flux moved back for air, she came at him equally hard and with just as much passion. His dick pulsed against his leg as Maggie moved her hips upward, lightly grinding against him. She was making cute little noises that were driving him fucking wild, and her hands alternated between gripping his hair and moving down to grab his ass.

"You're killin' me, Duchess," he rasped. His cock throbbed painfully, and he needed to ram it inside her heat and fuck her like she'd never been fucked before.

She moaned louder and gripped his butt harder.

Then there was a noise outside the stable, like something had dropped from high up. Maggie stiffened and Flux cursed.

"What was that?" she asked. "No one's supposed to be here."

"In a rodeo, someone's always around doing shit. It's probably just one of the stable hands.

"I guess."

He dipped his head down and before he could claim her lips again, there was another sound. "Fuck," he muttered as he pulled back and rested on his knees. He helped her sit up and suddenly Flux realized that the stable wasn't the place to be banging her for the first time. He wanted it to be special. *Special?* Yeah ... he'd think about breaking *that* rule another time, but at that moment, he wanted to make sure no one was spying on them.

He licked his lips, wanting to savor the taste of her. They were both still breathing ragged when Maggie looked at him as she ran her tongue over her bruised lips with a growing smile.

"Wow, damn …" The sentiment sat in the air between them. "That was …"

"Yeah." Flux cleared his throat, unable to look away from her glowing face. "That was something." His body still chomped at the bit to figure out a way to get his hands back on her and finish off exactly what they'd started together. Shit, if that was only the appetizer, he could only imagine what she'd be like when he got all her clothes off.

Arousal still buzzed inside him as he stood up. He rolled his shoulders and reached out to Maggie, who moved in the hay sluggishly. She grabbed his hand and the feel of her skin didn't help jack shit in trying to calm his dick down. He pulled her up then let go quickly and walked toward the barn's entrance.

"Did you hear that noise?" His voice was still thick with desire, and he hated that he needed her that much. "I'm gonna see if someone's around."

"It was probably something falling off the lofts. It happens all the time, but during the day no one pays attention to it."

"Maybe, but I don't go for guessing—I like to know exactly what's going on. I'll be right back."

Darkness surrounded him and the only sounds he heard were the shuffle of hooves and the chomping of mouths. He walked around the barn, then up and down the aisles, checking out each of the stables, but nothing was amiss.

When he returned, Maggie had the shovel in hand, back to work. She didn't look up at him, she just kept at it as if nothing had happened between them.

As quickly as they had come together, they had split apart.

*Damn.*

## CHAPTER SEVEN

# CHET

CHET STOOD IN the shadows watching his girl clean out the stall, working side by side with that biker asshole. He made sure not to make any noise this time as he crept back to watch Maggie make a damn fool of herself with that bastard.

When Chet had first seen them together at the bar, everything went red. *How the fuck could Maggie want him over me?* A well of anger pulsed inside him as he watched them clean out the stall. Neither of them spoke, and Chet wondered how long it would take Maggie to wise up and realize that Flux was nothing more than a man whore who only wanted to use her. When she finally grew a fucking brain, he had no doubt that she would come crawling back to him, begging for a second chance.

Of course, he'd take Maggie back—she was the love of his life, but she'd be punished for her indiscretions. Although, he couldn't really count on her wising up any time soon, especially since he'd seen that vulgar display of their lust just a short while before. So he'd have to make sure that she'd see the light—sooner rather than later.

*How could she let that vermin touch her?* If he hadn't made some noise, he was positive they'd have done it right there and then, in the hay with the stench of shit all around them. And to think that she rebuffed his advances only to roll around in a barn with that dirty biker just like a slut. *Oh Maggie, you've really fallen since you broke away from me.*

# FORGIVENESS

Chet had known Maggie was his from the second he saw her take on a barrel race. Her intensity was admirable, and he knew he'd enjoy taming her spirit and making her his protected and coddled play thing. She'd be the mother of his children and his future wife.

Just like any good stallion, all Maggie needed was a little taming.

But she wasn't going to get it from the low life pawing at her like a damn animal. Maggie was better than that, which Chet had tried to show her during their brief but oh-so important time together. He knew she'd only run away from their relationship because she was scared. What they had was something real, and it spooked her because she was worried about changing into something she didn't yet understand. *No worries, honeycakes. I'll make sure you're not scared anymore.* He'd help her and guide her in the ways he needed her to be—so that she could be better for them both.

If only Maggie would let him. *Stubborn little bitch.*

Chet pushed down the anger and tried to find an outlet for his rage that didn't involve throwing himself headlong into a fight with Flux while Maggie was in the way. She didn't need to see that side of him. That would hardly encourage her to trust him. And in order for his molding to work, Maggie needed to know she was safe, that *he* would take care of her completely so long as she abided by his rules. He was much better for her than that narcissistic asshole would ever be.

Honestly, Chet didn't see why all the girls went crazy for a shiny motorcycle, a vulgar biker with more tattoos covering his body than skin, and a stupid leather jacket and vest. Flux was an A-class jerk who treated women like playthings. Chet had heard talk about the biker and had even seen him in action during the last two rodeos they'd worked together. It was unbelievable and sickening, yet the women still lined up, just waiting to be used by him. *Why the hell are women so weak?* Chet knew the answer: Deep down, most women craved a strong man to take the lead, harness them, and take care of them. They didn't need a macho man for one good, solid fuck before being discarded for the next girl in line. No, they needed a loving man who could take charge and let them be free to do what women did best—please their husbands and have babies.

Chet shook his head. He had carnal desires, but at least he had the class to take that kind of business to a hooker instead of leaving it for a decent woman to pick up the pieces.

His lip curled with disgust, and just thinking about what an abomination Flux was made Chet wish he would've fucked with the biker's shiny pride and joy. Maybe without his toy, a woman like Maggie would rip the blinders off, and the loser's appeal would take a nose dive. All that asshole had going for him was the bad boy vibe and a damn Harley-Davidson. *Big fucking deal.* Flux was as far from a gentleman as it got, and it was up to Chet to make sure Maggie understood that so she would appreciate a real gentleman—*him.*

Chet shook his head. As long as he was playing secret babysitter, his girl would be safe, but eventually he'd have to lay down the law and make her see things his way. He figured at first Maggie wasn't going to like that, but after some time she'd learn just like every animal he'd broken from the time he was old enough to wield a rope.

"Excuse me, Chet? Can I help you?"

Chet swung around from his main focus and stumbled out of the barn. "Shut the fuck up," he hissed as he motioned the lowly employee to follow him.

They went away from the barn and back to the arena, then Chet stopped and his frown turned into a deep scowl.

The worker tucked his hands into his pockets and took a step backward from Chet.

*Fucking coward.* "Now what the hell do you want?"

"Just wondering if you needed anything. You don't usually show up here this late," the man stammered.

"I need you to mind your own business and get the hell outta here. Got it?" He sneered and the employee stumbled farther back, his eyes widening. "Do I need to put that in a simpler language that you can understand?"

"Uh, no, you're..."

Chet watched the stable hand grope for the right word, then he walked away, cutting him off. He hid himself behind one of the work sheds as he waited for Maggie. The image of Flux rolling all over his girl, his large hands touching her everywhere made his jaw clench. *He had his hands on her ass and she ... she was touching his too.* A low, feral sound leaked out between his lips.

Hardly the noise of a gentleman, but he was driven to distraction by the memory of Maggie dangling her wares and then cruelly ripping them away from Chet. *She acted like she was so innocent. What a damn liar and tease.* Since Maggie had taken a break from him—that's the way he saw it—he hadn't touched another decent woman as he waited for his girl to come crawling back to him. Of course, his visits to the occasional hooker didn't count because, after all, men had needs. Chet had abstained from decent women so he wouldn't hurt Maggie's feelings, but after he'd seen how disrespectful Maggie had been to him, she now needed to understand what it was like to watch him with other women. It was only fair, and when Maggie saw all the southern charm and gentlemanly attention she'd be missing, she'd trip over her feet in a rush to get back together with him, especially when the biker kicked her gorgeous ass to the curb.

Chet pulled out his phone from his jeans pocket. When he'd seen Maggie making a damn fool of herself over Flux at the bar, he'd reached out to a woman he'd met at the rodeo a few nights before. She'd been flirting up a storm with him and they exchanged numbers, but he had no intention of calling her until just a few hours ago. *That's what you made me do, honeycakes.* Chet flexed his fist and looked around for something to hit at the idea that his girl had kissed that walking STD. He spat to the side and brought up his texts.

It looked like his date would be right on time. The last thing she'd sent him was a small heart emoji a few hours before. He'd asked her to have a burger with him back at the motel. Of course, he could've sprung for something nicer, and for Maggie he would've absolutely gone to the trouble, but this wasn't about wining and dining this woman, it was about rubbing Maggie's nose in it. And there was no way to do that if she wasn't there to see it all go down, so having dinner at the motel where Maggie was staying was ideal. He couldn't wait to showcase their little flirt-fest in front of her. *You asked for it, sweetheart.*

Chet was just about ready to pocket the phone when it vibrated, and he took another look at the texts. With any luck it was his Maggie begging him to take her back right now.

**Rebecca:** *I can't do dinner tonight. I'm sorry. Something came up.*

Chet watched the little floating bubbles from Rebecca's screen and clenched his phone as he tried not to panic. She was still typing, which might mean that he could turn this around in time. He just had to buck up a little bit. He rolled his shoulders and took a long breath. The little bubbles abruptly stopped again. Then started. And … stopped.

"What the hell are you trying to tell me, woman?" Chet nearly threw down the phone before he got his head in the game enough to write back a reply of some substance.

**Chet:** *What's wrong, baby girl? Anything I can do to help you?*

More of those damn bubbles. They died down again. *What the hell's up with this bitch?* At that moment, he didn't have the patience to be Prince Charming, especially with a throwaway reject who wasn't his girl in the first place. He was half-tempted to blow Rebecca off altogether, but Chet had exchanged too many texts with this one and had put too much thought into his plans to not get at least a blow job out of it.

**Rebecca:** *Do you want the truth?*

Chet nearly drove his fist through the shed's wall, but he kept it together enough to compose a reply.

**Chet:** *Absolutely, baby girl. Honesty is the most important thing between a man and woman.*

More bubbles. He kept his gaze fixed on the barn door.

**Rebecca:** *Ok. I bumped into Roy Mullins and he asked me out. I'm totally into steer wrestlers, and I've been following him on the circuit for a while. I'm super sorry. I hope u understand. Maybe if u come back around some other time???*

Insecurity clawed and clutched the inside of his chest, and his head pounded as if he'd been struck by a sledge hammer. Humiliation burned across his hairline and the back of his neck as he re-read the text. He gripped the phone as his fingers flew across it.

**Chet:** *Not a chance in hell, CUNT.*

He carefully slid it back in his pocket, then walked over to a tree branch that was laying on the ground and picked it up. In less time than it took him to breathe, he let loose all the anger that'd been sitting on his chest since he'd followed Maggie to the stables.

Sweat dripped down Chet's face and back as he swung the branch at anything in sight until he became exhausted and dropped it onto the ground. Hundreds of splinters laid at his feet as he breathed heavily, his adrenaline soaring so high he barely felt the cuts and scratches that were sure to be on his palms. All he saw was Maggie. Every thought was Maggie.

Without missing a beat, Chet strode to his pickup and jumped inside. He turned on the ignition and moved it to a dark corner of the lot so it faced the stables.

When Maggie came out, he'd be ready.

## CHAPTER EIGHT

# MAGGIE

MAGGIE CLUNG TO the shovel as her head continued to float in the clouds while she imagined all the ways that kiss could have kept going between them. She couldn't remember a time when something had been so hot and intense with anyone. Flux's lips had set her on fire and made her forget what was right or wrong or smart ... or foolish. All it had taken was his demanding kiss and the feel of him pressing hard against the crease of her skirt.

He made her body come alive.

The truth of that pushed its way through her fuzzy mind as she threw a large bundle of hay on the ground and began to spread it around the stall. Maggie resisted the urge to take a quick peek over her shoulder. From the grunting behind her, she knew he was working hard, but she could also feel his intense gaze on her. *I won't turn around. I won't.* Flux would never know how shaken she was by his kiss and the feel of his arms; she didn't like it at all, not one damn bit.

"You doin' okay over there, Duchess?" His deep voice rattled her, making her body rev up a few notches.

"Yep," she replied as nonchalantly as she could muster.

"Just checking."

Maggie heard the shovel scraping on the dirt again, and she forced herself to stay focused on the task. Ever since she could remember, her life had consisted of practicing and competing, and it'd suited her just fine. When all of her friends had been primping and giggling about prom and homecoming games, she'd been working hard for an upcoming competition. Sure, Maggie had boyfriends, and she'd had lost her virginity at twenty years old to a sweet cowboy whom she thought she loved, but hadn't. After three months the infatuation had waned, and they'd gone their separate ways. But the intimate contact of being wrapped in Flux's arms while he rubbed against her made Maggie ache for more. She wanted Flux like she'd never wanted any man before. No other had ever made her abandon her senses like that. *I was even humping him! Ugh ... why* him? A more complicated man couldn't have dropped into her lap if she'd planned it. A groan escaped from her lips.

"What's that, Duchess?"

Maggie cleared her throat. "It's just the dust."

The answer seemed to have satisfied Flux because he returned to laying straw around several stalls. *I can't believe I was all over him.* As the blush in Maggie's flamed cheeks continued to climb, she groaned inwardly and dropped the shovel to fan her face with her hands. *It'd be nice to get out of an embarrassing situation once in a while without being so damn transparent. Shit ... everything's a mess. But you didn't try very hard to keep away from him, did you?* She should've cut things off when she was at the bar before giving Flux any chance of hopping into the cab of her truck and landing them in a bale of hay.

Maggie thought she had everything in hand when she picked the least sexy thing they could do to get to know each other without all the sexual tension getting in the mix. But the way he looked at her had eaten away at her common sense instead. There was no doubt about it—she really had no one to blame but herself. She'd egged him on, practically dared him verbally, and a man like Flux? He wasn't going to take a challenge lying down.

He had all but told her that before he took her lips.

Now, Maggie was left with the consequences of her actions. Damn adulthood. Since she'd begun competing, her sights had been set on the pro rodeo trail, and she didn't need anything veering her off course. The ruggedly handsome, muscular, and oh-so sexy Flux was a huge distraction. *And I work with him. What the hell was I thinking?* This was why she'd stuck to the hard-and-fast rule of not seeing anyone from work, so things like that didn't happen on the regular. The last thing she needed was a rumor going around the yard. Maggie knew well enough how quickly *talk* spread on the circuit—and about whom. She wasn't willing to tarnish her glowing reputation in the ring for one night of hot, crazy loving in the sack with a biker who had intimacy issues. She'd heard the buzz about how Flux was a "love 'em and leave 'em" one-nighter. After she'd seen him at the arena, several of the women in the office had told her about his sexual prowess and his asshole ways. *Yeah ... complicated all the way around. I just need to nip whatever is going on between us in the bud. Like—now.*

But for Christ's sake, they were two adults. There wasn't any reason they couldn't talk this thing through and come to some sort of agreement on the matter. There was no reason for her to play coy with her feelings now. Who the hell would that help in the long run?

Maggie straightened her spine and took a deep breath.

"You about done over there, Duchess?" Flux's hoarse voice made her blink a few times, but she managed to get her bearings.

She wasn't falling against his dick again. Not until they'd answered some all-important questions and everything was on the table between them.

"I'm spread out on this side. We should probably move to the next stall, don't you think?" he said.

Neither of them spoke again while Flux handed her his shovel and took the wheelbarrow into the next empty stall as she followed behind him. They had a good system worked out by this point. Good enough, that when he went to take back the shovel, she held it fast until he was forced to look down into her eyes with a confused expression. Then his attention shot elsewhere entirely, and he dropped his grip on the tool as if it had burned him.

"So, now you can't even look at me?" Maggie accused him, only slightly teasing. "This doesn't change anything between us, right?"

Flux's brows creased before his face shuttered into a perfectly stoic mask. It was a nice trick. Maggie had her own version, but she didn't plan on employing it tonight. Not with him. He had issues, and she knew that from the start. So, she would do her best to work with those issues rather than against them. She couldn't ask him to kiss her and then walk out on the situation as if she hadn't done a damn thing.

*A duchess has better manners than that, dammit.*

She put her hand on her hip and caught his gaze. "Do you agree with me or not that the kiss doesn't change anything between us?"

No answer.

"Well … do you?" She was almost frantic for an answer now, even though on the outside she managed to keep her cool. The longer the gap of silence between them, the more she could think of all the different things this meant between them. They hardly knew each other, had barely even begun to talk about their lives, yet their connection was more genuine than that of any man she'd ever let touch her in the past.

It was unnervingly inconvenient.

"It doesn't change things," Flux parroted back as he rested his palms above his head against the horse paddock wall and stretched—probably so he didn't have to look at her while they had this conversation.

Meanwhile, Maggie was stuck staring at the ink move on his delicious biceps and triceps as he became a walking poster boy for sex on a stick. And the way his shirt rode up a little bit to reveal his flat stomach and happy trail made her mouth water and her skin tingle. She quickly turned around just so she could keep her dignity. One of them had to keep talking, so she picked up the mantel again.

"We're still casual and if we go down this road … and that's a big *if* … it's a one-and-done. No catching feelings, no relationship mumbo jumbo—none of that nonsense. We scratch the itch, then it's out of our systems and we go back to business, agreed?" *What the hell! Did I really say that? Where did my fucking brain go?* She ran her eyes over Flux then darted them away. *Just a casual hookup wouldn't hurt. For him ... it's his style, and for me, it'd be a release of a lot of stress. Just once, then move on and back to business. That wouldn't be bad, would it?* For once in her organized, calculated life, she'd like to throw caution to the wind—no plans, no goals, just some naughty fun. And Maggie had no doubt in her mind that Flux would aim to please, but could she really do it?

"So..." Flux drew out the word and Maggie cringed, knowing exactly what part of that sentence he had caught onto and hooked his attention.

"Just because I'm considering the possibility and bringing it up in a normal adult conversation doesn't mean it's going to happen, okay? But we have to explore all the possibilities and options, otherwise ... well, it could be fucking chaos!"

"Watch your mouth, Duchess. You're starting to sound like me."

Maggie looked over her shoulder and pursed her lips as she looked at him.

"Sorry, didn't mean to interrupt your speech." He threw her a shit-eating grin, then folded his arms across his sculpted chest and winked.

The biker Adonis didn't need any help knowing he was a hot commodity. She was sure the string of women who flocked to his bed did enough of the talking for both of them. And she wasn't about ready to be another one—not until he understood the possible ramifications and the limits of their engagement.

"You can mock all you want, big guy, but at least one of us is taking the full disclosure route," Maggie huffed and dropped her shovel. "Tell me how you feel about it. Now."

"Demanding—I like it." Flux's voice was suddenly at the nape of her neck, his body heat lingering against her back.

If Maggie moved less than half an inch, she would be pressed back against him, and the small possibility drove her whole body into stillness. *No.* Not until she knew what was going on between them. Anything else was beyond idiotic. How was she even justifying it to herself in the first place?

"I can see your brain spinning, Duchess. You're practically giving me a headache." His voice was low and soothing and so sure of himself, but it didn't match his prior reaction. "I've got every fuckin' intention of seeing this through and agreeing to all your terms. We're casual. One night. We're friends. Check, check, and check. But I'm gonna let you sit with it for the night before we do anything rash after that kiss, which was fuckin' incredible. You deserve more than me hiking up your skirt, hoisting you up on my hips, and taking you hard and rough against the wall of the stall, although if that's what you want, I'm all in, Duchess."

The way he caressed her nickname made her swallow, and her flesh lit up from the inside out as all the arousal she'd been suppressing flared to the surface. Maggie's nipples hardened and her panties dampened as her breath caught in her lungs. A vivid picture of Flux lifting her up in his arms, slamming her against the wall, and taking her within an instant made her squeeze her eyelids together hoping to beat it back.

"Thanks," she whispered.

"Don't mention it."

Maggie instantly knew the second he took a few steps back and put space between them again. For a beat, the whole world was a little bit clearer. Taking some time was in their best interests, especially when she never went into sex with a selfish agenda like she was considering with him now. She was a relationship kind of girl, not a one-night stand sex bomb, so why the hell had she even suggested it in the first place? Everything about Flux was foreign territory.

Maggie heard the thud of his footsteps as he walked away. "Flux, wait!" She pivoted, and within seconds he was right back in front of her as if he'd never moved at all. Flux looked down at her, his black T-shirt streaked with dirt, and his hair still a mess from where she'd run her hands through it less than half an hour ago. His expression was unreadable, but Maggie sensed the same barely leashed arousal in him that ached in her core.

"Do you want a ride back to the motel?"

"No, I'll walk. But thanks, Duchess."

"Okay, sure. How about one more for the road?"

Before Flux could say anything else, Maggie gripped his T-shirt and yanked him down to her level, and they kissed until she couldn't breathe without the scent of him in her lungs.

## CHAPTER NINE

# MAGGIE

AFTER SHE FINISHED up in the stalls and shut everything down for the night, Maggie took a deep breath of the warm night air. She'd hoped some miracle would appear to help her better understand all the mixed up feelings swirling through her body and her mind. Instead, she was just as stuck as she'd been in the stables, which was unusual since it was a place where she'd always felt safe and secure. Maggie kneaded her shoulder and with no magical answer in sight, started walking toward her pickup.

She didn't make it far.

One second her truck was in view, and the next, Chet blocked it from her vision. He stood there with his chest rising and falling in sharp, choppy breaths. Chet's eyes were narrowed with a dogged intention that made her muscles seize up in fight-or-flight as all her alarm bells went off.

Maggie took a step backward and tried to sidestep him. Maybe she'd get lucky and could avoid the situation. Fat chance. He blocked her path each time she tried, and he kept walking forward, forcing her backward through the parking lot and toward the stable. Maggie's brain told her to run, but she didn't. There was no way in hell she'd give Chet the satisfaction of having that much power. No, she'd hold her ground. It was decided even as her body struggled to tell her stubbornness to take a hike.

One of the overhead lights illuminated him, and Maggie noticed blood covered one of his hands. Chet pulled his cowboy hat down low on his face so she could hardly see his eyes. An icy-cold shiver ran up and down her spine, and she suddenly wished she'd brought a shovel out with her, or that Flux had wanted that ride to the motel.

"Chet, what're you doing here? This has gone too far. You need to leave me alone, okay?" Maggie swallowed, somewhat proud when her voice came out evenly and not reed thin from the fear that threatened to tear apart all her reason and logic. "Just go back to the motel and let me leave. I'm tired … it's been a long day."

He took a step closer.

"If you leave now, I won't tell anyone." *Take the lifeline. Take it and move the fuck out of my way.*

"Just like you won't tell anyone that I'm lousy in bed, right, *Duchess?*"

Flux's pet name for her felt dirty coming from Chet's lips, and she flinched as she dug in her back jean skirt pocket for the keys to the pickup. Maggie quickly arranged them like a weapon between the splayed fingers of her hand behind her back. Luckily, Chet didn't seem to be tracking her movements, too lost in staring at her face.

"What're you talking about? I couldn't say anything about you in bed or out of it—we never had sex. And if we had, I'd never do something like that. What would be the point of it anyway?"

Maggie stumbled over his flawed logic, trying to connect the dots. Out of all the people in the world that could spread those rumors, why would she—the woman who'd rebuffed his sexual advances—turn around and trash his name all around the rodeo? *It doesn't make sense. He must've really pissed someone off and now he wants to blame me. Typical.*

"Chet, listen to yourself … You're not making sense right now."

"Oh, *I'm* not making sense?" he yelled as spittle flew from his mouth and she took a step back. "That's fucking rich coming from a little slut like you! You passed up the chance to be with me—a *real* man, so you can suck that asshole biker's dick. You're out of your mind! He's the fucking scum of the earth. If this is your sick and twisted way of keeping all the other girls off me so you can make me jealous with *him*, you've fucking succeeded, *honeycakes*."

His sneer was all that was visible beneath the harsh glow of the lights around the barn.

"Chet—" She fumbled for words.

He moved the barest inch and her back slammed against the side of the stables, making a few of the horses neigh in protest. *Shit, how did he get me this far back and I didn't notice it?* The back of her head smarted where it had hit the wood, but she welcomed the pain because it kept her reeling mind clear. She would need all her senses in working order to get out of this mess.

Chet dipped his head down and she could smell the beer on his breath. "Stop. Playing. Me."

Maggie tilted her head to the left, and her hand tightened to the point of pain around her keys, but she didn't want to resort to violence … yet. She didn't really want to hurt Chet—she just wanted him to go away, but if he pushed it, she'd jam the keys right into his eyes and twist them. Adrenaline licked up her spine and tingled through her fingers and toes.

"I need you to get a grip. Can you do that for me? Because if you can't and this goes down the way I think it might, Chet, I won't hesitate to bring a formal complaint against you with the rodeo commission and with Charlie. Do you really want a sexual harassment charge on your file along with all the other rumors I *didn't* start? Is that your damn goal here?"

Maggie put her hands on his chest and pushed him back, not caring that she still couldn't see all his facial expressions or his eyes. She could pretty much feel the anger and defiance radiating from him, and she didn't give a flying fuck about it.

"I really don't want to fuck up your day, but I'll make it happen if you don't let me get by you, do you understand me?" Maggie held up her makeshift weapon and poked him in the chest with it for emphasis.

The silence was eerie and dangerous. Pushing her fear down, she lifted her chin.

"I asked if you got my drift." Maggie wasn't calling his bluff—she wouldn't hesitate to trash his career if he didn't leave her the hell alone. Even though the rodeo may be a boy's club, she knew Charlie wouldn't tolerate one of his biggest barrel racing draws being harassed by a bull rider who didn't bring in half the crowds she did.

"We understand each other perfectly, *honeycakes*." Chet's low snarl made the small hairs on the back of her neck stand up on end. "By all means, enjoy the rest of your night. But don't think for one damn minute you and I are finished. Next time, we can have another chat somewhere more private." He moved back a little.

That was all Maggie needed, and she shoved past him and hurried over to the truck. Once she was in the driver's seat with the engine purring, she inhaled several sharp breaths before gripping the steering wheel. The high beams illuminated the shifty SOB, and without hesitation, she hauled ass out of the parking lot.

"Oh God," she said out loud. Her eyes blinked several times, but that didn't stop the streaming tears. "It's okay. You're okay. *It's okay.*"

A wash of numbness prickled across her body, and despite the mumbled mantra, she couldn't think straight. Maggie probably shouldn't have been on the road for any longer, as the shaking racked her body from the ends of her toes to the tips of her fingers. Shock was a delayed and strange thing. With a quick wrench of the wheel she bucked off the main road and came to a stop on the shoulder. Right now, getting ahold of herself was a top priority. There was no point in freaking out all the way home and putting other people at risk while she drove recklessly. Maggie put her forehead to the steering wheel and let the waterfall of pent-up terror flow over and out of her.

She surrendered to the bone-shuddering sobs that seized her shoulders as all her repressed emotions from the past several months of Chet's stalking came to the forefront. Damn, she could only be strong for so long, and now all of his bullshit had finally worn her down. "I don't need this!" She pounded her fist on the dashboard. Maggie was so close to the chance of competing in the National Finals Rodeo in Las Vegas, and she couldn't let Chet throw her off her game. He was nothing but a big, chauvinistic bully, and she'd be damned if she'd let him take her down.

Maggie grabbed a few tissues and dabbed her face before blowing her nose. The idea of going back to her room alone made her stomach cramp into knots. There was no way she could bear to be by herself yet. Not with that psycho possibly following her and fully aware of where her room was at the motel complex.

There was only one other place she could think to go at that moment. Tossing the tissues in a plastic bag, she checked the rearview mirror then pulled back onto the dark road.

## CHAPTER TEN

# FLUX

THE MORE FLUX stared at the bottles strewn across the kitchen countertop, the less he understood where he was going with his life. He could still taste Maggie on his lips and feel her delicately writhing beneath him. Nothing kept his concentration. He ran his hands through his hair and let out a long, slow breath. Maybe it was supposed to bring him back to his senses, but closing his eyes merely slapped a 3D montage of their make-out session across the backs of his eyelids.

He growled with the need to go back to the stables and possess every inch of that woman. *Fuck!* The whole thing had thrown him so out of whack, he didn't know up from down anymore. There had only been one time in his life when he'd felt so torn up about a woman and that was when he'd met his wife, Alicia.

Flux cradled his head in his hands. There wasn't a single fucking second that he didn't think about her ... about *them,* unless he was so damn high or drunk to feel anything. *High and drunk—sounds good to me,* he thought, especially with his memories threatening to open up wide and swallow him whole again. *Fuck!* He grimaced. He wanted to be with Maggie in the worst way. Duchess was different than all the other women he'd taken to his bed—from that revolving door of his sex life. She was—

"Don't say it, don't you dare fuckin' say it, asshole," Flux said, looking deadass serious in the mirror. "She's not special. She's a piece of tail, just like any of the others, and if you're smart, you'll stay the fuck away

# FORGIVENESS

from her for good and find someone who is more your goddamn speed. Some sweet piece who has more tits and ass than brains." Flux clenched and unclenched his jaw. "Fuckin' hell, get it together." He leaned against the counter and found himself on the floor, knees to his chest and head in his hands. His fingers tightened around his skull until everything ached.

The idea of getting close to someone again drove him nearly out of his mind with fear. Only one other person knew him on that level, and she'd been dead and gone since he'd turned nomad after the funeral. Alicia would be his one and only, because he sure as fuck didn't deserve anyone else. That's why he only chose women for fucking and getting his basic needs met, not for dating or getting to know them. That was bullshit, and after what he'd done, he didn't have the right to be happy and in a relationship.

Then there was Maggie, and damn, if she wasn't different. She was quality, and that was why the best course of action was either to fuck Duchess's brains out of his system or to ignore her completely and hope she took the hint. *Fuck. Nothing's ever easy.* He brooded without touching his stash, all the while aware that the longer he remained sober, the quicker his demons would come out—and they never played nice.

But the way he felt after he'd had Duchess in his arms, with her hard nipples pressed against his chest and her soft moans that'd driven him crazy, it was fitting that the demons should torment him. Letting his guard down with Maggie was stupid as hell, so it was only right to be reminded of the stark reality that he'd brought the people in his life nothing but pain and death … That he was a selfish, narcissistic asshole at the end of the day, who didn't deserve a second chance at any kind of life outside of being a walking skeleton. Flux needed to do penance for kissing Duchess and allowing his brain to think, for even a single second, that he was entitled to something for himself that made him happy.

How could he live with himself if he disgraced Alicia's memory? The memory of their daughter—

Flux balled his fists and slammed his left hand down into the badly chipped bathroom floor tiles. Again. Again. And again. A burning ache washed up his arm from the ricochet working up his muscles. But nothing mattered, none of it mattered anymore.

There was nothing left for him aside from misery and pain.

*Skank perfume still lingered all over his cut and jeans, soaking into the seat of his bike no matter how much driving wind ripped through his body. Flux had been gone on a charity poker run with the club. Alicia hadn't wanted him to leave, but they'd been spitting insults at each other for a few weeks and he was fucking ready to break the cycle.*

*Now, he regretted spending the night three towns over with his brothers watching a bunch of strippers grind and wiggle all over a pole while his wife was home alone with their daughter. The least he could've done was come home after the run had finished that day, but he was still pissed at Alicia, and he needed to unwind after a long three days to throw back shots and shoot the shit with his friends. He should've ridden home, admitted he was being a bag of fucking dicks, and taken one on the chin so they could've made up and things would've gone back to normal around their house.*

*The way Banger had made it sound over the phone, Flux didn't know if he would have the opportunity to make it right.*

*Banger had said it was bad. Really fucking bad. Hadn't offered much more info than that though—just told Flux to ride like the devil was chasing him until he was home.*

*Goddamn, he couldn't make it home fast enough. Early fall weather wreaked havoc with his brain and he'd ducked, dodged, and weaved around every slow asshole on the road to get to where he'd needed to be with one singular thought in his head.*

*Whatever had happened to them, it had to be okay. They would be okay.*

*When he'd pulled up outside his small house with the grinning pumpkins and plastic slide in the front yard, police cruisers were parked out front, lights flashing blue and red. The whole nine yards. A pit of fear dropped hollow and nagging into his stomach. Flux had barely stopped the bike and put it in park before he jumped off and dashed halfway across the front lawn.*

*People had tried to stop him. A bunch of them. All suits or badges.*

*It didn't fucking matter to him. He'd blown through all of them, their words were like gnats in his ears as he'd forced the front door open and pushed past the yellow crime-scene tape.*

*The smell. That was what had hit him first before anything else.*

*Like unwashed pennies and something deeper, earthier, like rot in his nose. He was a member of an outlaw MC and knew that smell intimately. The reaper had come to his home to collect—and Flux hadn't been there to stop the sonofabitch.*

*A jolt of shock had kept him locked in place. Disbelief. Denial.*

*The fucking badge's words from outside the house came flooding back to him: "killed ... sorry ... don't go in there ... things you don't want to see ... death."*

*Death. Death. Death.*

*The last one had pinged between his ears as a high-pitched ringing rocked through his skull like he'd been at a concert for too long.*

*Flux had walked like a zombie into the kitchen, following his nose.*

*Alicia was sprawled out on the hardwood floor, clothes ripped off her body, and so much fucking blood. Multiple stab wounds: chest, hip, back, hands. A disconnect had ripped through him while he tried to piece together what he was actually seeing in his family's home.*

*With the image of his wife still fresh in his mind, he'd vaulted through the rest of the house.*

*Emily. He had to find his baby girl.*

There was a sharp knock on the door. A loud enough noise that Flux jolted back from his memory into the present while the panic, guilt, and loss still ate him alive from the inside out. He scrubbed his hands down his face. If he ignored it, they would probably just go away. He tried to keep quiet while the ache in his veins blossomed until he was rocking back and forth, sitting on the bathroom floor.

But the pounding on the door didn't stop. It got worse.

Then, he wondered if maybe it was only his imagination, his own headache and guilt creating shit that didn't exist. The banging grew louder and more insistent, and it was like a damn freight train running through the middle of his head. He weaved up onto his feet and braced himself against the doorjamb.

More knocking—it just wouldn't stop.

"Fuckin' shut it, I'm coming!" he yelled, slowly making his way to the door like an old man.

When Flux opened it, he took a quick step backward and nearly knocked himself over by tripping on his own feet. While the memory of his wife and child was still murky within his subconscious, Maggie stood in front of him with her arms crossed and her head down.

"Yeah?" he asked gruffly, unable to change his demeanor, given the circumstances. Flux didn't remember how to interact with humans, let alone talk like one with the shock still fresh in his brain.

"I'm sorry. I shouldn't have … I just, uh … didn't know where to go …" she trailed off with a small sniffle, which alerted a protective part of his lizard brain that something was going on there. "I can go. It's no problem."

She made to leave and turned around before he grabbed her wrist. Maggie spun around as if he'd hit her, and he dropped her arm immediately, hands up at his sides. Her wary eyes studied his face, shifting up and down every area of his expression. At that moment, he was pretty fucking sure he was rocking the zombie look.

Flux grunted and moved to the side. A silent signal for her to get the hell inside or leave—her choice. When Maggie looked up at him and took a few steps into the room, he noted the red rings around her eyes as if she'd been crying. *Fuck.*

He shut the door, barely able to keep it to a loud slam.

"What happened? Tell me."

Flux's demand wasn't met with a cold shoulder or an abrasive look from her. Instead, his words seemed to deflate Maggie where she stood, as her shoulders folded inward and her hands covered her face. Damn, he was going about it all wrong. Flux was tongue tied and gruff, ripping through what was happening like an asshole with no sense of compassion. It was his demons that still ate at him.

They were both at a vulnerable place and, maybe, this was his chance to make whatever problem she was going through right now better, if she would just talk to him.

"You must've come here for a reason, Duchess. Tell me what's going on and I'll help if I can." The words sounded foreign coming from Flux as he cleared this throat and took a seat at the edge of the bed. "Let me ... be there for you."

Flux patted the spot next to him, inviting Maggie to join him on the rumpled queen bed. There was enough space between them that they weren't sitting on top of each other. He was thankful for the small favor. Fuck knows, he couldn't handle it if they touched too much right now. Not when everything inside him was raw, and they were both live wires begging for a grounding connection.

"Chet has been fucking with me for months." Her voice came out in a low, enraged accusation. "Tonight topped it all. He's been following me and downright stalking me."

"Whoa, wait a fuckin' second! He's been *what*?" Flux nearly jumped out of his skin as protectiveness reared deep within him.

"I should probably go back to the start of this story ..." Maggie licked her lips and continued to hug herself. "We'd dated for a little bit. Nothing serious. It was only a couple months, clearly not enough time for me to have noticed the extent of his level of crazy. But he'd seemed like a decent enough guy ..."

Flux scoffed and ran his palms down his jeans, focusing on her numbed-out expression while she looked straight ahead and told her story. Yeah, Chet was an entitled asshole. No doubt about it, but taking it to this level? Fuck. With all the scum he'd seen in his lifetime, this shouldn't have shocked him, but the idea that Chet would fuck with

Maggie still threw him. It enraged him down to a part of himself he never knew he could access.

"Go on," he gritted, gripping his knee caps so he didn't punch something and scare the ever-loving shit out of the woman who was opening up to him.

"And then I started to hear the rumors." Maggie covered her face again with her hands, and when she removed them, her expression was filled with a mixture of rage, pain, and regret. "He was a womanizing dick-bag who was terrible in bed and had a tab with the local brothel. He'd left a wake of women who hated him strewn all over town, and I was his next victim. I'd been stupid enough to fall for the 'good ol' boy' routine. I'm sure he peddles that crap to anyone who'll listen. Then I'd started noticing the girls who worked behind the scenes at the rodeo … and how they wouldn't go near me when I was with him. Women whom I'd made friends with, who'd said hello to me on a regular basis, were treating me like I wasn't even there anymore."

"Not a great fuckin' sign," Flux breathed out, his words were meant to help not hinder her story.

"It gets worse. One of the women, Darlene, had cornered me after a race a few months ago and demanded to see my phone. When I handed it over, she'd asked me to unlock it. I was wary, but we'd had conversations before and I figured Darlene was pretty trustworthy, so I did what she asked me. She'd found an app on my phone … a tracking one … Chet had put it there."

Maggie took a long breath and closed her eyes before breathing out again.

"Of course I'd confronted him about it, and when he denied it, I'd broken it off. But it seemed like he wasn't even hearing me anymore. He kept placating me—trying to touch me, soothe me, kiss me—until I'd pushed him off me, ran out of his room, and never looked back again."

"That must've been rough for you." Flux tried to be sympathetic while every fiber of his being yelled at him to get the hell up and pound the shit out of Chet so he could never ride anything again—a bull or a woman. "And he bothered you again, tonight?"

"He's just continuing the harassment—it never really stopped. Oh, there've been small periods where it's not as bad, but they're few and far between. He acts like he's this good man with all these decent values, and he's nothing but a hypocrite. The crazy part is that he's convinced himself that he's *that* guy. Anyway, he follows me around on the rodeo circuit. If he's not competing in one of the rodeos, he's still there in the stands watching me. It's creepy as hell."

Flux saw her shudder and he wanted to draw her close to him and wrap his arms around her, but he didn't budge.

"At the bar tonight, before you came in, I confronted him after I'd overhead him talking smack about women—barrel racers in general. I should've kept my big mouth shut and ignored him, but I didn't. I guess he didn't like the talking to in front of his friends because after you left, he—" She cut off and swallowed, closing her eyes again.

This time Flux only hesitated for a fraction of an instant before he took her hand and squeezed gently, a silent signal that he was there. She squeezed him back and that small touch jerked through his system, spreading a soothing warmth he wasn't expecting to feel ever again.

"You've got this, Duchess. What happened when I left the stable?"

"He confronted me. Accused me of trying to make him jealous with you so that he'd come back to me. He said I started the rumors that are going around about him. And he, he …"

"Did he fuckin' lay a hand on you?"

"No. It was close, but I got away from him."

Flux let out a breath he hadn't known he'd been holding and squeezed her hand again. He was willing to do whatever it took to get her mind off of what had happened tonight with the added bonus of making himself feel less helpless than he had in months, maybe even years. She had come to him, not her girlfriends, not her coach, not Charlie—*him*. That was something he couldn't take lightly—and something he never would've anticipated from another woman again. That type of raw trust. Even now, her small, calloused hand squeezed back on his own, still slightly trembling as she turned to face him for the first time.

"Thank you for trusting me, Duchess."

Silence stretched between them as their gazes locked together. And then Maggie launched herself at him and tackled him to the bed, her lips exploring his, way faster than he could process the motion.

## CHAPTER ELEVEN

# MAGGIE

"W HOA! SHIT, DUCHESS," Flux spoke through her eager kisses, but Maggie barely paid any attention, only knowing that she wanted to lose herself in this moment and scrub away the nastiness that Chet had left behind with something she chose—something that made her feel things were good and in control.

She angled her head again and laid a small trail of kisses along his neck leading down toward his pushed up T-shirt. "Do you really want me to stop?" Her words were muffled as she enjoyed the surprisingly soft, yet hard planes of his body against her mouth. "Please, Flux."

"I don't want you to stop, darlin'." Flux groaned and threaded a hand through her hair, bucking his hips. "Far from it. I'd love to pick up right where we left off earlier in the stables."

"Okay, good," she murmured before placing her teeth into his shoulder, eliciting a small moan from him.

"But hold up a sec," Flux grabbed both her wrists just as her fingers were tracing down the fine lines of his abs heading straight below the belt. "Duchess, before we do this, I ... uh ... Fuck. I can't believe I'm saying this, but fuck it. I need to be sure you know what you're doing, okay?"

Maggie blinked down at him, her lips still buzzing from the delicious contact with his skin. *Why does he want to stop this? Am I doing something wrong?* A million scenarios flew through her mind.

"No strings, right?" She breathed out, ragged breaths drawing through her lungs as her heart beat like a caged bird behind her chest. "We're both adults, and I want this, Flux." She ran her finger along his jaw. "I want you."

Maggie made sure she caught his gaze, and even though his pupils were dilated and his fingers formed claws into the bed covers, Flux looked as if he wouldn't touch her until he got an answer that satisfied him. It was sweet, very gallant, but not at all necessary. All she wanted him to do was rip her clothes off and give her a real man to think about for the next hour or so, not the one who haunted her nightmares.

"You don't think we're going too fast after what—"

Maggie stole his words away with another passionate kiss. She must've been doing her job right because a trickle of a growl escaped from Flux's throat as he wrapped his arms around her back and flipped them over so he was on top.

"Fuck, darlin'," he gritted against her ear, his hard dick already digging into the denim fabric of her skirt as she wrapped her legs around him, silently begging for more. "You won't regret it in the morning?"

"No. Will you?"

"No fuckin' way." He crushed his mouth on hers at the same time he struggled to rip his shirt off. Then he guided her palms back to his chest. "Have your fill, Duchess. Tell me exactly what you like and take what you need from me."

Kind words. Much nicer than she ever expected from the intense, introverted biker, who dodged death for a living. His even tone, so sure and certain, ripped all hesitation away. While Maggie's fingers tripped down his chest, trembling for an entirely different reason than before, she ignored Flux's racing heart and smiled against his lips.

Lost in the dark, earthy, and leather scent of him, Maggie glided her hands down the taut muscles in Flux's back. They tangled together like two people forbidden from one another. A part of it felt illicit, dangerous, and yet he would no more hurt her than anyone else she kept in her inner circle—and she knew that with certainty. Maggie didn't know why or how she was so sure of him, but her gut knew that this man, though broken, was genuinely good.

"Duchess, tell me what you like," Flux grated out the words, hissing as she lightly tugged on his nipple with her teeth. "Tell me what you want."

Maggie moaned and leaned her head back against the pillow, biting her bottom lip. "Take me. I just ... need *you*."

"That's not gonna work for me, Duchess. I need you to do the dirty work. You've gotta speak up, or this stops now."

Every nerve ending in her body went on high alert as she gave him an incredulous expression. A slow, wolfish grin broke across his face before his intense eyes darkened, and he took each of her hands from his body and pinned them over her head. Maggie's breath caught in her throat, her voice tight. Flux was taking away all her control, yet he wanted her to take it back from him: a weird power struggle that she'd never engaged in during sex. Nine times out of ten, she was used to being the aggressor, but she never had to ... speak.

"Flux," she whimpered in warning, squeezing her thighs around his waist.

"Duchess," his dark tone mocked her before he kissed the tip of her nose and meandered down the sensitive skin of her neck with the flat of his tongue.

She hissed and arched against his touch, hungry and desperate for more of him.

"Just say the words and it's yours ..." His warm breath lingered along her collarbone as he pinned her to the bed with his body weight, lightly squeezing her wrists with his one hand. "I know you've got it in you, darlin'."

Maggie gulped, strung out on the scent, the touch, and the taste of him as he completely engulfed her small body. Flux's free hand roamed idly over her exposed stomach, a light touch that belayed all of the sexual aggression he would unleash on her if only she learned to use her words.

"I need you to ..."

"Yeah?" Flux's voice became coaxing, his finger easing along the line of her skirt, barely brushing over the top button before he curved his palm around her breast through her bra.

Even that small touch sent a shockwave of sensation through her, and she writhed beneath him unable to do a damn thing so long as he had her pinned to the bed.

"Put your mouth on me," she whispered as she ground herself against him. "I need your mouth on my breasts ... everywhere ..."

She had barely finished speaking when he lifted up off of her body. *Oh shit, are we stopping? Did I say something wrong?* He stood between her legs and stared down at her splayed, still-clothed body as if she were some kind of work of art. She wasn't used to such smoldering attention as his gaze took in every single inch of her before his hands drew back to the edge of her skirt.

Their eyes locked and he licked his lips.

"Do you care about this top, Duchess? Not a favorite?"

"W-what?" she stuttered.

He nodded as if that answert was good enough for him. But she hadn't really said much of anything before his large, delicious hands ripped her top in half, leaving it to hang in ragged edges off her body. She shuddered from the pure lust that vibrated down her nerve endings and watched in awe as Flux bent down and circled her navel with his tongue.

Such a light, teasing touch shouldn't have had such an impact.

"I like that you haven't moved for me, Duchess. Good." Flux's voice rumbled up from low on her torso. "Keep your hands like that until I tell you to move them."

Maggie closed her eyes, trembling from his tongue as he licked a path from her stomach to up under her bra, lightly tracing along the edges of each cup. She sucked in air as if she were drowning, and the rest of their surroundings fell away.

"More—please, more." She didn't dare move her wrists from above her head, but she angled her vision so she could watch as his tongue circled and teased her. When their eyes connected, his gleamed with lust and something deeper.

"I like the sound of that, darlin'."

He nipped at her tight nipple through the bra and then undid the front clasp with one hand. No sooner had she taken a ragged inhale, his mouth closed around her nipple with the slight press of teeth. Maggie bucked with a low groan. He laughed, quite possibly the sexiest sound in the world, as he continued sucking and toying with her. By the time he moved onto the other one, she was a panting, wet, frantic mess.

His fingers flicked and massaged and pinched her hard nipple while his warm, wet mouth closed in on the other, leaving her breathless and nearly mindless from the multiple sensations. By the time he was done, it took all of her willpower to keep her hands anchored above her head. A final nip with his teeth made her gasp.

Maggie gazed down the line of her body as Flux slid lower toward her jean skirt. His look held a-million-and-one promises: dark, dangerous, and ready to please her; all she had to do was ask. She bit the inside of her bottom lip and rolled her hips upward, hoping that was enough of a signal while he kneeled between her legs, his mouth so close to exactly where she wanted him.

Flux arched a brow and made a soft chiding sound with his tongue.

"What do you want, Duchess?" he said in a low voice.

She swallowed, her body heavy with arousal and her mind not working quite right. Connecting sounds to her mouth seemed like the hardest chore in the world right now, and he was expecting her to speak to him? A small whimper came out of her lips. Flux grunted as his hands slid between her back and the mattress to unzip her skirt, and she moaned when he yanked it down to her knees.

"You gonna answer me?" he asked thickly. He pressed his hands into her thighs, drawing small circles with the rough pad of his thumbs.

She writhed beneath him, her mind numb with pleasure and anticipation of what was to come. "Flux," she panted.

"I'll take that as an answer 'cause seeing you flushed and so fuckin' ready is more than I can take."

Flux's words were stolen away as she watched his head delve between her legs, and then she sensed a warm, teasing wetness against her panties as he licked her through them. Small, little touches, offering nothing but torment to the real feeling that was building deep inside her as he played with her body.

Although she tried to coax him further, her legs were bound by her skirt. There wasn't much she could do but submit to his control of her body. Even a small arch was made harder by the caged fabric. She yearned to grab his head and drag it exactly where she wanted it—but that wasn't the point, was it? Instead, she challenged herself to take his pleasure-filled teasing and allow him to take the wheel, as much as he wanted her to wrestle it back from him.

The power exchange was new and charged with lustful expectation. Sure, she had thrown in a few dirty words and sometimes full-on sentences to ease a guy's nerves or to drive home that she liked something. But this? This was very different territory as Flux gently took her panties between his teeth and pulled them to the side, anchoring the soft fabric with his fingertips.

"I thought, you said … you couldn't wait …" Maggie groaned as Flux's breath ghosted across her sensitive outer lips, and the warm burst of air made her tingle and writhe as much as her trapped skirt would allow. "Please, Flux."

His name was whispered on a gasp as Flux flicked his tongue across her most intimate place and stars shot across the backs of her eyelids. She clenched her hands together so as not to move them, then he eased his tongue around her sensitive clit before catching her off guard and driving his tongue into her opening in a move that nearly had her sitting up.

"Oh God, yes. More."

These kinds of noises she could manage, if only it would keep him between her legs. Maggie alternated between trying to keep her eyes open so she could watch him, and closing them as he did something amazing with his lips, that tongue, and his teeth. She couldn't capture a specific pattern. Just when she thought he'd repeat a certain motion, he'd lightly nibble her clit or tongue her slit instead. None of it was the same in method or strokes or intensity, and keeping her constantly guessing brought her to the edge quicker than she was used to, as his other hand anchored her to the bed by her hip bone.

When a single digit slid into her wetness, she clenched hard around him. Torn between the lust that was making her feel wanton and greedy, and the blush that stroked beneath her skin, she submitted to his slow strokes inside her body as her muscles grew tight.

"That's it," he coaxed against her as she attempted to rock her hips up to meet his strokes. "Fuck, Duchess, you taste like heaven in my mouth."

Before Maggie could reply, he clamped his mouth around her hardened nub, setting her on fire. Goosebumps coated her skin as her thighs pressed together. Her hands desperately clung to each other, so she didn't make a single move that would make him stop this exquisite torment. Even the coolness from the clunky air conditioning unit blew insistently against her hard nipples, teasing all her exposed flesh as his hot warmth took her to new heights.

"I need ... more ..." she begged through her tight throat, quivering on the cusp of an orgasm and desperate for him to push her over the edge.

"Since you've been so good, darlin', I don't think that'll be a problem," he growled against her aching nub before turning away and gently biting her inner thigh. "Stay exactly as I've put you, understand?"

Maggie nodded, silently frustrated with his need to move at all while she watched him quickly throw her skirt on the floor, shuck his clothing, and walk over to the nightstand and pull out a foil packet. She closed her eyes again and tried to catch her breath. Her body reeled with desire, fueled by only one single objective—Flux inside her while she clung to his shoulders.

"Are you ready, Duchess?" Flux's cock twitched against her thigh and he ran himself between her folds, lightly teasing her opening, exactly as he'd done with his lips, tongue, and teeth. "Tell me when you're ready. I want to hear the words."

He slid across her wetness, extra slick from her arousal and the condom he'd just rolled on. His dick was thick and big and so damn hard—and she figured he was reveling in his ability to make her bend to his will.

"Please, Flux, I'm ... ready."

"What was that? I don't think I quite—"

Maggie's whole body shook and ached for him, every nerve-ending doing the talking when she couldn't say a coherent word. She was out of her mind with need for him. She arched her back in anticipation, hungry for Flux to touch her again. Biting her lip, she silently demanded that he sink inside her wet heat.

Flux looked down at her, his eyes glazed with masculine pride and heady arousal as his dick bobbed against her thigh before he started teasing her all over again. She spread her legs wide and bucked up toward him.

"Fuck me. Now," she ordered.

"That's it, Duchess." Flux chuckled as he arranged himself over her body. "Wrap your legs around me and hold on tight."

There wasn't time to agree. With one chaotic beat of her heart he worked himself against her outer lips, and then in the next, he was buried deep inside her as she rocked her hips up to meet him. They joined in a chorus of sounds. His groan sent a flurry of shivers down her spine as she gasped and spasmed around him, grinding upward into him so he could sink himself even further.

"Fuck, darlin'. You feel so damn good. So tight ... so perfect," Flux murmured against her neck before biting her tender flesh and sending her into a spiral of pleasure as his hips picked up the pace.

True to his word, she had to hold on to him. There was nothing slow and easy about his deliberate, claiming thrusts. Her thighs ached, clinging to him and she fought to match his rhythm as they drove each other over the edge.

"Fuckin' touch me," he rasped against her lips before pushing his tongue inside her mouth.

Maggie moaned and released her hands from the death grip around each other, and then raked her tingling fingers through his hair. That quickly switched to driving her nails down his back when he plunged into her deeper, thrusting in and out so damn fast and hard that it left her breathless and craving for more. Never had she felt this much rapture or intensity or anything even close to this during sex.

Faster. Harder. Deeper.

God, she would never get enough of him. His hot, flexing muscles worked beneath his flesh as he forced pleasure through every inch of skin. Maggie squeezed and felt up and mauled every inch of Flux that she could get her hands on, and by the way Flux groaned and grunted, she knew this was as intense for him as it was for her.

"I fuckin' love your tits." When he moved his mouth back down to them, she arched her back again, offering herself to him with a bone deep sigh of bliss.

"So ... close," she whimpered, threading her fingers through his hair and yanking a bit, urging him to go a little harder.

Flux didn't disappoint. His teeth closed over her nipple at the same time his hand clasped around her ankle and brought one of her legs to rest on his shoulder. The intimate angle shifted at the same time his strokes became more frenzied, eating away at what was left of her rational mind. Before, Maggie thought he had brought his A game, but he'd been going easy.

Now he rocked into her so hard that the part of her that was barely aware wondered if they would break the cheap motel bed. Then all at once, there wasn't a thought left in her head as she tensed, and then shattered. Maggie gasped against his lips, moaning as she eased her own down his neck. Her arms and legs flexed around him, her toes came to a point against his shoulder while her muscles contracted and she lost all sense of reason.

"Oh fuck!" she cried out as the edge she'd been riding since Flux first started teasing her rocketed to a fine point where everything became crystal clear and jumbled all at the same time. A series of small quivers clenched through her abdomen before they released into a wave that wrung out her body beneath him.

"Almost there, Duchess. Give me ... one more. I'm not fuckin' asking ..." Flux panted, grinding against her hypersensitive core as he bent forward, deepening the angle.

Maggie clung to him, writhing from her first orgasm as his hand fumbled between them and deftly played against her clit. No sooner had he started rubbing in small circles together with his relentless thrusts than she fell again into the deep void of ecstasy where her brain completely shut off.

And this time Flux groaned and swore, his hips bucked abruptly as he followed her orgasm with one of his own while his hands clutched at her hips and her breasts and pulled at her hair.

"I can't fuckin' get enough of you, Maggie," he whispered, panting above her and still joined together as they both slowly came back down. "That was ... yeah ..."

"Uh-huh," Maggie panted, swallowing through her parched throat and maneuvering him back down so she could kiss him. What started off as frantic and hungry fed into something more tender and unexpected as their tongues delicately danced together.

"That was what I needed," Maggie muttered, stretching beneath him as all the little aches and pains from riding fell away against her post-orgasmic bliss. "Ugh, don't move yet."

Flux went to get up off her and he blinked in a dull, still slightly hazy surprise; but before he settled all his weight back on her, she readjusted her leg and wrapped it back around him like a blanket.

Their heartbeats echoed each other against her chest as he burrowed his face into the side of her neck and let out a long sigh that seemed to release years of tension he'd been carrying in his body. Flux mumbled something that she couldn't quite hear before he scooped her up and carried them both higher onto the bed until her head was surrounded by pillows. He rolled off the mattress and walked into the bathroom, and she pulled the covers snug around her. Her eyelids had just started to close when they snapped open as he crawled under the sheets and drew her to him. Secure under his arm, her skin shivered under his light touch as he ran his fingers through her hair.

"Sleep, Duchess. I'm not moving." He nuzzled into her neck, lightly nipping at her ear.

They stayed entangled that way until she drifted into a gentle, soothing sleep.

## CHAPTER TWELVE

# FLUX

FLUX WOKE UP to Maggie's gentle snores, his arms wrapped around her as he cradled her against his chest while he slept on his back. A stab of white-hot terror momentarily stunned him dumb. For something that was supposed to be casual, this was pretty fucking intimate. Warning bells went off in his head, fast and hard, as he surveyed the rest of the room.

He'd made sure Maggie was okay with everything that went down between them. That was more important than anything, especially after what that asshole had made her feel the previous night. But hell, maybe he hadn't looked at his own feelings before things went down between them. He wiggled a little in discomfort, annoyed by the fact that he even had feelings to examine.

No strings. Casual. One and done.

All of his rules flew through his head, but as Maggie burrowed harder into his chest, he knew with a resounding level of deep-seated fear that there was only one other woman he'd woken up to this way, and he'd married her. *Fuck.* Any other girl who came in and out of his bed didn't get this treatment. It was a silent agreement that they would be gone after the deed was done.

He swallowed thickly and forced back the pounding headache that had taken residence in his skull the second he opened his eyes. He had a fucking hangover from not having a hangover. *Goddamn it!* He scrambled to figure out what to do next considering that the past six years he'd spent his time alone and avoided anything like this in the first place. Maggie muttered in her sleep, her golden blonde hair fanning out over his chest.

"Shit," he mouthed, clenching his jaw.

She was achingly gorgeous in the morning light, covers half splayed off her naked body so he could trace the lines of her curves and drink her in for as long as he wanted to without getting sick of the sight. *That* was part of the fucking problem. After the night before, he didn't know if he could handle a repeat, but that was all his body wanted right now.

While this wonderful woman had given him everything the night before, he was still the fucked up, head case who was dead inside. But as much as he hated to admit it, Maggie had brought him back to life again, even if for a small period of time, and that's exactly why he couldn't do it again. No, not when his emotions were too close to the surface with this one.

Maggie threatened to bring him to his knees if he allowed her to get any closer—and no one could take Alicia's place. He owed his dead wife that much, if not every damn breath in his fucking body. He didn't deserve happiness or forgiveness, and any part of Maggie that could erase the memory of Alicia needed to stay far away.

Another time, another place—

Flux jerked upward too violently before he caught himself and kissed Maggie's temple as she murmured something and rolled over, falling back to sleep. Fuck, he hated to be this asshole, but he couldn't be anything other than what he was at his core. Walking out on her now was what they'd agreed on, and it was a good warning for her not to get near him again. He'd only bring her pain.

With an exaggerated carefulness, Flux eased out of the bed and threw on his clothes as he tried to make as little noise as possible. He never should've agreed to fucking her without getting his head on straight first. But she wanted and needed him so much, and Flux craved her with a hunger he hadn't known for a very long time. He shook his head. *It was just one night of mindless fun. There was nothing else to it, and it wasn't supposed to be anything else. Duchess wanted it that way too.* So why did his brain insist on perverting it and making it all emotional and bullshit? He spiked his fingers through his hair, unable to rip his attention away from Maggie's gently breathing form.

He picked up the keys from the dresser and walked to the door. It was better for both of them. A selfish dick move, but she needed to know what she was dealing with, and he didn't have any better way to show her than to be exactly who he was. It was better she knew now than have any bullshit expectations.

The thought that he'd abandoned Alicia when she'd needed him most flitted through his mind, but he pushed it back and refused to deal with it. Flux clenched his fist on the doorknob and steeled himself to skulk away back to the fairgrounds. Maggie deserved a man without his kind of baggage: a man who moved from day to day as if nothing mattered and nothing existed. He didn't have any roots, and he simply went where the road took him. *Fuck, she doesn't even know me that well.*

Well, now Maggie never would, and she'd be better off for it. He only had to look at his track record to know that, clear as fucking day. He walked out of the room and into the hot morning air. Squinting against the sunshine, he made his way across the parking lot.

★ ★ ★

MAGGIE KEPT HER eyes screwed shut while she heard the door gently close behind him. When the rumble of his motorcycle dissipated, she sprawled out on the bed and took a deep breath, hating how she loved that his wood and leather scent lingered in the bedding. He was everywhere she looked and tasted and touched as he seeped into her skin.

She had no regrets, even if her heart had pounded watching him go and not being able to say anything to bring him back. Maggie gripped her sides and shivered, closing her eyes. His side of the bed was already cold. Still, the heated montage of everything they did together the night before played in a loop on repeat in the front of her mind, so there was no way she could forget a single second.

But she wasn't naive or stupid. There was no way she didn't know what she was taking on with his intimacy issues. He was a rumor unto his own in the rodeo fairgrounds, and he went through women like other men went through chewing tobacco. Fast and hard, his addiction was never sated, yet neither was that haunted look in his eyes.

Maggie wasn't his savior or therapist.

The night before had been life changing, but when he'd violently jerked this morning and had woken her up, she sensed his heart-rate shift and gallop in his chest and knew waking up to a woman wasn't an everyday occurrence for him. Flux's fingers had trembled beneath her as he angled to get away from her and the bed. He'd fumbled to get his clothes on judging by the soft, jerky footfalls, the way his belt buckle had clanged, and how he'd muttered a curse because of it.

Everything about their night together had been so perfect, and in the morning light it had suddenly drawn to a close as she witnessed all of his imperfections on display. The last thing she wanted to do was rip his pride from him when he was at his most vulnerable. No need to rub salt into the wound or start a big, overarching conversation that would lead neither of them anywhere.

So Maggie played it cool, as best as she could, and let him have his moment sneaking out the front door. If she happened to see him later when she hit the fairgrounds, she'd say hi. They'd act like friends, like nothing had happened between them, and things would be normal.

Maggie sighed and curled up tighter in the sheets, squeezing her eyes together.

"It'll all be fine," she whispered into the silent darkness of the room as the air conditioner shuddered out a blast of icy air.

After making sure no one was around, Maggie sneaked back to her room for a quick shower and a change of clothes then made her way to the rodeo.

An hour later, Maggie left the stables after taking her horse, Odysseus, for a practice run in the ring before the match, then she stalked by the bull fighter's area. It didn't count as bugging Flux if they weren't dating. And she actually did have to go that way to get some of her cleaning tools to rub her horse down before their barrel run that night.

It was all logical and her reasoning was sound, but explaining it to herself made everything weird. She shouldn't have to make excuses to see a man, especially one who was a friend—one whom she'd slept with the night before—and whom she worked with to boot. Maggie mentally chided herself for even surpassing her first instincts and sleeping with him when she knew damn good and well at the very beginning that there'd be possible consequences. *What the hell is the matter with me? There aren't any consequences right now except the ones in my head. We had a helluva good time last night. Great. Finished. Done. I need to stop thinking about it.*

For all she knew, Flux wasn't even there—

*Shit!* The rugged biker stood outside one of the bull pens talking to his boss, his usual bandana tied around his head instead of the token cowboy hat that almost everyone preferred in the rodeo. One hand was in his pocket and the other balanced him against the fence post. He looked more worn down than usual, his stance slightly off. His boss nodded once, Flux did his version of a nod, and then his boss headed off in the other direction.

"Hey, stranger, how's your day going?" Maggie made it sound as casual as possible, and she stayed where she was so she didn't overwhelm him.

"Fine." Flux sounded monotone, and he didn't even look in her direction before he started walking off somewhere else.

"Hey, are you okay?" Maggie pressed her luck and followed behind him, trying not to take it personally that he was giving her the cold shoulder. She wanted to give him the benefit of the doubt, but he didn't even turn to acknowledge her presence.

## FORGIVENESS

It was entirely possible that he was having a bad day. *Yeah ... that's it.* The problem was that Flux wasn't being subtle in ignoring her as she fought to catch up with larger than normal strides. This was getting a bit ridiculous. Maggie made a noise of frustration that she sure as hell didn't try to hide from him.

It wasn't like she was being overly clingy or weird about their night together—she hadn't even brought it up at all. All she did was ask him about his day as politely and non-threateningly as she could, short of the silent treatment, which was what he appeared to be sporting with her at that very second. It was childish and beneath him to just keep walking while she followed behind him, and she felt like a pathetic doormat loser doing it.

"You know what? Fine. When you feel like talking, you know where to find me. I hope whatever crawled up your ass dislodges itself soon," Maggie said, stopping about halfway across the yard before she headed in the opposite direction.

Maggie entered into the covered back area of the fairgrounds, paused to retie her hair back, and tried not to take personal offense to Flux's behavior. After all, hadn't she wanted a man who could go about his business without stalking her day and night after they'd had sex? Wasn't she the one who said if they got together it would be a one-time thing with no strings attached?

It appeared her wish had been granted and she'd gotten more than she'd bargained for—and then some. There was no reason for his rebuke to hurt. She would try again later, and if he still wanted to be an ass, well, she'd learned her fucking lesson, hadn't she? With a bucket of reality mixed with resolve coursing through her veins, Maggie went to retrieve the items she needed for Odysseus and put her head back to where it should have been in the first place.

Men were distractions. So long as she could keep her head in the game and her heart in the ring while she rode Odysseus, nothing else really mattered in the long run. She should be cherishing every single day she got to do what she loved for a living. Nothing else would ever be as important—certainly not a one-night stand with the rodeo *Lothario*.

As the day went by, Maggie's anger grew and Flux's rebuff ate at her, so by late afternoon, Maggie stalked away from the stables in search of Flux. It was so obvious that after the awkwardness by the bull pens, he'd gone out of his way to not see her. Each time she'd caught a glimpse of him earlier that day, he'd disappear and that pissed the hell out of her. As Maggie looked around for the rugged biker, she kept telling herself that he wasn't important in the grand scheme of her life, but she knew that was a damn lie. *I screwed up big time last night.* She brushed the sweat from her brow and marched forward. There was something about their night together that made her feel all mushy inside and *that* burned her ass to no end.

*I want to spend more time with him.* The thought took her by surprise and her gasp bounced off the concrete walls. Whether Flux wanted to admit it or not, there was a strong connection between them and it'd been there from the moment they'd danced that first night at the bar. *And I ran to him after Chet upset me. I didn't go to Larissa or Sandy. Ugh ... I'm sick of all this shit.* Just thinking about Flux created a mess of opposing feelings: warmth and affection spread through her while hot, vulnerable rage burned in her belly.

*No one, absolutely no one, disrespects me on my turf.* As the bull pen area drew nearer, pride told her that Flux was like any other man she went toe-to-toe with over the years, just a guy who needed some verbal sense slapped into him. *Once I'm done saying my peace, he can ignore me all he wants and I won't give a shit. I'm stronger than that. So the sex was mind blowing. My feelings are clouded by that. I just desire him and wouldn't mind a repeat performance. I'm mixing affection up with pure lust.* Of course, she shut down that damn inner voice of hers and kept walking.

With the mental pep talk invigorating her, Maggie pinned her shoulders back and strode into the stables. She had one more thing to do before she could seek out Flux, although it was more for her own well-being than her horse's. She always kissed the tip of his nose for luck, and before confronting Flux, she felt like she needed all the luck in the world.

"... see, shit's never fuckin' easy. Connections? Fuck it, you know?"

Maggie halted in her tracks and narrowed her eyes. "You've got to be kidding me," she murmured under her breath, worried she was hearing things that didn't exist out of her own anxieties.

"What the hell am I doing talking to a motherfucking horse?" Flux groaned and she heard a loud bang as if Odysseus had stomped his hoof down in agreement.

Maggie swallowed and inhaled a deep breath. *Why's he with Odysseus? And he's talking to him. Has he lost it?* She heard Flux murmuring, but it was too low for her to make out any of the words. She slowly approached Odysseus's stall, figuring that she should make a noise or something. As much as she didn't want to ruin the moment and take him by surprise, he would probably keep yapping and she needed to talk to him.

Maggie coughed then heard the shuffle of footsteps then silence. Turning the corner, she saw him standing in front of Odysseus. "Flux, what're you doing in there?"

## CHAPTER THIRTEEN

# MAGGIE

MAGGIE'S HORSE POKED its head out of the stall followed by Flux's confused expression, which quickly turned guarded as soon as he saw who was speaking. He cleared his throat and tucked something into the pocket of his cut.

"Is that a flask? Are you drinking on the job?" Maggie felt like a school teacher wagging a finger at a student. "What's going on with you?" There was no way to keep her accusatory tone on lockdown.

Flux grunted and hid from view, making her outrage simmer to a low hum of disbelief that made her ears ring. *What kind of child did I sleep with last night?* How could he put himself in danger by drinking when he spent a majority of his day surrounded by huge bulls that could spook with the wrong movement and flay him in an instant?

Instead of talking, Maggie unlocked the paddock door, grabbed Flux by his cut and dragged him out into the narrow hallway that separated all the stalls. Once she'd locked up after petting Odysseus on the nose, she flung her full attention at Flux.

"Explain. Talk. Make words happen. Now." She squared off in front of him, planting her feet shoulder-width apart with her hands on her hips. "I know you know how to have an adult conversation, so break out the good stuff now or I'll out you so fast your head will spin. Got it?"

Maggie hated the idea of resorting to being a rat fink, but that was the only threat she had in this fight. She didn't have a clue if she'd get anything out of him without it, given their screwed-up emotional circumstances. Flux leaned against the wall and crossed his muscular arms, straining his tight black T-shirt as he crossed his legs at the ankles. The guy even refused to wear the usual cowboy boots, and instead went for steel-toed shit-kickers. Maggie's gaze skittered over his body as she absorbed how far away he was from her normal type, yet how right things had felt the night before between them.

"Don't fuckin' threaten me, *Duchess.*" He jammed his hands into his pockets, and she saw a muscle jump in his jaw.

Flux's look went through her with an icy blow, but Maggie pretended to shrug it off. He licked his lips, shaking his head with a snort through his nostrils.

"You wanna talk to me so badly that you're throwing threats at me? I don't go for that. Doesn't seem very friendly to me, now does it?"

"I think we passed friendship about four hours ago, big guy." She glowered at him, ignoring the wild beating of her heart.

Maggie had never in her wildest dreams felt as pulled in by this biker than she had by any of the upright, cowboy types who'd fallen in her romantic path over the years. And that was the trouble. Sure, she'd only known him for a short time, but he was like a burr stuck on the bottom of her foot that just wiggled its way deeper into her skin. No matter if they ignored each other for the rest of eternity, the way he'd touched her, the way he'd talked to her—it would all be etched in her head as "the bar," and good luck to any other man who tried to compete with it.

"Yeah ... I guess we did." Maggie started to say something but he cut her off with a scowl. "You wanted to listen to me, so fuckin' listen 'cause I'm only saying this shit once."

She nodded and dropped her hands down to her sides as a burst of adrenaline made her lightheaded. Whatever was coming, it had to be some kind of turning point. Maggie tried to mentally prepare herself the best way she could while Flux rubbed a dirt-streaked hand along the back of his neck before cracking his knuckles.

"Nothing about being near you is fuckin' easy, you know that,

Duchess?"

Maggie didn't make a sound. She was too afraid to break whatever spell allowed him to talk to her without walking in the other direction.

"Last time I checked, I wasn't a billboard, so I don't need to advertise myself to anyone. No one gets to demand jack shit from me, except my brothers in my MC. Do you see any of them here right now? Because I sure as hell don't, but I'm here talking to your perky little blonde ass because you asked me to. Shit."

"That's it?"

Flux splayed his hands on his thighs. "Whaddya want me to say? That I've been a fucking dick all day?" His gaze flew to her face, but the anger in his eyes had been replaced with something infinitely softer.

*Tenderness? It couldn't be.* Maggie moved her boot around the dirt in circles. "Yeah, because you have been a fucking dick."

Flux exhaled a long breath like he'd been holding it for a while. He blinked at her. A muscle tensed, then loosened in his jaw. "Yeah, well … fuck … this isn't easy, Duchess. I thought it would be like all the others and fall right back into place—with the two of us on the same page that what we shared was nothing more than pure sex. But fuck, that isn't what happened and we both know it." He cracked his knuckles again and moved his head from side to side like he was working out a kink or something, then he tilted his head back. "Whenever I close my eyes, I see you staring up at me. I fuckin' hear your greedy little moans in my ears. And your scent, you fuckin' marked me up last night, and all I can taste past this goddamn whiskey is your lips."

Flux's gaze never wavered. He watched her intently as if gauging her response, and Maggie had to keep herself locked in place so she didn't go to him. Now wasn't a good time, even if every muscle in his body seemed to strain beneath the burden of airing everything out that was inside his head. He turned around and put both his hands on the top of the stall, leaning his weight against the wood.

"What I did this morning and this afternoon was fuckin' wrong of me—you didn't deserve it." He breathed out an audible exhale, a whoosh of air that made Maggie tense again, wondering what could be coming next. "But you don't know me, Duchess, and you need to walk the fuck away right now before you get to know me."

"Flux, I don't need you to make cho—"

He held up one hand to stop her from speaking, and Maggie forced her lips closed while everything inside her longed to argue with him. But he needed this space to air out his shit. If she didn't give it to him, who knew when he would clam back up again and re-erect all those walls.

"It's my fuckin' job to do everything in my power to keep you the hell away from me. You don't have a goddamn clue what darkness I got inside me. You and I would never fuckin' work. I don't want any woman in my life. I'm a nomad, choosing to live in solitude. I stayed away from you today for your own fuckin' good, even if you don't see that right now, Duchess."

"I don't believe that for a second, Flux. For some reason you've decided that you should live a life of pain and loneliness and that's batshit crazy. I don't understand why can't we be friends. It's not like I'm proposing marriage here." Maggie threw her hands up, at a loss for why he would want to completely cut her out of his life when they had a good thing going between them. "I just want you to acknowledge that I exist and, maybe, go out for a few beers once in a while, okay?"

Flux pursed his lips and shook his head. "No, it's not okay. That's how shit starts with us. It'll never be one or two beers and then we're done, it'll be one or six beers and then we're fucking in your truck or I have you pressed up against a tree with my hands in your pants. This isn't something I can escape or get rid of or scrub from my damn head." He was breathing heavy as he turned around to face her and the rawness that sculpted his features took her breath away.

"Something changed last night. I know you know what the fuck I'm talking about so don't play dumb, Maggie. I can't come back from that place. And you don't wanna know why I can't go there with you ... You don't wanna know me at all because you won't like what I bring into your life. Just be satisfied to leave me in the one-and-done category, and let me get on with the rest of my fuckin' existence."

"Flux, the fact that you're opening up to me right now is a huge sign that we can be something other than what we were together last night. You're manning up, but you're also being vulnerable with me. I need you to know that I appreciate it, and I get how hard it must be for you." Maggie didn't want him to just slip away from her—she wasn't ready for that, not now ... maybe not ever.

Flux flinched as if she'd struck him, but then she watched the mental wheels turn in his head as he digested the magnitude of her words. There *was* hope for them. If he could break himself down to her right now, at least work on stripping down his walls like this, then he couldn't be nearly as bad as he thought he was inside.

"There's nothing wrong with us being friends and casual sex partners. Neither of us will toe the line and we can keep it all separate. I'm a big girl."

Flux looked skeptical as he stomped his boots in the dirt and glared in her direction.

Maggie took a step forward as a soft smile brushed across her lips. "Do you really think I would risk breaking one of my hard-fast rules of not getting intimate with anyone I work with if I didn't trust what we have together? We keep it honest and you double down on the communication instead of hiding from me and we'll be golden."

"Are you trying to convince me or yourself of that fact, Duchess?"

Now, it was her turn to flinch and look at the facts he was laying down for them both before she jumped into anything without a parachute.

"If we do this, are we seeing other people?" Maggie asked the question as if his answer didn't matter. "I think that's important to figure out."

The best thing they could do was outline the parameters. As long as she knew her course, she could stay in the lines. That was how it worked with barrel racing and that was how it would work with him. *"Know your boundaries."* Her coach's voice echoed in her head. She'd been hearing that since she was a kid.

Flux's eyes narrowed, his lips becoming a grim line. "You wanna fuck other people?"

"Do you?" she countered, tilting her head to the side.

"No," he replied gruffly, the single word portraying a slew of emotions. "I want just you."

Suddenly Flux's intentions blazed through his expression, every inch of him telegraphing a masculine sense of possession that made Maggie take a step backward. A warm blush flooded her cheeks and she chewed at the inside of her cheek and crossed her arms. His intense gaze never let up, and she hated showcasing to him exactly what was on her mind.

Polite wasn't really his thing. To a degree, she appreciated the gruffness. She would never have to wonder where they stood with each other and that alone was refreshing. Still, she wanted nothing more than for the blush blazing across her face to go away. Or she would at least settle for the sudden ability to speak, which had gripped her vocal chords out of nowhere.

"Duchess. You haven't answered your own question." Flux licked his lips while his primal intensity made her lungs squeeze tight in her chest.

"No, I don't plan on seeing anyone else," she whispered.

"You don't plan on it or …"

Now he was being an asshole and giving her a hard time, but the teasing brought a grin to her lips as she relished the fact that he was getting back to his old self.

"I'm not seeing anyone else. If that changes, I'll send you a courtesy text." Maggie tossed her hair over her shoulder.

## CHAPTER FOURTEEN

# FLUX

*D*AMN THIS WOMAN *gets my blood boiling.* And that was one of the many things Flux liked about Maggie, but he wasn't going to think about it because what they'd just agreed to was casual fucking, and that meant no thinking about shit like *how she made him feel* or *what he liked the most about her.*

Flux's mind kept telling him to get on his bike and get the hell out of Dodge after the show that night, but he didn't want to and that's when he knew he was asking for trouble with this arrangement. *No doubt about it.* But they'd had their heart-to-heart bullshit and he had to trust that Maggie knew what she was doing in the grand scheme of things. Flux could only trust himself so far. The only thing he knew was that this decision could turn out to be the worst mistake he'd ever made by opening the door he'd kept closed since Alicia and Emily had been murdered. Murdered. The word alone burned a hole through him like acid.

"What's going on?"

Maggie's soft voice saved him from falling through the demonic rabbit hole. *Shit ... what was I thinking when I agreed to do this?* His gaze snapped to hers and he stepped forward. "Are you hungry? We got some time before the events start. I thought we could grab a bite to eat now that everything's sorted out."

Maggie eyed him suspiciously, then nodded. "Yeah, I could eat. But we're splitting the bill. This isn't a date."

"Whatever, Duchess." Flux fixed the way his cut hung on his chest. "Let me go wash up and I'll meet you by your truck—you're driving."

He was happy when she nodded, turning without a word to head toward the parking lot.

"Any reason we're taking my ride and not yours? I feel a little gypped not getting to be a bike bunny or whatever you guys call those women."

"Back warmer, biker chick, biker babe—take your pick."

"What do you call them?"

Flux shrugged. "Nothing—I don't take chicks on my bike."

Maggie's eyes widened. "You've never had a woman on the back of your motorcycle?"

Alicia's red tendrils whipping across his face and her soft body pressed against his back flashed through his mind. "Only one"—he saw curiosity light up in Maggie's eyes—"and I don't wanna talk about it. I'll meet you by your truck in ten," he said as he walked toward the washroom.

Fifteen minutes later he saw Maggie leaning against one of the concrete walls and looking down at her phone. Flux ambled over and her gaze flew up to his face; for an instant, it looked like fear, then it morphed into relief. *She thought I was that fuckin' Chet.* Anger crackled through him.

"Ready?" She threw him the type of smile that went straight to his dick.

Flux turned away, not wanting her to see what a horny bastard he was. "Yeah. I thought you'd be in the truck. It's so damn hot out here."

"I don't mind the heat as long as it's dry."

The gravel crunched under their boots as they walked toward the pickup.

"Am I ever going to get to ride on your bike?" she asked as they shuffled along.

Flux looked at her from the corner of his eye. "What is it with chicks and bikes?"

"I don't know. Maybe it's the idea of doing something dangerous and rebellious. And I bet it's fun and exciting to experience the world in a way you never could in a car." She paused for a beat, then gave him a mischievous look and added, "It's also pretty damn sexy... and a powerful Harley has that bad-boy mystique written all over it."

Women craved a ride on his bike and that didn't surprise him at all. Most chicks fawned over his metallic-green Road Glide, and he was guilty of hinting at long rides for his own sexual advantage more times than he could count, but damn, if the idea of Maggie clinging to his torso didn't make him hard all over again. Her hands on his body, squeezing right where he wanted her to be until he took one of her palms and moved it a little lower and right to his—

"Hey, big guy, where do you think you're going?" Maggie laughed, her voice dragging him out of his fantasy world.

He'd walked halfway across the parking lot away from her truck. Flux shook his head and backtracked as coolly as possible. There was no fucking way to maintain his outlaw credibility if he kept acting like a damn pussy around her all the time. Of course, there was always the chance that she would grow weary of his rough edges and his resistance to fit into her world, and she'd push him to the side in favor of a more polished, suave cowboy.

Even the idea made Flux cringe inside, but he couldn't walk into this arrangement like a blind man. Soon enough Maggie would find herself a Duke, and when that happened, he'd be back to bottles of Jack and half-burnt joints for company. At least he knew what he'd be getting if and when shit hit the fan. He'd move on to another town, another job—not the rodeo because he needed a break from it—and another chick in his bed. *But she won't be Duchess.* Flux pretty well knew that after Maggie, no other woman could compare to her. With that thought, he jacked himself up into the passenger side of her truck's cab.

"You're driving, you pick. Ladies choice."

"How chivalrous." She teased him before putting the car into gear and rocketing them onto the main road.

"You drive this thing like a pro." Flux jerked on his seatbelt and looked at her out of the corner of his eye.

"That surprises you?"

"Well, I don't see many women who can handle a pickup this big unless it's a minivan loaded with a bunch of soccer balls in the back of it."

"Oh, sick burn." Maggie taunted him with her laugh, another thing about her that went straight to his dick. "I learned to drive a truck when I was twelve. My dad needed me to help him on the cattle ranch, and he didn't want me working directly with the cows, so I got truck duty. I would ferry things out to my family when they were in the fields and pick things up that we needed during a rigorous work day. You name it and I was the girl for the job."

"How the hell did you see over the dash?" Flux tried to paint a mental picture of a younger Maggie and all he got was the blonde hair, nothing else matched up.

"I was tall for my age. It seemed like I sprouted up all at once and then stopped. Anyway, my dad taught me on a lot of the unused roads, and I mostly stuck to those while running errands, it still being illegal and all."

There was a moment of lapsed silence and he didn't really feel the need to fill it. Sitting in her presence while the intense afternoon sun beat down on his arm as he pressed his elbow against the window was enough to make him want to close his eyes and take in the rare bit of peace. Immediately, that emotion shattered as soon as he'd realized contentment flitting across his brain.

"Tell me more about you." Flux really did want to know about Maggie—from the littlest things to the bigger, life-defining moments. She was ... different. That was for damn fucking sure. He watched her with naked interest, concentrating on the smallest details, like the tiny hitch in her breath when she inhaled too deeply, and the way the small hairs at the corners of her temples were stick straight, but the rest of her hair was wavy.

"What're you doing?" she breathed out, taking a somewhat jerky right turn that jostled them both in their seats before she kept driving straight. "I can see you looking at me—there's no two-way mirror in here."

Flux quirked his lips and looked away. There was no reason to make her think he was anything like Chet, the leering asshole. At the thought of the SOB, Flux's thighs clenched tight and his lip twitched in a protective snarl. What he wouldn't give to have fifteen minutes with the fucker in a dark alley, or a lit barn stall. It didn't really matter where so long as he could sink his fist into that cocky asshole's belly.

Flux swallowed and shook his head, trying not to allow anything to screw up their time together. Even if she didn't require it, he still felt like he should at least be kissing her ass a little bit for being a bastard that morning. After all, he did have some decency left in him even after Alicia—

"I'm returning the question. Your turn." Maggie threw on her turn signal and checked her mirror a little too long than what made him comfortable.

"You checking for that asshole behind us? What does he drive?" Flux looked over his shoulder but didn't notice anything unusual.

"Why are you dodging my questions?" she fired back without missing a beat.

"I'm not dodging shit," he grumbled. Flux rubbed a hand across his mouth. He figured he owed her some information since he'd been buried inside her the majority of the time the night before. Still, the idea of opening up at all made his shoulders tighten, and he rolled them, cracking his neck. *One fucking step at a time.* Maggie was more than worth it. He blew out a breath and looked out the window, watching the sun burn hot in the bright blue sky as stucco houses with red tile roofs flew by them.

## FORGIVENESS

A loud, dramatic sigh made him glance over at Maggie. She clucked her tongue then gripped the steering wheel a bit tighter. "Okay, I'll start this." She cranked up the AC a bit even though it was fucking freezing in the cab and flicked her gaze from the road to him then back to the road. "I've never been on a motorcycle before, but I bet you've never been on a horse."

"You'd lose that bet. I grew up riding horses. I started rodeo bullfighting when I was in high school."

"Oh, yeah? Where're you from?"

"A small town in Texas—Johnson City. The biggest events around that area were the rodeos, but once I got my ass on an iron horse with the engine vibrating between my legs, I was hooked. Where're you from?"

"Greeley, Colorado."

"No shit. I used to work on a ranch, too, back in Colorado. That's where I was patched." Flux rolled the window down and stuck out his hand, wiggling his fingers into the hot air that slapped through his palm.

Maggie looked over. "Are you cold or something?"

"I just like the wind blowing on me. I'm not really fond of cages."

"Okay … you lost me."

"A cage is biker lingo for a car. If you want me to close it I can."

"No, that's all right. I can just turn the AC higher. So your club's in Colorado?"

Flux rested his head against the seat and enjoyed the breeze blowing over him. "Pinewood Springs."

"What a small world. I love Pinewood Springs. My family and I used to go there a lot when I was a kid to visit the hot springs and swim in the mineral pool. Some of my friends and I celebrated my eighteenth birthday there. We had fake IDs and we went to the Neon Cowboy and had a blast. Did you ever go there?"

"Yeah, my wi—" Flux shifted in the seat. "I used to go there often. It's a great place."

"Wouldn't that be a kick in the ass if you were there when I was?" Maggie giggled.

"Yeah, but I definitely would remember if I ever saw or met you before, Duchess. You're not the kind of woman a man forgets too easily."

A light red painted her cheeks and he grinned, loving how damn cute she looked when she got flustered or embarrassed. *Watch it. This is just casual, remember?*

"Why aren't you still in Pinewood Springs?" she asked.

"Some shit went down and I decided to go nomad. Been on my own for about six years now, doing my own thing, and occasionally going back if my MC needs me."

"Sounds lonely," she sympathized gently, but with less pity than he expected, which was a nice touch.

"It is what it is." Flux stretched out his legs as best he could in the cramped quarters.

"How old are you?"

"Too old for you."

"I don't think so. I'd say you're around thirty-one or two."

"Thirty—like I said, too old."

"How old do you think I am?"

"You look around twenty-two."

"I'm twenty-five, so you're not too old for me." She chuckled and glanced at him. "Your name is unusual. Did your parents give it to you or did you change it?"

"You like asking questions, Duchess." He tipped his head out the window and let the air blow through his hair.

"And you hate answering them."

He pulled back into the cab. "My parents named me Jared—my last name is Hughes. Flux is my road name. The brothers gave it to me because I was a rodeo kid turned biker. I traded in my horse for a motorcycle. The first year I prospected I went through a lot of bikes until I found the one that spoke to me."

"The name fits your lifestyle. I mean you're constantly moving from town to town and job to job." Maggie drummed her fingers on the steering wheel as they waited for the light to change to green. "Do you miss living in Pinewood Springs?"

"Yeah … sometimes." Flux pulled at the seatbelt. "And I suck at poker." He tacked on as an afterthought, hoping she wouldn't dig too deeply into the *wheres and whys* of him leaving behind his brothers at the clubhouse.

"I'll be sure to add strip poker into our next night together, then."

The quip was light and he snorted from the cockiness. He clamped his mouth shut and tried to keep any snide comments to a minimum as they pulled into the parking lot.

"Seriously? You're not going to say anything? That was a gimme, Flux."

Maggie parked the truck and stuck the keys in her pocket, lifting her hips off the seat. The small movement had him eyeing her up and down from those tits that he'd sucked and kneaded, to the hips that he'd kissed and licked, to her ass that he'd squeezed and bit most of the night before. He held back a groan.

"Really? You're not going to say anything now? Are you back to not talking?" Maggie huffed and frowned looking at the front door of the Happy Rooster Diner.

"Fine. Would it make you feel better, Duchess, if I told you that I regret giving you the choice to pick our spot for lunch?"

"Why?"

He shook his head. *This woman really has no damn idea. She just doesn't fuckin' get it.* Maybe he would need to fix that. Without missing a beat, Flux leaned over the console until his lips were at her ear.

"Because I can't get the idea of eating your sweet pussy out of my head … seeing all the clever ways I could make you scream my name. It seems like a helluva better use of time than sitting at a diner with slightly cold, soggy food and forced to act all polite."

Flux watched as Maggie tensed and shuddered, her lids fluttering as she inhaled. He pulled back and as she glanced up at him, her eyes sparked a flame that burned right down to his crotch. *A job well done.* He did a mental pat on the back, then placed his index finger under her chin, tipped her head back, and stole a kiss that left her gasping.

Flux's other fingers wound through her gorgeous hair, with all of its thick softness he loved, anchoring her to him as he took her mouth the way he'd been thinking of doing since waking up that morning. Part of his hightailing it out of the room had been because he'd watched her lying there like some kind of goddess, and he knew if he hadn't left, they'd still be fucking up a storm in his bed.

Flux made sure to put everything he couldn't—or wouldn't—say into the kiss as he claimed her mouth with enough ferocity that he was shocked they didn't both burn up in the truck. Maggie's small, deft fingers clung to him, little moans leaking from her lips as he teased them with his tongue before thrusting forward and taking what he thought of as his. When he pulled back, she was flushed and panting, her fingers still wrapped up in his black T-shirt.

"Well, at least we know we do *that* well," Maggie spoke through choppy breaths. She opened the cab door and a blast of heat slammed into them. Then, he watched as Maggie strode across the lot, her sexy round ass wiggling with each step.

## CHAPTER FIFTEEN

# FLUX

BY THE TIME their food had come, Maggie had managed to get a few more details out of Flux. The more he let go, the easier it was to give her the small stuff. Silly bits like his favorite color being green, or the fact that he didn't watch TV but kept it on in the background at night because the voices helped him fall asleep. Real amateur bullshit. But Maggie ate it up as if he were feeding her filet mignon. It baffled the hell out of him, but it gave him plenty of wiggle room to ask some questions of his own.

"Why do you hitch a little bit when you take a deep breath?" Flux put another nasty ass bite of overdone strip steak into his mouth and chewed until his jaw hurt.

He watched as she stilled, her fork hesitating over her salad before she caught herself and shoved the utensil into the dish so loud that the noise seemed like it ricocheted across the diner. Maggie winced, tucking her shoulders in before chewing the bite for too long. Putting the fork on her plate, she looked at the table and wiped away imaginary crumbs before speaking.

"One of the first professional matches I competed in when I started racing didn't go well." She left it at that and Flux blinked, completely unsatisfied with the answer.

"Yeah, I'm gonna need more than that, Duchess."

Her eyes narrowed as if she was trying to judge how far he was going to take things. Flux had no intention in letting up until he got the full answer. Double standard? Fuck, yeah. Did he care? Not one fucking bit.

After probing for the next several minutes, Maggie finally threw back her head in frustration then glared at him. "Enough already." She took a sip of water. "My first horse took a turn too quickly and missed one of the barrels. I overcorrected with my hands at the reins, which was a stupid newbie mistake. Totally my fault ..." She paused, playing with the fork in her salad. "When I pulled my horse too tight, he tripped and floundered, and I went flying into a fence rail. I suffered a bunch of bumps and bruises, and one of my ribs punctured a lung, so the doctor said I'd probably have to do some therapy to get it back to working properly."

Maggie wouldn't look at him. The aversion made him tense as their moods shifted, and he tried to think of what to say since Maggie was obviously upset. *I shouldn't have pushed it.*

"Let me guess, you didn't do the therapy?"

"It interfered with my training schedule." She gave him a brief little smile before her emotions closed up again. "My horse went lame. He had to be put down because we couldn't guarantee his quality of life, and I didn't have the money to pay for his upkeep as well as my new horse's. It fucking sucked." She went back to brushing away crumbs that weren't on the table.

Flux leaned forward. "You feel guilty."

Maggie's gaze snapped to his. "Wouldn't you, if you took a life like that?"

He plopped another shitty steak bite into his mouth, giving him an excuse to avoid her scrutinizing look or answering that question. No need for Maggie to know the nitty-gritty of the outlaw lifestyle. She didn't have to know Flux had killed many times before and it hadn't been animals. That shit could stay where he'd left it, with the Insurgents, until he needed to pick it back up again.

"Hey, Maggie, I didn't think I'd see you here today. What luck for me to see my pretty girl."

Flux stiffened as anger pulsed through his veins. He didn't have to turn around to know it was Chet. Flux looked at Maggie and her face was tight and pale, but her eyes pleaded with him to ignore the fucker, so Flux took a large gulp of Coke and stared straight ahead.

Then, Chet stood in front of their booth with a cocky smirk plastered on his face, but his brown orbs shot daggers at both of them. "I've seen you two around together lately, so our girl here must've gotten sick of good dick and gone looking for something easier. And to imagine, she decided to go slumming instead of going with the obvious choice."

"Clearly you weren't the superior choice," Flux growled before he slowly rose from his seat. "And if you know what's good for you, you'll apologize to the lady and get the fuck outta here. It'd be a shame if you couldn't compete for that prize money tonight."

Flux took a step forward into Chet's personal space. To his credit, the fucker didn't back down, but then Flux didn't think he had much in the brain department—too many falls on his head in the arena, he supposed.

"Flux," Maggie said gently, almost a warning.

Too fucking late.

He took another step until he was standing right in front of Chet. Flux watched out of the corner of his eye as the diner's owner stepped behind the counter and signaled for the waitresses to stay behind as well. Flux wasn't planning on making the diner a blood bath, he'd do it on the concrete in the alley.

"Let's take this outside, and I'll fuckin' teach you how to respect a woman."

Chet's face clenched down and Flux watched a hint of uncertainty ripple through his expression. Yeah, Flux was fucking used to that: big boys always wanted to puff their damn chests out until Flux called them on it. The majority of the pussies ended up backing the fuck off, and he figured the cowboy asshole was going to talk some shit before he took off in his pickup, forgoing the alley entirely. Too damn bad—Flux was itching to beat the shit out of him.

Flux cracked his knuckles then clenched his hands into fists. "You apologizing to the lady, or are we gonna settle this in the alley?"

Chet stood up straighter and thrust his chest out. "Hell, no. I'm not saying jack shit to your biker bitch. You want my leftovers, you take 'em. But you better believe she'll be thinking of me when you're between the sheets." He wrinkled his nose and fixed his gaze on Maggie. "Trash should be with trash."

Flux shot a look at Maggie to check how she was handling everything. She was tense in her seat, hands clasped in her lap as her lower lip trembled.

"And trash like you needs to be taken the fuck out." Before Chet could reply, Flux nabbed Chet's jacket as the guy tried to shake him off with surprise written all over his movie star mug.

"Get your hands off me," Chet snarled, batting away at Flux's grip as he escorted him farther away from Maggie.

"You need to leave her the fuck alone. What you did to her last night will never happen again. Do you fuckin' understand that?"

Chet's brows popped up and he blinked a few times. It seemed like the asshole didn't think Maggie would confide in Flux about what he'd pulled. Then, Chet ran his gaze over Flux as if he was sizing him up again. Chet's fists tightened and he moved from foot to foot with a curl of his lip.

"You can have the slut," Chet snarled.

That was it. Without Flux uttering a word, his fist sank into Chet's belly, and the cowboy bowled over gasping for breath.

"No one calls my girl a slut," Flux said through gritted teeth.

Flux's knee came up and slammed into the fucker's chin.

Chet cried out in pain.

"Maggie's done with you, asswipe. Grow some fuckin' balls and move on." Flux delivered the final blow—a karate chop to the back of the jerk's neck. Chet crumpled down on the checkered linoleum floor.

He was out like a light.

Pappy, the owner, rushed toward them, wiping his hands over and over on a dish rag. "Did you kill him?"

"Nah, he's just unconscious. Throw a bucket of cold water on him and he'll come to." Flux stalked back to the table, ignoring the stares from the diners. When he reached the booth, he stopped short when he saw the look on Maggie's face: eyes wide, mouth open, face blanched. She leaned back against the booth like she was ready to bolt out of her seat and flee from him.

"You can be pissed at me all you want, but there's no way I was gonna just stand there and let him fuckin' trash you. The asshole got what he had coming." Flux picked up his glass and gulped down the rest of the Coke. "Let's get outta here."

Maggie slid out of the booth and he tucked her hand in his and walked over to the cashier. They stepped over the sprawled out cowboy, and Flux noticed the asshole had started to regain consciousness. If Flux had been in the alley with the fucker, the fight might have escalated to where Chet would've been lying dead instead of knocked out. Years of studying karate had given Flux the upper hand in most fights, and he knew the exact amount of pressure to use to either kill a man or knock him out with a blow to the neck.

Flux paid the bill and Maggie didn't even protest; she was still in a daze. He didn't want to fight in front of her, but Chet left him no choice. No man acted like that with Flux and didn't get a few or more punches thrown at him. No one fucking messed with him or the people he cared about.

When they arrived at the truck, Flux jumped into the passenger's seat and waited for Maggie to turn on the ignition. She moved sideways to face him, and her brows drew together as her mouth turned grim.

"What the fuck did you expect me to do back there?"

"Since when am I *your girl*?"

Flux's stomach hardened and he grimaced.

*Ahh, Fuck!*

## CHAPTER SIXTEEN

# MAGGIE

MAGGIE LICKED HER lips and played with the ends or her hair while she waited for Flux to answer. Given his knack for avoiding questions, she didn't expect much from him. When she'd first heard him call her "my girl" a funny sensation fluttered in her stomach, and she had to admit the whole territorial thing was hot and endearing.

Maggie thrummed her fingers against the steering wheel, but Flux stared out the window without any hint of talking any time soon. She watched him wondering how their agreement to a casual sex relationship had turned into a possessive thing. There was no way she'd ever have consented to *that*. A boatload of nervous stallions bucked and galloped in her belly as she sat still as stone. *Do I want more with him? Is he just going to sit there all day without talking. What the hell?*

Maybe it would be best if they both pretended like he'd never said she was his girl and just continue like it was no big deal. Yeah ... that sounded like a nice option.

Maggie cleared her throat. "Maybe we should—"

"I was just—"

They each broke out at the same time before Flux bit off a curse and shifted in the seat.

Maggie switched on the ignition and turned right onto the street. Neither of them said a word the whole drive back to the rodeo parking lot. By the time she'd killed the engine, her shock at seeing Chet again had worn off and terrified anger had taken its place. She cradled her stomach and stared out the windshield. There was no way she could keep letting him get away with following and harassing her every day.

"You're thinking about that asshole, aren't you?" Flux's gruff voice broke the silence, startling her.

"Yeah."

"Do you want me to put him permanently outta commission?"

Maggie glanced at him from the corner of her eyes and saw that Flux was serious. "Uh … thanks for the offer but I'll pass on it."

"Then you need to talk to Charlie about the fucker."

"I don't know if that'll do me any good," Maggie muttered and turned to face him. "But I know one thing—he sure as hell isn't scaring me away from my career."

"Fuck no," Flux said as he looked out the window then back to her. "Other than exterminating the bastard, if you need me to watch over—"

"Stop right there, big guy. If you're going to go twenty-four seven bodyguard on me, let me save you the trouble. I stood up to him last night, I'll do it again. I can handle it. I'm a big girl."

Flux put his head back and closed his eyes.

"Won't hear me arguing that point, Duchess."

"Then trust me."

"Trust doesn't have shit to do with this, but I'm reading you. Hands off. Roger. I'm not an idiot."

Maggie kept the smile off her face, but just barely before Flux looked over at her and winked. She averted her gaze and smoothed her hands over her jeans. Her mind churned with possibilities for what she should say to keep her from climbing over to Flux's side to mount him.

"You look like you're thinking too hard, Duchess. You want me to take your mind off it?" Flux said in a low voice, his suggestive tone a dead giveaway that they were both locked onto the same idea.

When Maggie's breath hitched and she choked a little, his laughter was warm, rich, and a burst of sound that made him look a little less hardened and like the years of shit that had marred his life were slipping away. It was ... nice. Maggie grinned as she scooted over in the seat.

"You really want to know what you can do for me, big guy?"

"I'm at your service, Duchess."

"If you see Chet again, don't rearrange his face for my honor."

"I can't make that promise, but I can say I won't start shit first."

"I don't want you to get in trouble on my account."

"Trouble and me have been fuckin' best friends for as long as I can remember. Don't worry about it. I won't mess with him unless he starts shit with you ... and me. No way a man could let that pass."

Maggie pressed her lips together and kept his gaze. "Is that the best you can promise me?"

"Yeah, and for me it's a lot considering how badly I wanna make your problem go away."

"Then I'll take it." Maggie blew out a breath. "Chet's not the kind of man to take on a giant when he could pick on someone smaller."

"He's a pussy and a fuckin' waste of space, and there's no way in hell I'm letting him pick on you." Flux rubbed a hand over his mouth. "You call me if the asshole fucks with you again. Hell, if he so much as breathes in your vicinity, I wanna know about it, we clear?"

He locked eyes with her, and Maggie felt her legs go to jelly again, only this time it wasn't out of fear. She found it entertaining and very much like him that he didn't ask her if it was a deal. *An assuming, arrogant ruffian.* She smiled. In the short time that she'd known Flux, it seemed as if he was only cocky in the things that he could back up with reason.

"Come to my room later tonight."

Maggie weighed the car keys in her hands, acting as if spending time with him again was a decision she had to make instead of his assumption.

"What? Do I have to win you over again, Duchess?" He ran his fingers up and down her arm.

Maggie laughed then pulled away, opened the door, and slid out onto the asphalt. Flux remained seated as if he had all the time in the world to wait for her answer.

"We have ten minutes to get back to work," she said.

"I know. So after the show, I'll see you at my room. We can order in."

Maggie tossed her hair over her shoulder. "If you're going to stay in the truck, don't forget to lock the doors when you leave." She winked at him, feeling extra bratty.

Before he could answer, she strode off to the stables without answering his question that wasn't a question. Let him stew on the answer for a little bit, at least until she showed up in front of his motel room later that night.

## CHAPTER SEVENTEEN

# FLUX

*Five days later*

SILHOUETTES OF SAGUARO cacti dotted the landscape as the sun dipped behind distant mountains, painting the sky in orange and purplish hues. Flux hung a left into the parking lot filled with F150 pickups and pulled into a space reserved for rodeo employees. He jumped off his bike and scanned the area, looking for any badges before he took out a blunt and lit it. Inhaling deeply, he tilted his head back and blew out tight rings of smoke, wanting to get a good buzz on before he went inside and faced the bulls ... and Maggie.

The sassy cowgirl, who was supposed to be a brief interlude in his life, had quickly come to be so much more to him. The sound of her voice, the feel of her against him, the way she laughed, and the fucking feel-good sensations he got when he was around her floored the hell out of him. *How the fuck did this happened?* He rubbed the roach into the ground with the heel of his boots. A stab of guilt assaulted him because for the past few days Maggie had been on his mind, crowding out Alicia. As hard as he tried, Maggie's blue-gray eyes replaced Alicia's bright ones, and her blonde mass of waves edged out his dead wife's frizzy red hair. The nightmares had subsided as well since Duchess had been tucked against him during the night. A part of Flux welcomed the thread of joy that wove through him, but another part wanted the pain. Losing the bitterness and anger seemed liked a betrayal to Alicia and Emily.

"You going in?" Pete asked as he lit up a cigarette.

"Yeah. How's the crowd?" Flux replied.

"Good. It's pretty damn well sold out." A puff of smoke encircled the two men.

"How's your knee doing?" Flux asked. Pete had taken a bad spill the night before, and his kneecap looked two times its regular size.

"Hurts like a motherfucker, but I got my pads and knee guards so I should be good."

Flux nodded then glanced at the time on his phone. The bull riding event would start in about fifteen minutes and he needed to put on the plastic vest that protected the bullfighters' front, back, and sides. "I'll see you in the arena."

"Sure, dude." Pete exhaled another cloud of smoke as Flux walked to the back area.

Glancing through the wooden slats, Flux saw a sea of cowboy hats in the stands. The bright rodeo lights made the arena look like daytime, and the colorful Western shirts the "buckle bunnies"—rodeo groupies—wore reminded him of the kaleidoscopic quilt his mother had made for him when he was a child.

Flux saw Stan staying right in position, bareback on the bucking bronco. Above the music of the arena band and the excited play-by-play of the announcer shouting "Ride 'em, Stan, ride 'em! Show 'em what you got!" Flux heard the back hooves of the horse as they slammed to the ground. Dust circulated everywhere, which made him cough as he turned left toward the locker area.

Ten minutes later Flux took a quick drink of water, the sign above the fountain warned—No Spitting—and he headed for the chutes. He saw Chet astride the bull, his eyes cast downward on its back. Flux walked out into the arena and lifted his chin to Pete and Hank. Pete grinned but Hank ignored him, which didn't surprise Flux since the bullfighter and Chet were good friends.

The spectators in the stands leaned forward and the wave of tension and excited anticipation washed over the rodeo. The bull riding was always the last event of the night, and it was the one most of the crowd came out to see.

The rush of adrenaline shot through Flux as it always did before an event; the harsh reality was that he risked his life every time he stepped into the arena. It was something he'd been accustomed to with his biker lifestyle, and as a rodeo bullfighter, he'd been launched air born for sure—it came with the job sometimes. There was no fear in Flux. It went away the day he'd buried his wife and daughter. Life had dealt him a cruel blow and he now embraced the rush of facing a 1,700-pound bull in the ring. His focus was laser sharp and the bullshit demons from the past had no place in his head during a show. He respected the danger each and every time; otherwise it would kick him in the ass—maybe for the last time.

Everything was still, like the calm before the storm, and then the gate opened. The bull bellowed and shot into the air, then paused for an instant and crashed down again, nearly a ton of muscle and bone hitting the ground hard enough to cause major injury to the rider. Chet thrust his chest forward when the bull leaped ahead and the crowd jumped to their feet in a cacophony of whistling, yelling, and clapping.

"Chet is holding on strong at the five-second mark, but is he going to make it to the prized eight seconds?" The loudspeaker system crackled as Flux watched Chet ride out his time clock, hoping the jerk would be thrown on his pathetic ass.

Flux watched as the bull snorted and glared, a sure sign that shit was going to go down hard. He looked to Pete and Hank, and noticed Pete was struggling to get his ass closer in the ring. Chet still clung on, but Flux knew he wouldn't last much longer.

Then Chet was flying in the air as the crowd roared, and the excitement was so fucking palpable that Flux swore if he reached out, he could touch it. The possibility of carnage always made the spectators go wild. *Gore getters.* He'd come up with the name after the third bull riding show he'd worked.

## FORGIVENESS

Chet landed inches in front of the bull's stampeding, pissed-off ass, and without a second thought, Flux rushed toward the bull. Chet was lying on the ground, barely breathing, and Flux figured he'd probably had the wind knocked out of him. But the snorting bull didn't give a flying fuck and kept moving toward the rider.

Flux and Chet locked eyes for a split second.

In a flash of an instant, Flux measured all the ways this could go wrong for him if he let the bull get Chet. Adrenaline mixed with anger pounded through his veins as Chet scrambled in the dirt. Such a damn easy target for a bull, and all nice and wrapped up with a pretty bow.

Fear laced Chet's eyes as the bull came straight for him. Flux growled and hurled himself between the animal and the rider, kicking Chet to the side and rolling him over. The heated beast's eyes locked on Flux like a homing beacon. Flux wiggled his fingers in a "come-hither" gesture, already on the move as the bull's focus found a new target.

"Come to Daddy. Let's tango, baby," he muttered under his breathed as he saw a dazed Chet stand up on wobbly legs. Three backers hurried over and escorted the rider out of the ring.

The bull kept coming as Flux dodged the agitated beast. Every second ticked down slower than dripping molasses. He counted in his head, zigging and zagging, keeping the charging bull off his game as Flux surged toward the fence himself. *What the fuck's up with this asshole? He's not even slowing down.* Normally, the bulls would give up the chase by now, but this one seemed bound and determined to skewer Flux on his horns like a goddamn kabob.

*Shit! Where the fuck's Hank?* He darted his eyes toward the fence where he saw the bullfighter watching Flux doing a damn death dance with the enraged bull. Flux glared at him, but the bastard showed no signs of jumping in to help.

"Dude!" Flux cried out as Hank hooked his fingers through his belt loops and looked away.

The bullfighter's code was to help whoever was in the ring—period.

Full stop. Flux threw himself in diagonal toward the fence gate again. He was running out of steam; his legs burned and his jaw ached from clenching it so tight.

From the corner of his eyes, he saw Pete limping toward him from across the way, and he didn't know he'd been holding his breath until a large whoosh of relief swept out of his lungs. Pete waved his arms and wiggled his body, and the bull turned away from Flux and headed for Pete. Flux watched as the bullfighter took the animal in a number of riveting, long circles across the ring.

"Fuck," Flux muttered as he hauled himself over the ring fence and nearly fell to the ground on his ass. His eyes narrowed as he scanned the ring and then the crowd looking for Hank, but he didn't spot the fucker. *What a fuckin' pussy.* Flux rolled his shoulders and did a mental examination of every inch of his body. Once he was convinced everything was in working order, he looked back at the ring where the bull was trotting into the holding pen. It looked like Pete had gotten over the fence without too much trouble.

Flux cleared his throat, wiped his palms on his jeans, and strode forward toward the area behind the arena where most of the performers hung out before and after each show. *That motherfucker's gonna be sorrier than hell.* Flux balled his hands into fists at his sides and ignored everyone who spoke to him. His adrenaline flared across his scalp and his heart pounded in his ears while he charged forward toward a small group of bullfighters who'd gathered together in front of the bathrooms.

Hank was in the middle, neck arched back in a belly laugh that couldn't be heard from the other noises in the area. *Fucker won't be laughing much longer.* Before he knew what hit him, Flux ambushed Hank, striding into the center of the group and clocking the asshole in the face at the exact time the bastard's head righted from laughing. The SOB didn't even have his eyes open, and there was no way he could've seen it coming—much like Flux was fucking blindsided by Hank's betrayal in the ring.

The asswipe stumbled backward with his hand to his face, then wobbled on his legs as he righted himself and glared through one good eye at Flux.

"Don't act offended, you fuckin' pussy. What the fuck was that about out there? What's your goddamn problem?"

Flux didn't give Hank time to answer any of his questions before he went in for another solid swing—but his arm didn't connect because Chet grabbed his elbow. Doubly enraged by the situation, Flux growled and lunged with his non-dominant hand and swung it around in a tightly planted half-circle until his other fist connected with Chet's jaw and knocked him on his ass. The guy mus've seen cartoon stars or some shit because he sat in the middle of the floor, blinking and holding his head. Served him fucking right and, man, did it feel good.

"Feel better now, Chet? Fuck, I just saved your sorry ass. The least you could do is stay outta shit that's none of your goddamn business."

Chet groaned, baring his teeth, as he struggled to rise to his feet.

"I fucking hate you, you pussy ass biker."

"Who the fuck are you calling a pussy, cowboy?"

Without missing a beat, Flux squared off with the bastard. If Chet wanted it to go down, right here, right now, who was Flux to say no to a prime opportunity? With the excitement and terror from the ring still flowing through his system, Flux steadied his stance as Chet threw himself at his midsection and tried to bring Flux to the ground. Instead of going down, he landed a solid blow to Chet's kidney, and the bull rider cried out as he doubled up. Flux didn't let him regain momentum; he hit Chet again in the side of the head and launched a glancing blow toward the back of the rider's spine to push him off balance. By now, the surrounding crowd had gathered around the fight with enough spectators to choose sides and probably start a betting pool. Flux knew exactly what he would use his winnings for when he handed Chet's ass to him.

"Think you got more in you, pretty boy? Or are you all outta steam? Did I tire out the fuckin' pussy?" Flux taunted, shifting back and forth on the balls of his feet.

Sure, he could have laid the fucker out flat in a one-two punch combo that would have left Chet dazed and drooling, but Flux didn't want to make it easy for the cowboy. If they were going to go at it, Flux wanted it to be a proper fight and give the asshole an outside chance to face him like a man for everything he'd put Maggie through over the past few months. If that meant Flux got in a few more painful blows? So much the better.

He watched like a hawk as Chet righted himself and tried to make a tight circle around Flux, attempting to box him into place and decrease his hitting range. *Fuckin' rookie move.* The bull rider hadn't even landed a damn punch and he was angling for the offensive. Flux's upper lip curled in disgust as he made an agitated noise in the back of his throat.

"Come on, asshole, fight like a man." Flux surged forward and landed three jabs to Chet's abdomen, chest, and shoulder. "Fuck, I forgot—you're a pussy. No wonder you fight like one." Flux chuckled.

"Shut the fuck up!" Chet cried out, launching himself at Flux at the same time the biker sidestepped.

Chet's blow landed on the side of Flux's right shoulder before he went for an upper cut, and Flux grabbed his wrist, dragged him down, and switched gears. *I'm tired of this shit. Now, it's time to fight dirty.* Flux locked both his hands on the back of Chet's head, and using his own momentum against him, he drove the cowboy's face into his knee as he raised it and connected it with Chet's nose. There was a harsh, gargled scream when Flux made contact as he felt the bones crunch against his leg.

Flux backed away.

"You motherfucker!" Chet yelled as he clutched his nose.

One final blow and this would all be over. "This one's for Maggie, asshole. Flux took a sharp, deep breath that echoed through everything in him. Shit, it'd been a long-ass time since he'd felt this alive. It wasn't that often he'd get a good reason to pick a fight these days. A majority of the time it was only his fists and some inanimate objects that may or may not have survived the wrath of his anger and pain.

Chet would survive, but not without his share of bruises to remember Flux by over the next few days. Flux cracked his busted knuckles, licked his lips, and watched as a winded Chet swayed while trying to regain his concentration through the pain as blood ran down his face from his nose. With a low grunt, Flux took two quick steps forward, swept his leg under Chet, and knocked the fucker onto his back.

The sound of the cowboy's head connecting with the ground was a satisfying slap as Flux knelt over Chet and grabbed a fistful of his hair. He made the fucker lock eyes with him. The other man tried to spit in Flux's face, but only managed a pathetic dribble that wound up sliding down his chin as Flux slapped him on the side of the face and then the head.

"Have you had enough, asshole? Do you fuckin' get now what it's like to constantly have someone go after you, like you do to Maggie?" Flux smacked the man with his open palm, again and again, in a relentless set. "That's what it feels like for her when you won't take the fuckin' hint. So, I'm here to serve it to you, got it? Leave her the fuck alone from now on, or this won't end with humiliation—it'll end with your dead fuckin' body. Don't think I won't enjoy doing it either, so don't fuckin' tempt me."

"Flux? What're you doing? Oh my God!"

Maggie's voice from behind him drew him up short, as he immediately dropped the rider's head and staggered to stand up and face her with barely a scratch on him. He turned his back toward Chet. No threat was there anymore, and if one of the cowboy's cronies wanted to come finish what Chet had started, his biker radar would sense them and he'd tear them apart.

Flux locked eyes with Maggie and noted her crossed arms. She chewed the corner of her bottom lip and kept dropping her eyes to Chet on the ground and circling back to Flux. He cleared his throat, wiped his hands, and stood in front of her without a damn thing to say that would make what she was looking at any better.

"I suppose he started it," she said dryly.

Flux heard Chet's buddies pick him up and haul him off to the on-site EMT that was always on standby for any injuries in and out of the ring.

"What the hell happened?"

"The fucker got into my business. I had a problem with Hank—the asshole left me high and dry out in the ring with a madder-than-hell bull ready to impale me. I showed Hank what I thought about what he'd done, and Chet intervened." Flux shrugged. "It's really pretty simple. The asshole wanted a fight, so I gave him one."

Maggie's mouth hung slightly open and she shook her head. "Oh, Flux. Thank God you're okay."

Before he could say anything, she flung herself at him. Her well-muscled arms dropped around his neck and she squeezed him tight, as if the idea of actually losing him weighed heavy on her heart. Flux blinked a few times then wrapped his arms around her waist, locking her toned body to him from shoulders to toes. He squeezed her so tightly that they almost couldn't breathe. Maggie let out a small, content sigh.

"I'm so glad you're okay," she whispered, featherlight against the tip of his ear. "And that the big, bad cowboys didn't hurt you."

Her laughter caught in her throat as he tipped back her body and claimed her mouth with a primal noise that echoed all the way down to his soul. He took her with all the pent-up violence that still rode through his system and funneled the energy into a passion he hadn't thought would ever exist for him again after Alicia's murder. When their lips pulled apart, he grinned at her glazed-over eyes.

"I better talk to Charlie and explain what happened. He doesn't like any fighting on the grounds." Maggie rested her head against his chest.

"Yeah ... I guess I didn't think too hard about getting my ass canned when the bastard came at me."

"What'll happen if Charlie doesn't listen to reason. From the way Chet looked, I don't know if he'll be able to ride tomorrow night."

Flux kissed her forehead. "Don't worry your pretty head about me. I'm not attached at the hip with this job, it just gives me money for booze, weed, and chow. I've worked a shitload of jobs in so many cities and towns that I can't even remember them all." He brushed his lips across hers. "I'm a nomad, darlin'. I go where my bike takes me."

"I'm not ready for you to go," she said, burying her face in his shirt.

Warmth crawled up his spine and he held her closer. "Neither am I, Duchess. I can pick up some work while the rodeo is still in the city." A small sniffle hit his ears. "You're not crying on me, are you, Duchess?"

A small shake of her head.

Flux ran his hands up and down her back. "That's good 'cause I don't ever wanna make you cry." A smaller sniffle. "I'm fuckin' starving."

"Me too," she said in a small voice.

"Pete told me about a great barbecue place downtown."

"I like barbecue." Her words were muffled against his shirt.

"Darlin', I can't believe you got your face buried in my shirt 'cause I smell like ass. I gotta go to the motel and take a shower."

Maggie tilted her head back and looked up at him. "I'll find Charlie before he leaves."

He bent his head down and kissed her gently. "You don't have to do that for me."

"I know, but I want to. I'll come to your room in a half hour."

"Sounds good."

Maggie untangled her arms from around him and smoothed down her tight-fitting Western shirt. "I'll see you soon." She started to walk toward Charlie's office.

"Duchess?"

She turned around. "Yeah?"

"What're you doing tomorrow after practice?"

"Nothing much. I thought I might go shopping at the Tucson Mall with Larissa and Sarah. Why?"

"I wanna take you for a ride on my bike, but we can do it another time."

A wide grin spread across her face and her eyes sparkled. "No way, big guy. I wouldn't pass up a ride on your Harley for anything. I'm in." She spun back around.

Flux's jeans grew tight while he watched that familiar sway of her hips and the jiggle of her rounded ass as she walked away. Arousal crashed through him and he growled.

Once Maggie had disappeared from sight, Flux made his way to the parking lot, knowing a cold shower awaited him.

## CHAPTER EIGHTEEN

# MAGGIE

"WE'RE ALMOST THERE, Duchess," Flux shouted from in front of her as his Harley chopped through the hot, dry air the next day.

Riding on the back of the motorcycle, every noise was amplified and drowned out at the exact same time. The wind whipped tears into Maggie's eyes, and her hair tangled against her face as the desert landscape blurred past. She clung to Flux's hard, gorgeous body beneath his token black T-shirt, and every bump sent her hands scrambling, loosening them a fraction. Her heart jumped into her throat, and more than a few times she'd groped for a makeshift handhold and had found her palm tightening around his dick through the rock-hard bulge in his jeans.

Maggie loved the feeling of Flux's body tensing beneath her fingers whenever he moved to maneuver the bike, or when her hands wandered over his shaft. It was almost as if he and the bike were one and the same. If someone had asked her, Maggie wouldn't have thought she was missing out on anything by not riding a motorcycle, but as her body molded to Flux's and the scent of sage and sweet earthiness wrapped around her, she knew she would've been wrong. The most intense nature hike of her life, the closeness to Flux, the speed of the bike ... all of it was more exhilarating than she could've ever imagined.

Every one of her senses was on overdrive. It was a more intimate experience than anything she had ever done—pretty similar to flying on the back of a galloping horse, only faster and with twice the adrenaline. Maggie held her breath and clung to him as they took a hairpin turn, and it seemed like his wheels had left the road. Her laughter erupted out of nowhere, and the wind ate it as soon as the sound came out.

No wonder Flux lived for the ride. She understood him better now than if he'd ever tried to describe his love of riding with words. It was similar to the way Maggie would get lost in her horse, ducking and weaving, executing each small movement with a precision that made everything else in the world disappear, yet she was still aware of her surroundings.

At that moment, the feeling of flying was insanely amazing and something she would never forget, and she was thrilled they were sharing it together.

Her mouth went to his ear and her teeth toyed with his earlobe before her tongue licked the slightly salty skin of his neck. Flux threw a sharp look at her over his shoulder, and the heat in his eyes made her shiver and giggle. Maggie rested her head against his back and, once again, watched the world fall away into a smear of colors and shades: red, pink, brown, and green. Her heartbeat echoed through every inch of her body, and her thoughts were lost to everything but the moment.

"Are you ready?" Flux shouted, his voice falling away as soon as he spoke. "Hold on tight, Duchess."

Her hands clamped tighter around his waist until her fingers ached, and then Flux did something that made the bike roar and shoot forward like a bullet. The sudden increase in speed made her cry out as her stomach dropped, and it felt like she was a kid again on one of the free-falling rides at an amusement park. A million tiny pinpricks of fear rushed through her body, and Maggie was acutely aware of her mortality and testing fate; nonetheless, she felt free.

When the motorcycle took another sharp corner, Maggie's fingers scrambled again, but that time they dropped down onto Flux's hard bulge. She smiled and squeezed—three quick teases and he squirmed against her touch.

"Fuck."

Maggie felt, rather than heard, the rumble in his chest.

"Watch it, Duchess. I've got to concentrate and you're making it fuckin' hard."

Maggie smiled and leaned in closer to his ear. "That's not the only thing I want hard."

Flux threw her a heated stare then slowed the speed down a few notches. They were climbing, and soon pine trees replaced the desert's rock formations, and the hot air morphed into clear coolness. Flux turned down a small road, and fifty yards later, the bike stopped and he killed the engine. The quick shutdown left a void of sound in her head. For a few seconds, all she heard was ringing in her ears when Flux dismounted and offered his hand. Their fingers interlaced and his simple touch drew desire tight in Maggie's belly and clouded her head with a lust that nearly made her clench her thighs together. Her eyelids fluttered and she licked her lips, feeling out of place to have both her feet back on solid ground.

A lush forest of trees surrounded them, and in the distance, hundreds of saguaro cacti looked like miniatures in a Southwestern diorama. A flush of pleasure and a heady rush of excitement made Maggie squeeze Flux again in a tight hug from behind.

"You like it?" he asked gruffly and opened one of the containers behind the seat.

"It's beautiful." She pointed at the compartment. "Is that the trunk?"

Flux chuckled and took out a blanket. "Yeah, but it's called a saddle bag. I fuckin' love it up here, and I wanted to share it with you."

When he moved around her, she scooted to get out of his way, and they ended up doing a small dance as they both went in the same direction. Laughing, Flux took her shoulders and gently planted her in a spot opposite from him. Maggie's cheeks warmed and she looked away. Since they'd hooked up, everything was hot and heavy and so good between them, but it seemed right to her that they still had their little awkward moments: the small blips across the radar so it didn't exactly feel like a perfect romance novel. If it was too good, Maggie would second guess herself into screwing it up. She smiled as she watched him close the compartment. *Even when things aren't perfect, they're so much better than I could ever imagine with anyone else.*

Flux held out his hand and she tucked hers into it, following him to a grassy patch with a scenic overlook. He unfurled the blanket and shook it out before he walked over to a shaded spot under the trees and spread it. She stared at it, admiring the burgundy and rust-colored Navajo designs.

"Are you coming or what?" he asked with a wink.

"You're such a romantic." Maggie rolled her eyes in an exaggerated manner, then chuckled when Flux threw her a hard expression. She ambled toward him, and he caught her arm and yanked her flat against his body. "I was just playing around, big guy. No need to get bent out of shape." Maggie suppressed a giggled.

"Uh-huh." His hands wandered from her hips to her ass, where he squeezed gently then slapped her right cheek hard enough for her to jump. "Looks like I'm gonna have to teach you a lesson on manners."

Tingles ran down Maggie's spine and she kissed the side of his neck. When her lips found his pulse, she ran her teeth over the skin, admiring how his heart rate skittered and then skipped before raging forward again. She loved the effect she had on him. It was proof that she was beginning to break down the many walls he'd constructed around his emotions.

Still gripping her ass, Flux sat down and Maggie toppled along until she straddled him to regain her balance. The thrumming vibrations from the motorcycle still pulsed through her muscles, and her flesh felt like a live wire beneath his touch as he gently brushed back a rogue bit of hair on her cheek.

"You're fuckin' gorgeous, Duchess." His intense stare bored into her.

Maggie looked down and hid her face as a telltale blush crept up her neck and into her face. The way Flux complimented her was so real ... so *matter of fact*, and none of that kiss ass, want-to-get-in-your-pants crap she'd heard from most guys. Maybe it was because Flux was so sincere that embarrassment swept over her more times than it ever had with any other man.

Maggie leaned toward him for a light kiss, barely a brushing of lips as her fingers traced down between his pecs.

"You're an anomaly, Flux. What makes you tick deep down inside?" Maggie figured Flux would squirm with *that* question. Since they'd gotten together, he'd dodged a lot of the things she'd asked him, but she vowed to herself that he wouldn't pull that off today. The night that Hank had left Flux high and dry in the ring brought home the reality of the dangerousness of his job. She could've lost him that night, and the thought scared the hell out of her. At that moment, it'd never been more important that she understood the man who'd made his way into her bed and was quickly becoming the center focus of her heart.

Flux remained silent, pressing his forehead against her own with his eyes closed, as if even thinking about the question pained him. She squeezed her lips together and gently stroked the back of his head. Whatever it was, it was hard for him—that much was clear. Maggie moved her head away only to lay a small kiss on his brow before returning to their intimate embrace.

She wrapped one arm around his shoulders and stroked the side of his neck. "Whatever it is, you can tell me. It's okay," she reassured him, hoping he didn't sense any pressure in her words.

Flux didn't answer, he just stared over her shoulder at the expanse of desert.

"I want to get to know all of you," she whispered.

When he didn't answer, pricks of anxiety nipped her spine, and Maggie feared she may have overstepped her bounds. *I won't push him.*

Resting her head against his shoulder, she listened to his strained breathing.

## CHAPTER NINETEEN

# FLUX

MAGGIE'S QUESTION DIED in his ears, her voice still ringing through his skull as Flux tried to sort through the millions of thoughts running through his brain. As soon as he'd found *them*, he'd shut down, not talking to anyone about it, not even his brothers. A sharp wince made his muscles shake and tense, but even though Maggie must've sensed the shift in him, she didn't back down. Instead, she ran her hands over his, trying her best to soothe him like he was some sort of spooked horse or something.

Though Flux couldn't deny the ghosts from his past were spooking him—they always did. He didn't revel in the idea of bringing all that shit up right now, especially when things were so new between Maggie and him. But she was fucking right; she'd asked more than a few times about his story. Who was he to bury his cock in her all night, protect her from assholes like Chet, take her out on his bike, yet deny her such a large part of himself.

Flux let out a long, ragged sigh. The sound seemed to come up from deep within, an endless well of pain that had gnawed on his insides until he numbed himself out with anything and everything. Grief licked at his core and he inhaled a shaky breath, his palms flat against his thighs.

*It's fuckin' show time.* The moment seemed as good as any to show Maggie his damn scars and hope to hell she wouldn't run for cover once she realized that his fate was all his own goddamn fault.

"Flux, are you still here with me?" Her voice cut through the muck clouding his mind.

"Yeah, Duchess," he croaked through the lump in his throat. "Fuck, I don't even know where to start anymore..."

Words stuck in his throat and Flux groaned in frustration, gnashing his teeth together as Maggie gently shushed him and continued stroking the top of his hands.

*The kitchen. Blood splattered from wall to wall.*

*Alicia. Naked in a pool of blood. Stab wounds crisscrossing her body like a checkerboard.*

*Emily. Fuck... Emily. Face down. Lifeless. Covered in angry, deep slashes.*

Like snapshots against a flashbulb, Flux saw every single graphic picture in his mind, in full-fucking-3D color with all the trimmings. His stomach rolled and he nearly gagged as Maggie pulled back and tilted his head up until he looked into her eyes.

"It's okay, Flux. I won't leave you. Talk to me," she said softly.

The steadiness in her eyes reminded him that he was in Tucson, on Mt. Lemmon, surrounded by pine trees and not in his home on Redwood Drive. Flux nodded, wordless, while he groped for the beginning of his story.

"I met Alicia when I'd just turned twenty. It was right after I got my full patch with the Insurgents." Flux swallowed, the words thick in his throat, but he refused to close his eyes so Maggie wouldn't see his pain. He needed to maintain their connection while he broke down all his walls. "She was the best." A small smile ghosted across his lips as the image of Alicia eating watermelon on the seat of his bike flitted through his mind. *I was so pissed that she was gonna make the seat all sticky, but she just winked at me and laughed, and then we made love—right there on the bike.*

"Was Alicia from Pinewood Springs?" Maggie's voice dragged him back from the past.

Flux quirked his lips while shaking his head. "No. She was from

Johnson City. That just fuckin' blew us away. We were both from the same town in Texas, but we didn't know each other until we met in Pinewood Springs. She used to say it had to be fate because it was too much of a coincidence." He shrugged. "I don't know … maybe it was. When I first saw her at a country western bar, I had to have her. She felt the same way about me and we started dating. Six months later, we got hitched. The brothers thought I was fuckin' crazy for settling down with one woman at such a young age, but Alicia was everything I ever wanted or needed. She was the perfect old lady, the perfect woman, she completed parts of me I didn't know were busted and broken open."

Flux darted his eyes around until they landed on Maggie's. He ran his knuckles softly over her cheek. "Shit, I shouldn't be talking about this with you. Forget I said anything, okay? Just … fuckin' forget it." He jerked his hand away and made to get up before Maggie's fingers cupped the side of his face in a gentle gesture that soothed his demons.

"Don't shut down on me now," Maggie said.

"Shit, Maggie. You don't need to fuckin' compare yourself to a ghost, and I'm a damn bastard for making you."

"Shh, that's not what this is about, baby. I asked you to share, and Alicia was a part of you."

For a beat, Flux searched her face and traced the lines of her expression for any kind of pain. When he was satisfied there was none, he nodded and coughed before starting again.

"Alicia liked the biker lifestyle, and she was cool if I hung out at the club or went to the parties as long as I didn't fuck around and made time for her. We had a real rhythm going." Flux shut his eyes tightly, fending off his unshed tears that burned his eyes. "A couple years later, we had Emily." He chuckled and shook his head. "Fuck, she was cute. She was more perfect than both of us combined. I couldn't stop holding or kissing the little one. I felt so lucky to have Alicia and her in my life …"

"Something happened to them," Maggie spoke softly, kissing him lightly. "Tell me."

"The sick, fuckin' bastard slaughtered them. Alicia and me had been going through a rough patch a few weeks before. She had a problem with one of the new club girls—Rosie. Now, Rosie's a flirt and she's a looker, and Alicia got it in her mind that I wanted her, which I didn't. I never wanted anyone but my wife. Anyway, I don't go in for cheatin'— I'm not that type, and Alicia knew it, but she was being insecure about Rosie and I don't know why." Flux glanced over at Maggie.

She shrugged. "Us women sometimes get insecure, especially if things are too ordinary. We think that a man may be getting bored and want some variety. Maybe that's what she was feeling."

"Maybe. When the charity poker run came up, I told Alicia I was going. She was cool with it at first, but then as it neared, she told me she didn't want me to go. When I asked her why the fuck not, she couldn't give me an answer—just told me I couldn't go. I don't like anyone telling me what I can do, so I told her I was going. Period. I was actually looking forward to getting away for a few days and putting some brakes on our bickering. So I left—we didn't even kiss goodbye that day 'cause we were both too pissed off. When I came back they were gone. Butchered."

He choked on his pain and shook his head, unable to continue. The visions of their bodies assaulted him and he couldn't get enough air. Maggie's voice faded in and out. In and out. He couldn't make out what she was saying to him anymore. Everything was melting together—his pulse skyrocketed, he felt his chest being squeezed like a vice, and he was going to burst or suffocate.

"Oh, Flux ..." Maggie's cool hands stroked his face, his neck, and his arms.

Flux blinked and Maggie's touch disrupted his flashback and slammed him abruptly back down into the present moment as if he'd been squished by a hammer. Their gazes caught again and he licked his lips, still wrestling with what his heart and his fucked-up brain were telling him.

"You couldn't have known what was going to happen to your wife and daughter," Maggie said.

"If I was there it wouldn't have happened. I fuckin' abandoned my family because I was too damn proud to have my woman tell me what to do. I let the fucker do horrible things to them."

"You can't blame yourself, Flux."

He jerked back and narrowed his eyes. "But I do. I don't want to forgive myself. I think if you're guilty of something, you should live with it. All this bullshit talk about getting rid of it blows. How the fuck can a person—*can I*—get rid of a real guilt? I need to live with it and face up to it."

Maggie grasped his hands and squeezed them. "But you didn't do anything on purpose. I can see what you're saying if you did something that would purposely hurt your family, but this was just a horrible, senseless murder that you couldn't control. Even if you'd been there that day, who's to say that they wouldn't have been killed at a time when you were away at work or at the clubhouse?" Maggie brought his hands to her mouth and kissed them tenderly. "Was the one who did it a stranger?"

Anger shot through Flux. "No. The fucker was the boyfriend of our next-door neighbor. Alicia was friendly with Barb, and the no good bastard moved in with her a few months before he destroyed my family. The SOB was at Emily's second birthday party the week before. Fuck! I wanted to tear him apart, and give him a million times more pain than he gave my family."

"Is he still in prison?"

"The fucker killed himself while in the pen." Flux clenched his jaw.

"I can't even begin to imagine what you've been through, but I'm pretty sure your wife wouldn't have wanted you to torment yourself for the rest of your days. You knew her. Do you think that's what she would want from you?" Maggie kissed his hands again.

Flux bristled and winced, unable to look her in the eyes. His thoughts and emotions were a mixture of pain, bitterness, tenderness, and joy all melded together and infused in his heart, warring with each other.

"Flux …" Maggie spoke his name on a whisper, bringing her lips to his and doing her best to erase the pain.

Flux groaned into her mouth wanting to leave the past behind and to lose himself in the present. He took Maggie's mouth with all the passionate longing that swept through his body, channeling all of his anger and frustration into a consuming desire as he locked his arms around her waist and ground her down onto his hard cock beneath the fly of his jeans. To let her understand exactly what she did to him, regardless of the situation.

"I fuckin' need you, Maggie," he grated out against her lips in between their heavy make out session that left him lightheaded and growing even harder by the second. "Ride me. Let me make you feel good."

"Are you sure?" she moaned against his mouth as he captured her bottom lip with his teeth. "I don't know if it's—"

"Don't fuckin' say it, Duchess. Don't make me ask again. Put your pretty pussy on my cock and ride me like there's no tomorrow, understood?"

Maggie whimpered and drew away from his lips, panting as her tits and pebble-hard nipples pressed into his chest through her bra.

"All right, big guy, but don't say I didn't warn you when your eyes roll back in your head and you're begging me to ease up. I ride stallions like you for a living, you know."

With a cheeky little wink, Maggie slipped off him and he groaned, mourning the loss of her heat smothered across his body. She tossed her clothes in the grass and was back next to him, unzipping his fly then pulling him out of his pants.

"Fast and dirty, huh?" Flux grated out, biting her neck.

"That's how I want it." Maggie threw him an impish, sexy grin and his cock twitched in her hand. "Ready, big guy?"

Flux dug in his pocket and took out a packet, and Maggie snatched it away from him and tossed it on the ground.

"I want to feel you," she said without breaking eye contact.

A slow grin cracked his face. "Just so you know, Duchess—I'm clean."

"Me too." She bent her head down and swept her tongue over his dick's head. With a wicked glint in her eyes, she cupped her breasts and lightly pinched her nipples as she slowly climbed on top of him.

Flux licked his lips, mesmerized by her as she straddled him.

*Damn.*

## CHAPTER TWENTY

# FLUX

FLUX WATCHED IN awe as Maggie lowered herself down until he was deep inside her wet heat, his back arching up to meet her at the same time that she flung her head back with a moan.

"I didn't think it was possible to miss that so much. Didn't we just do this?" Maggie murmured, tugging on his hair to arch his neck. Her hungry lips demanded his in a dominant act that made him growl with pleasure.

"Doesn't fuckin' matter, we can keep doing it all day, every day," Flux groaned into her mouth and anchored her hips with his hands.

Maggie was smooth and burning hot against his palms, and when she started to rock against him, he let her set the pace. She ground down on his lap and the friction from his jeans must have teased her clit, because her eyelids fluttered and she licked her lips, increasing her thrusts while her hands explored every inch of him.

"That's right, Duchess, take what you want from me," he said, arching up to meet her frenzied thrusts.

Maggie's wet heat contracted over him as she plunged herself down and her thighs tightened on either side of him. Flux held on for the ride, loving how Duchess used all her skills from riding a horse to buck all over him.

"Fuck, darlin'," he rasped as her walls molded around him.

Maggie's cheeks flushed and her lips parted as she slipped her hands under his T-shirt and ran her nails down his chest—hard and demanding. Flux's gaze roamed around each delicious curve, dimple, and bend on her body, reveling in the fact that they were so in tune with each other. She knew how to fuck him, and the way she cried out and writhed when he made her come told him she was more than satisfied with the way he fucked her too. The thing that blew his mind was how much he craved her. It seemed like he could never get enough of Maggie and was always left wanting more. Yeah, there was no doubt about it ... he was fucking addicted to her body, the feel of her, the way she smelled, the way she tasted ... all of her.

With a possessive noise deep in his throat, Flux gripped her hip until she cried out, biting her lip and thrusting her down even harder. His other hand glided over her tits before he cupped one and sucked her peach-colored nipple into his mouth with a tight tease of his teeth. Maggie arched into him allowing him better access. Flux slid his palm in between where they were joined as she went up and plunged back down. When she hit his palm, he rubbed her sweet button with his thumb. Small, short strokes. A wolfish grin tipped up his lips as their stares caught and her breathing hitched with a secret smile.

Maggie moved harder, faster, edged on by his teasing into a frenzy as her nails bit in the back of his shoulders. Flux traced her mouth with his tongue, loving the small whimpers that escaped from her parted lips.

"Tell me when you're about to come, baby." He nipped her neck and kept up the pace with his thumb, gauging her for any sudden movements indicating he needed to switch it up.

Fuck, he was delicate with her and treated her like a prized possession, showering her with compliments and taking her pleasure into account over his without missing a single, fucking beat. When was the last time he'd done that? The answer alluded Flux—he'd been utterly selfish in bed for the past six years. He only needed a woman for one night, to get his stones off, and then to pass the fuck out. Hell, he couldn't even remember half his encounters with all the women he'd fucked. But here and now with his Duchess, none of his past mattered, so long as she came long and hard, passing out on top of him.

"Soon, Flux. Soon," she cried out, breaking her rhythm and strokes down into his lap.

Each time Maggie came down onto his cock he could feel her tense up around him, her muscles begging for release as she milked him. Her juices were starting to soak through to his jeans as he gritted his teeth and used his grip on her hip to help her out, slamming her down harder onto him.

"Fuck, Duchess. You're tight as hell. Keep going, I wanna make you come," Flux murmured against her tits as he flicked one nipple and then the other. Maggie bucked, threw her head back and moaned, and he reveled in how responsive she was to his touch.

"Please, Flux ... please, so close ..." she begged as his thrusts upward became more brutal, rougher with her little pleas ringing in his ears.

He loved doing new things to every inch of her and watching her reactions. The small jerks, movements, and intimate facial expressions made something in his chest tighten every time he looked at her, cherishing her while she took what she deserved from him. He wanted her on the edge, ready to topple into a million pieces. All because of him.

Without a doubt, Flux wanted to be the one to make her see pleasure the way she'd never seen it before because he'd given it to her for the first time. He wanted her to never forget him the way he'd forgotten countless other hookups. Flux wanted to burn every second of their time together into his memory bank so he could dig it out when he was alone. Once he moved on, he'd need it to help him through the shit times when he'd want to take one more drink or one more hit.

If Flux could hold on to Maggie and hold on to himself for one more second, maybe there was hope that this was his reality: that he'd somehow been granted a reprieve in the hellhole that was his life and given a chance to grab on to this woman and keep her, not wreck her whole life like a house of toppling cards.

Maggie's face was lost to bliss, her eyes rolling lightly in the back of her head as her hands skittered across his back, losing their grip on his shoulders.

"Now," Flux whispered, watching as her legs quivered around him and her hands folded into fists at the fabric of his T-shirt hiked right above his chest. She whimpered and bit her lower lip, almost losing her rhythm. "That's it, Duchess, let it all go."

Maggie orgasmed around him, her inner walls drew up tight around him, and her moans rose to his ears. While she lost herself in the sensation, Flux drove his hips upward fighting her tight, slick heat in a bid to drive her even higher. Each inch seemed like heaven as he fought through her body's orgasm and continued thumbing her sweet spot, landing small kisses along her neck and collarbone to balance out the epic sensations riding inside her flesh.

Maggie's face lit up and glowed with pleasure. A grin spread across Flux's face as she blinked back into reality, still arching her back and moving to his well-timed, quick, and deep thrusts from beneath her while she wrapped herself around his body.

She made a blissful noise in his ear, sitting up to kiss him as her nails gently teased down his inner thighs and she leaned back, deepening the angle. *Fuck, she's gonna be the death of me.* There was no way he could hold on much longer when the view was this damn good.

"Fuck, baby. Your body's so beautiful. Don't stop what you're doing, keep exactly like that, and I'm gonna come until I pass the fuck out," Flux groaned and used his leverage to aid her swift hip thrusts downward onto him.

A shudder rolled up his spine and pressure mounted in the small of his back. His brain turned to fucking mush as his fingers gripped Maggie's hips until she cried out, biting his lip at the same time that his orgasm flashed across his whole body. Strong jolts propelled through him along with the vague notion that his woman was still working herself on his palm between their legs as he rode out the exquisite sensation that wrung out of every pore of his body.

"I want... to go... for number two," Maggie said, her voice strained while continuing to move against him.

"That can more than be arranged, Duchess," Flux took his hand back and cupped her ass and her shoulder before he shifted so she landed in a surprised heap under him on her back. "Did you just squeak at me?"

"Maybe," she looked down, sheepish, and suddenly shy.

"Good. I fuckin' loved it." Flux rose above her, surveying his territory and knowing full well he would enjoy finding out exactly *which* little spots, curves, and buttons *did what* to her extra sensitive flesh.

He crushed his mouth on her while easing his fingers between her legs. *Fuck!* Maggie was so damn wet against his fingers as he slid two of them inside her and started working her up again.

"Let's see how many other sexy sounds I can get from your perfect mouth. It'll be a game and it's not stopping until I'm fuckin' satisfied that you can't get a single second's more pleasure. Understand the rules, baby?" He bent down and flicked her hardened nipples with the tip of his tongue.

"Oh God, Flux," Maggie breathed as she shimmied her hips to match his finger strokes. A wave of satisfaction broke over him so hard and so quick, he caught his breath looking down on the delectable woman spread bare before him.

Flux didn't know what karma he'd earned to get her in his life, but whatever the fuck it was, fluke or not, he hoped he did it again and again so he never had to lose her.

## CHAPTER TWENTY-ONE

# FLUX

*Two weeks later*
*Kremmling, CO*

THE ROAR OF the Colorado River filled Flux's ears as he cut through the canyons and entered into a lush valley surrounded by tall mountain peaks. Grazing cows and sheep blurred past him as he made his way toward Kremmling. Each August, the tiny town burgeoned with people as the annual rodeo got underway. RVs and tents littered the valley, and Wranglers, cowboy boots, Western shirts, and Stetsons became the normal attire.

Flux spotted the Super 8 motel sign and turned into the lot, scanning it for a cherry-red pickup. The only truck he saw was Chet's, and he was the last person Flux wanted to run into at that moment. Flux slipped his phone from the pocket inside his cut and checked for any messages from Maggie.

It'd been a week since the rodeo had ended in Tucson, and he and Maggie had gone their separate ways, promising to meet up in Kremmling. She'd invited Flux to come to Greeley with her to spend a few days on her family's ranch, but he wasn't into meeting parents and getting the third degree, so he declined. But stepping inside his motel room, he wished like hell Maggie was with him, and he couldn't wait until he heard the hum of her pickup's V-8 engine as it pulled into the parking lot.

Flux threw his bag on the bed and lit up a joint. It'd been a while since he'd been back in Colorado, and the cool air blowing in through the open door felt good after the stifling heat of Tucson. *The only thing missing is Duchess. Fuck.*

Leaning against the doorway, he stared at the rippling waters of the Blue River that cut through the town. After spending all their days and nights together in Arizona, being without Maggie for the past seven days was damn hard, and every inch of him felt the fucking loss. Yeah, Flux was more than ready to get his hands on Duchess again.

He inhaled deeply then slowly blew out. He'd had sexual droughts before, but never for longer than forty-eight hours over the past year and a half while his grief had been especially hard to tame. Now that grief wasn't his main motivator, his feelings were even harder to hang up and ignore than they'd been before, because it seemed like Flux was feeling things all the damn time. The fucking floodgates were open and a part of him would give anything to dam them up. Before, his life had been a steady flow of predictability and pain, with chasers of drugs, booze, and one nighters to numb things up nice and good. Now? A whirlwind of emotions swirled inside him like he was on some fucking out of control Tilt-A-Whirl ride.

Flux raked his fingers through his hair. It'd been a long time since he'd missed someone, not since ... Alicia. *Fuck no—I'm not going there.* He flicked the blunt on the ground and smothered it out with the toe of his boots. *Damn this woman.* Since he'd met Maggie, he'd been breaking his cardinal rules all over the place and paying for it every time he scanned the lot for Duchess's truck. Whenever he'd turned into the dirt lot in Tucson and saw the cherry-red pickup, it'd immediately put a dumbass grin on his face. *I'm fuckin' hopeless*—a damn lost cause when it came to Maggie and wanting to hear her voice, to smell her skin, and taste her on his lips.

Flux shut the door behind him and headed out to the rodeo setup to check out the stalls and tack area. *I need to get my shit together.* If he didn't get his feelings on lockdown, there was no way he would be able to make Maggie think things were still nothing but casual fucking between friends. *But it sure as hell didn't feel casual between us in Arizona.* And the way she'd pretended not to cry when they parted ways after the rodeo made him think they'd crossed over the friends-with-benefits line a while back.

Flux killed the engine, hopped off his bike, and made his way to the fairgrounds. Once there, he made a quick, brisk walk through the area, noting that Maggie didn't seem to be anywhere, and he ignored the disappointment that wrapped around him. *Fuck that.* The screech of wheels exploded behind him and he spun around and saw Chet kicking up dust with his truck. Loud country music blared from the open windows, and Flux turned around and walked toward the back area, wanting to avoid a confrontation with the cowboy. Flux had narrowly escaped getting canned after he beat the pussy's ass in Tucson, and if Maggie hadn't pleaded his case with Charlie, Flux would've lost about two grand in wages.

He pivoted outside of the stables, and his brain tracked something out of the corner of his right eye. Something shiny. Flux spun around and his gaze landed on a row of Harleys, six of them. *What the fuck?* It was damn surprising to see any biker at a rodeo, no matter how slow of a night it might be … but *six*?

A shuffle of footsteps made Flux hustle away behind one of the stalls, and he watched as a tall, lanky dude in jeans and a leather cut walked over to one of the bikes. The biker had a wrench in his hand and he knelt down and started fussing with the rear axle nut. The guy stood up and turned around then bent over one of the saddle bags. It was at that moment when Flux's eyes widened and his initial surprise morphed into a scowl as soon as his gaze fell on the dude's cut and MC patch—Satan's Pistons, Arizona. All the small hairs on Flux's neck stood on end. There was no fucking way the rival club's assholes were here to take in dinner and a goddamn rodeo show. *Something's not right.*

Flux ducked back into the stalls so the fucker wouldn't see him, and as he walked to the far back area of the ring, his gaze darted around just to make sure none of the other assholes were about. He stepped into a small room at the end of the twist of hallways, fished out his burner phone, then punched in Hawk's number. Flux thrummed his fingers against his thigh as he waited for the VP to pick up.

"Hey, bro. Where the hell are you?" Hawk's deep voice rumbled through the phone.

"In Kremmling. I'm still on the fuckin' rodeo circuit."

"I didn't know they had rodeos there."

"Well, you're not exactly in on the rodeo grapevine." Flux chuckled.

"Yeah, I don't even know what the hell they're about." Hawk laughed.

"Right, so why the fuck do you think six Satan's Pistons would have their fuckin' asses here in this tiny-ass town? I saw six of their damn bikes in the rodeo lot. My gut's telling me this shit stinks real bad."

There was silence on the other end of the phone for a long pause. "What the fuck? Those assholes are in Colorado?"

"And at the rodeo. See why I'm calling?"

"Yeah. Those fuckers are up to something on our turf. Banger's outta town with Belle and the kids, but I'll give him a call. I'll call Steel too. The Night Rebels practically annihilated the fuckin' Pistons last year. Steel's not gonna be too happy to hear they're back and pulling shit."

"I'm not sure what the hell they got going on with the rodeo, but I'll keep a tight eye on that shit and see what I can find out." Flux cracked open the door and his gaze swept up and down the aisle, double-checking for anything off.

"Can you get your ass to Pinewood tonight?" Tension etched Hawk's voice.

"Yeah. I'll head over as soon as I get a chance after the show tonight. Cool?"

"Yep. See you then, bro. Watch your back."

"Always." Flux coughed and crossed his arm, staring off into the distance as the silence between them spread thick. "I was gonna tell you I was back in Colorado—"

"Don't start with the mushy shit, dude." Hawk cleared his throat. "It's good to have you back."

"Yeah," Flux answered gruffly, his throat choked with emotion.

Neither man didn't get to say anything else because Hawk terminated the call, and Flux stared at the small burner in his palm. His fingers clenched hard around it until the parts bit into his palms from the pressure, and he was forced to let it go or crush the thing into bits.

Not until that moment had he realized how much he missed his brothers and the club life. How the Insurgents were still his home. *It's been too long.* The thought was sobering while he stood in the middle of the empty room blinking into space. Flux really thought he'd left all his good emotions behind after the murder of his family, and he never expected to feel this way about anything or anyone again. But without missing a beat, his heart yearned for his club. He wanted more than anything to hop on his bike and head over to Pinewood Springs. He chuckled thinking of the looks on the members' faces when he strutted inside the clubhouse. There'd be a kickass party in his honor without a doubt, and Rosie would definitely make a beeline for him. *But the only one I want wrapped around me is Duchess.* Fuck, if he got any sappier, he'd have to sign up for a role in one of those Lifetime movies Maggie watched.

Flux rolled his shoulders and pocketed the phone. Now was the fun part. Playing it cool and acting like nothing was doing while not letting the rival MC get a whiff that he was sniffing around them. Plus, he still had a full rodeo set to work tonight. During the steer wrestling competition was as good a time as any to root things out and see if he could find out why the fucking Pistons were in Insurgents' territory.

Flux shrugged off his cut and folded it carefully. For a while he had to be just one of the rodeo hands and not an Insurgent. He opened the door and strode down the hallway toward his locker.

★ ★ ★

AN HOUR LATER and Flux was finished setting up the area he was in charge of. He'd broken down and sent Maggie a text asking where the hell she was, and she sent back some smiley faces and told him she was running late but would be there in a few. Elation at seeing her again battled with anger at having contacted her first like some lovesick pussy. Before he could figure out what the hell was going on with him, he heard several sets of footfalls behind him. Without turning around, he stepped aside, and three Pistons shoved passed him.

"Stay outta the fuckin' way, cowboy," one of them snarled as they kept stalking toward the back of the fairgrounds.

Flux was amused for a split second that the fucker would mistake him for a cowboy. He waited until they disappeared before he followed their footsteps, which led him to the normally empty backrooms in the rodeo that some of the staff occasionally used to have illicit hookups. Each rodeo had rooms in the back for the performers to relax between shows or decompress before they had to go on, but more times than not, they were used to fuck buckle bunnies or carry out clandestine affairs. A few times, Flux had walked in on the married owners' of various rodeos banging one of the secretaries or a sweet young thing. *So why the hell are the Pistons in this part of the arena?* He doubted that they came all this way for a quick fuck.

Flux quietly walked down the narrow, dimly lit, and abandoned hallway. *The Pistons must've gone into one of the rooms.* It was like some cop show or some shit. All he needed was freaky, stressful piano music. A majority of the doors were wide open, but the first closed one Flux came upon, he heard plenty of grunting and moaning so he knew what was going down in there.

The next closed door was still the slightest bit open, as if someone had closed it so quickly, it didn't have time to latch. Without any hesitation, Flux saddled on up to it and put his ear to the slight space.

"… you would pay premium for this kind of juice anywhere else, but since you're repeat customers, I'm willing to knock a little off."

Flux's entire body tightened as he listened to the same Piston's voice who'd cursed him just a while before. The fucker kept extolling why he was peddling his shit at the rodeo, and Flux put two and two together all kinds of quick: they were juicing the damn bulls. No wonder the one that came after him in Tucson had Hulk tendencies. Bigger bulls meant better performances, which meant better shows, which meant more bets and, ultimately, more fucking cash in the riders' and bull owners' pockets. A little under-the-table deal or two didn't hurt the damn profit margins.

White-hot anger shot through him and he willed himself to stay put and not barge into the room and beat the shit out of the three fuckers. *Play it cool. Detach your emotions from what's going on. You're here to get info to give to the club.* He inhaled and exhaled several times then focused back on what was going down in the room.

"Same stuff? No bullshit? It'll make him grow even bigger?" Another, higher-pitched voice broke out, and Flux recognized it as Eddie's—one of the owners of several top-rated bulls. It was one of his who practically gored Flux in Tucson.

The veins in Flux's temples throbbed. *Play it cool, dude!*

A tall, built biker with long black hair moved to the side, and Flux could read the patch on the front of his cut: "Demon." *President.*

"The fucker'll look like Arnold Schwarzenegger and Vin Diesel combined. Should make you some serious money," Demon said as he rocked back on the heels of his boots.

Flux moved away from the door since the asshole had stepped in his line of vision. He plastered his back against the wall behind him, his pulse pounding out of his skull as he fought to hear what else was going down in that room.

"Yeah, we want it to go down just like in Tucson, except I don't want to be on the fucking bull. That would be ideal," Chet drawled, his accent a little more nasal after getting his nose bashed in by Flux's fists.

Flux wiped the corners of his mouth. *Of course, that fucker's a part of this scheme.* What about this shit *wasn't* up the asshole's alley? Chet was a greedy, no-morals pussy who had to feed bulls steroids as a way to make himself feel like a man. Flux had heard the talk among the women staffers about Chet's lack of prowess between the sheets. It had only reinforced what Flux had already thought about the lame ass excuse for a man.

"You got anything else that we talked about for my uh, performance?" Chet asked.

If the guy was buying Viagra, Flux was going to lose it and blow his entire cover.

"We got plenty of Adderall. No need to get the shakes on me. We're delivering some premium grade shit to some of our customers, too, mostly meth, if that strikes your fancy, pretty boy," Demon said, irritation creeping into his voice.

"No, the pills are fine," Chet croaked.

"That's right, I figured you weren't one for the hard stuff." The three Pistons laughed.

Flux blew out a long, silent breath and tried his best to contain the need to bust into the room and rearrange Chet's face all over again. Clearly the bastard didn't learn his lesson. He doubted a second beatdown would make things any simpler for him either. There was the unmistakable sound of footsteps in the distance, and Flux ducked into the nearest empty open room, shutting the door behind him.

As soon as the footfalls died away again, Flux made his way to Charlie's office and told him he was sicker than hell and blamed it on the chili he'd eaten the night before. Since he'd never called off work before, Charlie believed him—hook, line, and sinker—and told him to take the night off.

Flux scanned the parking lot again, hoping to see Maggie's truck, but it wasn't there. There was no way he could wait for her to show up, club business took precedence, so he revved up his bike then hauled ass out of the parking lot and drove like a bat out of hell to Pinewood Springs. The shit that Satan's Pistons were doing in Colorado was totally unacceptable, and it would change the entire underworld landscape of his club. As he put miles between the rodeo ... and Maggie, there wasn't a doubt in his mind that nothing was more important than the Insurgents.

## CHAPTER TWENTY-TWO

# FLUX

WHEN FLUX ARRIVED in the parking lot of the Insurgents' clubhouse, he checked his phone and saw that Maggie had left a simple message asking him if he was doing okay. He tried to remember the stupid, light-headed-bitch-boy glow the text gave him as he headed into the clubhouse to piss all over everyone's parade with the news about the damn Satan's Pistons selling dope in Insurgents' territory. More than anything, he wanted to text her back. His fingers were practically itching with the need, but he knew she'd have a slew of questions, and there was nothing he could share with her about any of this since it was club business.

Three other texts came in right as he was about to open the door to the clubhouse. Flux's mouth went into a grim line and he switched his phone to silent before stuffing it into his pocket. The second he was out of there, Maggie would know it. That was a promise, but at the moment, he needed to keep his shit screwed on tight and help out his brothers—that took priority. Flux squared himself up, pushed through into the clubhouse, and smiled when the familiar smells wrapped around him: weed, booze, and pussy. *I'm home.*

"Fuck! Is that you, Flux?" Throttle asked as he slipped off the bar stool and strode over to him.

"Who else were you expecting?" Flux joked as he let Throttle pull him into a bear hug.

"Hawk said you'd be here tonight. Damn, it's good to see you, bro.

How've you been?"

Flux followed Throttle to the bar and picked up the shot of Jack that stood waiting for him. He threw back the whiskey, wincing as it burned down his throat. Several members seated around the club's tables jumped up and came over to greet him as if he'd come back from the dead. Everyone wanted a hug—including a few of the club girls, who rubbed all up on him like he was a fucking corn cob and they were a stick of butter. From the corner of his eye, he saw Rosie crossing the room, her low-cut top leaving little to the imagination. Flux lifted his chin at the prospect who put down another whiskey neat in front of him.

"Long time no see." Rosie's sultry voice washed over him as the strong floral scent of her perfume wisped around him.

Flux took a step back and Rosie's hand fell from his forearm. "Yeah ... how've you been?"

"Okay. How long are you here for?" She took a step toward him.

Flux took another one backward. "Just today."

"Too bad." She ran her fingernail down his black T-shirt. "You're looking real good, Flux."

"Thanks," he mumbled then picked up the glass and brought it to his lips.

"Go on and get outta here, Rosie. We got shit to discuss with Flux," Smokey said as he came up beside him.

Rosie nodded then leaned into Flux. "Later," she whispered in his ear then sauntered away.

"She's got the best damn fucking ass," Smokey said.

"What about Tania?" Animal asked as he sidled up to the bar. "You don't know Tania," he said to Flux. "She's been with the club for a year now. Damn, is she hot."

"But Rosie's still got the best ass." Smokey brought the beer bottle to his mouth.

*No, Duchess has. She's got the best of everything.*

"You can get some sweetness later," Rock said. The sergeant-at-arms clasped Flux's shoulder. "Good to see you again, bro."

"You too," Flux answered.

"Maybe he can have a quickie. I bet you're tired of those rodeo bitches. You need a club girl who knows how to please a biker," Puck said, and the other men guffawed.

"I'm good," Flux replied.

Club girls. Puck was right about how they knew how to make a biker feel like he was a damn king. Flux had loved all the attention they'd given him, and before he'd married, he loved all the fucking he could do with so many different women—it'd blown his mind. But not anymore. The only woman he wanted to be inside of was Maggie, and the realization of that startled him.

"What's with the fuckin' monk act?" Throttle handed Flux another glass of Jack filled to the brim.

"Maybe more whiskey will loosen the pipes," Rags added as the others whistled and laughed.

"I'm just tense is all. Seeing those fuckin' Pistons took me by surprise." He took a sip. There was no way in hell he was telling the guys about Duchess. He didn't need their ribbing, and he didn't need to be reminded that he was acting like a damn wuss over her.

"Swearing off pussy? Now I'm fuckin' concerned, bro." Throttle clapped him on the back so hard that the blow stuttered through his jaw and down into his toes before he grunted and shook off the attention.

"No way. I get enough on the road. Chicks love a man with a cut and a Harley."

"Fucking amen." Smokey lifted up the beer bottle.

"I'd love to keep chatting like we're in some fuckin' sewing circle, but I gotta talk to Hawk. Is he around?" Flux put down his empty glass and pushed away from the bar.

"In his office," Throttle replied. "We're gonna have church once Banger gets here."

"I'll see you in a few," Flux said as he walked out of the main room.

He knocked roughly on the vice president's door until Hawk called out and told him to come in. Flux opened the door and closed it behind him.

"You got here early." Hawk blew out a thick cloud of smoke and tossed a joint at Flux. "Banger's stuck and can't get here until late, so he wants us to proceed without him. I'll go round up the brothers—it's church time."

Flux tucked the joint in the pocket of his cut and followed Hawk out of the room. Soon, all the members sat around a large table in the conference room. Flux tipped the folding chair against the wall and closed his eyes. Surrounded by his brothers in their sacred space, Flux could almost forget the horrors of his past—due to the simple fact that he was where he'd always felt the most comfortable—with the Insurgents. But there were shadows beating on the doors of his subconscious, everywhere he looked in the clubhouse. A small smile whispered across his lips as he remembered Alicia and him fucking on this very table. If Banger had known, his ass would've gotten a beatdown, but Alicia had loved the excitement of doing something that was so taboo in the biker world. *You could be so fuckin' crazy, babe.* The memory made him grimace, and he put his head in his hands.

"Church is now starting." Hawk knocked the gavel against the wood block on the table. "You all know we got a damn problem with the fuckin' Pistons. Flux spotted them in Kremmling and he's here to tell us what the fuck he found out." Hawk jerked his head at him. "The floor's yours, brother."

Flux shook away the cobwebs from his mind and rose to his feet. It didn't take him long to establish the situation. Satan's Pistons were selling on the Insurgents' home turf without an agreement, which was a major breech of respect. The rival club was selling to locals as well as out-of-towners, which could bring danger to the Insurgents MC if someone accidentally overdosed and word got back to the damn badges.

# FORGIVENESS

The Insurgents had a tenuous relationship with the badges to keep hard drugs out of their territory and the badges would look the other way on some of the shit the MC pulled. The Night Rebels, the Insurgents' affiliate MC in southern Colorado, had the same type of relationship with the badges in their county. The fact that the Pistons had set up shop in the same county where the Insurgents national headquarters was, opened up a ton of headaches and potential problems for the MC. The fact that they were being *disrespected* by the fucking Satan's Pistons took their rage to a whole new level.

"This isn't something we're gonna stand for. I don't even think we need a vote, am I right?" Hawk asked.

There were various grunts and yells and curses of outrage around the table.

"The dirty rotten bastards are gonna pay for their disrespect!" Wheelie said while pounding his fist on the table.

"Damn straight," Axe added.

"Steel wants a part of this too," Jax said. The president of the Night Rebels MC had an ongoing feud with the Pistons.

"We're gonna show them what happens to fuckers who disrespect us and try to set up shop in our county." Smokey crossed his arms over his broad chest.

"When are we gonna show them who's boss?" Animal gritted.

"We're gonna handle this situation quickly, quietly, and with as little mess as possible while still sending a blunt fucking message," Hawk replied.

Flux cracked his knuckles and leaned back in his seat, hands behind his head. "Are some of the Night Rebels gonna help us out?"

"Diablo, Steel, Army, Goldie, Muerto, and Sangre are on the way as we speak. They'll stand by us. Our Colorado Springs chapter is ready to jump in too, but I think we can handle the pussies on our own." Hawk steepled his fingers. "How many fuckers are in Kremmling?"

"I only saw three but there were six bikes out in the parking lot,"

Flux replied.

"Sounds like we got enough back up," Rock said.

"Yeah… Banger wants me, Rock, Throttle, Smokey, Animal, Wheelie, Jerry, Hubcap, and Tank to go. With the Night Rebels and Flux, we should be good. We should head out first thing in the morning and handle this shit before it gets even more out of hand. Of course, we're gonna kick their asses in the dark of night—we don't need witnesses or fuckin' badges interfering. We'll get a lay of the land and what the situation is all about. We'll take our cages and get dressed like fuckin' rodeo dudes." Hawk's last words got a rise out of the members and they guffawed and joked about looking like cowboys.

Flux cleared his throat. "No offense, but there's no fuckin' way any of you are gonna pass for rodeo spectators. I suggest a couple of you hang out in the stands, but if you all come it'll totally tip the fuckin' Pistons off."

"I didn't mean for all of us to show up in a group," Hawk said, shaking his head. "We got this under control, dude. If there isn't anything else, then church is over. Don't get fuckin' wasted tonight. We gotta bring all we got tomorrow."

The strike of the gavel signaled church had ended. Chairs scraped against the concrete floor and the members shuffled out of the room and headed to the main part of the clubhouse.

Flux stood up and stretched as he looked at the departing members. A tremor of something like grief, but deeper, squeezed tight in his chest. He massaged his hand over his heart.

"You good?" Hawk bent down and took a beer out of the mini-refrigerator then handed it to him.

Flux downed it in three long pulls.

"More?"

"No, that's good," Flux replied.

Hawk nodded, and Flux glanced around and saw that they were the only two still left. He looked down and then back up again. He had a sinking suspicion that shit was about to get real between them. But anyone would be a fucking fool not to notice the signs of the siren's call working its way through his bloodstream, the lifestyle flaring back to the forefront of his brain.

"You know, you can only fuckin' deny it for so long, bro." Hawk's penetrating stare bored into him. "Eventually all that shit you got buried will eat you alive if you let it."

Flux grunted.

"I know going nomad was good for you." Hawk took a gulp of beer. "Is all that shit inside you still fuckin' with you?"

"Yeah, but it's not as strong as it was."

"Good to hear that. You needed a fuckin' break, but we need you back as an active member. Seems like being on the road's helped you deal with all that tragic bullshit that went down with your family."

Again, Flux grunted, knowing that only one thing had helped him. *Maggie.*

"Think on it. It'll be good for you to be back with your MC and riding with us."

"Yeah." Being back for just a few hours showed Flux how much he missed the camaraderie and belonging to something so real and so loyal.

The rattle of glass against metal jarred him, and he looked up as Hawk turned away from the trash can.

"You staying the night?"

Flux shrugged. "Maybe."

"I'm heading out. I have to pick up my kids from day camp."

"How're they doing? And how's your old lady?"

Hawk chuckled. "The kids are ornery as fuck, and Cara's busting at the seams with our third kid."

Flux heard the love and pride in the vice president's voice, and for a split second, he regretted his nomad life, but he pushed down the feelings and smiled. "When's the due date?"

"In a month."

"Congratulations. You gonna have a boy or girl?"

"Boy." Hawk walked toward the door. "I'll see you in the morning. If you go back tonight, lay low and watch your fuckin' back." With a lift of his chin, Hawk walked out of the room.

Flux stared out the window at the Rocky Mountains, remembering how many times he'd ridden around the back roads with Alicia pressed against him. Then Maggie's face filled his mind and he wished like hell she was with him now so he could take her on a ride to Crystal Lake and they could screw under the tall fir trees. Maggie was slowly chiseling away at the armor around his heart. She was patching up the leak that created the nightmares from the past in his brain. A part of him mourned the dissipation of pain because it had been his way of life for so long, but another part rejoiced in the freedom of letting it go.

*Duchess, I fuckin' miss you.*

Flux walked into the main room and joined Rags, Smokey, Tank, Animal, and Hubcap at the bar. Without asking, the prospect placed a bottle of beer and a shot of Jack in front of him. He picked up the shot, clinked glasses with his brothers, and let the liquid slide down his throat.

## CHAPTER TWENTY-THREE

# MAGGIE

"What're you doing?" Maggie hissed at her phone, devoid of messages before she shook it angrily and stuffed it back in her pocket. Normally she didn't get bent out of shape if she didn't see a man she was dating for more than a week, but no matter how hard she focused on other things, all she could think about was Flux. *Why the hell don't you call me?* Maggie had scoured the motel parking lot and the fairgrounds, but he was nowhere to be found, and he hadn't answered any of her texts in the past several hours. While she was independent and he had a reputation for being elusive, after what they'd shared in Tucson, she had every right to think he would text her back in a timely manner so she could make sure he was okay. His motorcycle was gone too, which made her stomach drop whenever the notion of him being in an accident crossed her mind.

*Maybe he doesn't think he owes me an explanation as to where he is.* Maggie shook her head. The truth was pretty evident. Every time they made forward strides in their arrangement, which had evolved into so much more on her end, Flux freaked the hell out, or at least that's how it appeared to her. She didn't know if she could handle hiding the growing feelings she had for him—not when they must be obvious as hell. There was no way Flux could really think what they had together was casual—but then she hadn't heard anything from him.

He was baffling. One second he was shoving his deepest, darkest secrets at her, and the next, he was either retreating emotionally or physically as if she'd hurt him. And that was the last thing she ever wanted to do to him. Maggie bit the inside of her cheek and leaned against Odysseus's stall. She hated the fact that his absence was starting to affect her performance. As much as she hated to admit it, her barrel racing career wasn't her only concern anymore. She'd let Flux in and she'd never felt such need or want for another man as she did for the biker.

The way Flux looked at her was as if he never wanted anything or anyone else but her. It was intense and humbling all at the same time. Maggie knew he treated her differently than the other women he'd been with, mostly because they were one-night stands, but also because a few of his hookups who worked the backstage circuit had gone out of their way to talk to her about him.

Some of them were well-meaning and sweet, others were bitter and sad, still others were pitying their time with Flux. But with rumors spreading like wildfire, there was no doubt in Maggie's mind that they all shared a common thread—no one got more than a night with the guy. After that, he booted their asses to the curb the second he was done with them.

A few of them had asked what new moves Maggie had tried on Flux to get him to stick around and she'd shut them down pretty damn hard. That was absolutely no one's business. Besides, if she knew why Flux was still sticking around, other than for the amazing sex, she'd have a few of the answers she was looking for herself. And yet, here she was with him pulling back again. *He's ignoring me. Oh, Flux. Damn you!*

Maggie sighed and closed her eyes. Despite everything, and regardless of how logical she tried to be about things, she'd gone and fallen in love with him. Stupid move on her part, but it wasn't anything she'd planned. Actually, Maggie had gone out of her way to convince herself he was just very good at scratching an itch without any emotional attachment. *What a fool I've been.* She'd been hoping that Flux felt the same way about her, but that'd clearly been a delusion and nothing more on her part since he didn't give enough of a shit to let her know that he was all right.

Her phone went off and she dug in her pocket, nearly dropping it as she fumbled to the main screen.

**Flux:** *With friends. Won't be back 'til the morning.*

Curt, short, and straight to the point. Damn it, what was wrong with him? Why was he so hot and cold?

**Maggie:** *What the hell? Where r u?*
**Flux:** *I told you—with friends.*

She groaned in exasperation.

**Maggie:** *R u in Pinewood Springs?*

A long pause.

**Flux:** *Yeah. Gotta go.*

"Fuck you!" Maggie said out loud as she shoved the phone back in her jeans pocket. Licks of anger made her tremble, and she needed a place where she could be alone to clear her head. If anyone saw her face now, they'd immediately know the deal. She was never a good poker player and word was all across camp that she and Flux had a thing. The last thing she needed was a bunch of bullshit questions about what was wrong and where was Flux.

Maggie glanced at the big clock above the stands and saw that she didn't have time to go back to the motel and veg for a bit. Deciding to go to the backrooms where employees went to screw, Maggie stalked down the hallway as she pushed down the well of unspoken feelings that beat against her ribcage. She pushed open a door and burst in on what looked like a meeting of some kind.

"Oh, shit, I'm sorry," she sputtered, looking at the circle of men, one of whom was holding a prescription bottle in one hand and a boatload of syringes in the other.

The guy wore a biker vest, was tall as a redwood tree, and looked ready to kill. Maggie had no doubt in her split-second assessment that he wouldn't hesitate to fuck up her day or slit her throat for what she was witnessing at that moment.

"What the fuck are you doing in here, *Princess*?" the biker growled. "Go the fuck back to where you belong."

But Maggie stood like a statue with her mouth opening and closing while she digested the biker and Chet, who was standing next to Eddie.

"What the fuck?" Chet lunged forward and Eddie grabbed him by the arm.

It was enough of a distraction that when she heard more footsteps coming up from behind her in the hallway, she whirled around to them. With any luck, they wouldn't be an enemy. Maggie fumbled out of the doorway then slammed the door behind her before she started down the hall at a fast jog.

She heard a door jerk open behind her but didn't glance back. Any kind of pause would be the difference between danger and safety; she instinctively knew that with an absolute certainty.

"Oh fuck," she cried out, startled as she ran headlong into Jack, one of the rodeo clowns, who was leading a girl by the hand.

"I'm sorry. Hi … uh, I'm just going to … uh—"

"I didn't see you, Jack. Sorry. I'm off to the stables." Maggie pointed past him down the hallway and tried to move around them, but froze in her tracks when a light whisper brushed against the back of her neck and she sensed another warm body at her back. All of the hairs on the nape of her neck stood on end. She bit back a whimper and brought her hands into fists at her sides.

"Don't think I'm letting this go, bitch. You'll pay for putting your fucking nose where it doesn't belong," Chet said in a low voice that was almost a growl.

His words made her whole body go numb, but she was sure Chet had a smile plastered on his face so that if Jack noticed him, all he'd see was a rekindle of Chet and Maggie's old flame. Certainly nothing dangerous.

"It's okay, Maggie. I'll see you later." Jack dodged around her with a nod. "Hey Chet, you're back here too, huh? Guess the rooms are getting used up pretty good." Jack snickered.

Maggie didn't wait to hear Chet's answer before she flew down the hallway with only a little bit of regret that the asshole saw her flee from him in fear—again. But if it was going to come down to her safety and her pride, it was no contest.

It wasn't until Maggie was outside that the rest of what she'd just witnessed came back in stark clarity. *If only I could rewind all this and never have gone into that damn room.* Covering her mouth, Maggie tried to take it easy as she power-walked across the parking lot. The last thing she wanted was to look too suspicious in case anyone came out with a mind to silence her before she had the chance to tell Charlie what she'd seen.

Chet and Eddie had been in the middle of a drug deal with the biker. Maggie shook her head wishing it would do the trick in erasing the memory completely from her brain. Nope, that wasn't going anywhere, anytime soon. Eddie was doping his bulls and Chet was using. *Asshole!* Maggie swallowed down her revulsion as she walked toward her truck for some peace and quiet. *Now it makes sense why he was so off his rocker and way too full of rage when we were dating. It also explains how he can stay on those pumped up bulls for as long as he does.*

The rush of relief and awareness that she'd escaped the situation before things escalated left her achingly exhausted as she hauled herself into the driver's seat and shut and locked the door. Suddenly, her whole body longed for Flux's strong arms to wrap around her and his deep voice telling her that she was safe. *I need you, big guy.* Maggie closed her eyes and sank into the quiet space inside her head, where she went to relax and zone everything else out.

A screech of wheels made her lids pop open, then she saw Chet striding across the parking lot and all her ideas about serenity swirled down the drain. Chet looked as if he didn't have a single care in the world, but she noticed his right hand never strayed far from his pocket, patting it idly or sticking his hand in it. *Must be where the jerk keeps his stash.*

Maggie rubbed her throbbing temples. *There's no way they're going to let me get away with knowing what they're up to. I've got to report it to Charlie.* The trouble was that she didn't know if she had the guts to report it. Calling Chet and Eddie out on illegal drug use was huge because Chet was one of the top riders in the amateur circuit and Eddie had been involved in the rodeo longer than Maggie had been alive. A good part of her worried that Charlie would doubt the validity of the claim because he and Eddie had done hundreds of events together. It would end up being her word against theirs. She brought her thumb to her mouth and chewed on the cuticle until she drew blood.

*If I report Chet, he'll make my life a living hell.* Since Flux had come into her life, Chet had stopped stalking her, and resorted to throwing her lewd and glaring looks whenever Flux wasn't with her. And even though Maggie had been strong and stood up to Chet before Flux had become so ingrained in her life, the good ol' boys' club was still alive and well in the rodeo world. The last thing she needed was to start shit all over again with Chet she'd ratted him out, and Eddie wouldn't take too kindly to her betrayal either.

The more Maggie mulled it over, the clearer it became that there wasn't any good way out of the mess thrown at her. Maybe she'd talk about it with Flux when he got back the following morning.

*Yeah ... that's what I'll do.*

But the next morning seemed like a lifetime away.

## CHAPTER TWENTY-FOUR

# MAGGIE

*Later that day*

"THAT WAS A good run, but next time try reining in sooner and into the opposite side of where you think your horse is heading, that way he's anticipating one thing, but you're feeding him something else. It'll re-train him and let you do what you want with him in the ring. Does that make sense?" Maggie asked the dusty woman, who was slightly younger than her twenty-five years, as they hung out at the fence's edge after the younger woman's ride. "You're fierce, but you have to know when to give them the right feedback."

The woman nodded. "Thanks for taking the time to help me out."

Maggie smiled at the newcomer in the barrel racing event. It was nice to be appreciated for all her hard work, and Maggie was more than happy to mentor anyone in the sport. There needed to be other women out there vying for the big leagues too. She couldn't create a movement of women barrel riders breaking barriers like herself, if she alone kept all the good information and didn't spread the love around.

"You're welcome. Just remember—you're the one in control at all times. You're good out there and that's half the battle."

The woman smiled. "Thanks, that means a lot to me. I'll try that in practice next—"

"Excuse me, I hate to interrupt." A man she hadn't seen before tapped the younger woman on the shoulder and looked at Maggie with a sheepish smile. "The a couple of sponsors want to see you backstage.

They have a few questions and want to run some new ideas by you."

Maggie sighed then smiled at her protégé. "You know where I'll be after the show if you think of anything else you want to ask me."

"Yes. Thanks." The woman grinned, tipped her hat, and limped away.

Maggie glanced at the man and made a gesture for him to lead the way, and she followed close behind him.

It wasn't unusual for sponsors to take in a rodeo show from the stands and then restructure their branding and marketing plans once they saw how their audience responded to various stimuli. Over the years, Maggie had gone to a few of those meetings. The last one had been a debate on which hat color she should wear in the ring. While it seemed ridiculous to her most of the time, the sponsors wanted to use every bit of her to stick their product in people's brains so they would remember to buy it. The fact that sponsorships were financially lucrative didn't hurt either. So, if it involved wearing a pale pink hat, which was the color of their clothing line, versus the fawn-color she normally wore, then so be it. The money she received went a long way in sustaining her riding career because a life on the rodeo circuit was filled with expenses.

"Just back here, miss. Thank you." The man led her past the hookup hallways, the ones where she'd witnessed Chet make his drug deal, and took a sharp right into a part of the building she hadn't been in before now. "They wanted to pick a more discreet room today because the competition is also here; their ongoing battle with one another has gotten worse since you last spoke to them."

Maggie nodded even though his words didn't make sense to her, but before she could analyze them, he opened the door and used his hand on her lower back to guide her into the room before shutting the door. Her lip curled at the odd touch still lingering at the small of her back. The room was weirdly dark and cavernous.

"Hello? Where is everyone?" Maggie called out, wiping her suddenly sweaty palms on her jeans. Her stomach tightened with a niggle of fear.

She licked her lips, vainly searching through the blackness before someone hit a light switch somewhere, and a bright light flooded the space.

Maggie winced and blinked as she tried to adjust to the abrupt lighting. In the far corner of the room, a figure stood still, clinging to the shadows. All her senses went on high alert and she tensed, gingerly fumbling her way backward toward the door. Her hand searched behind her for the knob, knowing it could make or break the moment for getting out of this screwed up situation.

Maggie knew that the "meeting" sure as hell had nothing to do with sponsorships or promotions—she'd been duped. Then Chet stepped out of the shadows just as her hand gripped the cool doorknob. Maggie wrenched it with all her might, and half-turned to swing it open so she could get the hell out of there, but the damn thing was locked. Her mind whirled. *Fuck... this isn't good. What the hell am I going to do?* Maggie spun around and kept her back against the door's fake wood grain. Her brain scrambled for a way out, while the rest of her body switched from panic to anger to shock, which left her numb and tingling at the same time.

"Chet, what the fuck's this about? What're you doing? I'm sick of playing your stupid mind games, and if you don't let me out of here, I'll scream bloody murder until security busts down the damn door."

Truth be told, Maggie had no idea if security even went this far back into the building. *I was an idiot to follow a stranger back here. Okay, stop. Now isn't the time to beat myself up. I've got to stay vigilant and on my game.* The situation reeked of danger and she didn't have anything close to a weapon nearby. Maggie had to get out of there, but she knew if she made one mistake, Chet would be on her like a targeted bull. There was no room for error.

"Honeycakes, you saw something you weren't supposed to, and I know you're not going to forget it. So, that puts us in a little predicament that needs to be solved quickly and without a whole lot of fuss."

Maggie swallowed and felt all the blood drain from her face. "Let me out of this room, Chet." She threatened, low and fierce, allowing all her anger to show past the fear that was making her insides quiver.

A cruel smile curled up on his lips. "No can do, *honeycakes*. I've got to keep you here until some of my associates show up. But as long as we're alone together, waiting, and bored … we might as well have some fun, right?"

"Chet, this is insane. You're being a jackass."

Maggie rattled the doorknob again in vain, hoping that she might be able to break it, but it wasn't budging even an inch. A small whimper built in her chest and she squashed it down, unwilling to let Chet sense her fear as he moved through the shadows at the corner of the room and into the full light.

"Chet, you need to think of the consequences here. You're doing this on rodeo property, if someone found you or found out …" Her voice died away as her throat grew tight with panic. "I won't tell anyone about what I saw. It doesn't even have anything to do with me. Let me leave and I'll take it to my grave, okay?"

"No, you little biker whore, it's not okay. Everything is very fucked up, and the way I see it, the root of everything going wrong in my life starts and ends with you. So, what we're going to do here is teach you a nice little lesson and that way you won't disgust me quite as much once I'm done with you."

She curled up into herself while Chet cornered her against the door and threw his hat on the floor.

"I thought you were too good for me before, but I didn't get it back then. Now, I do—*I'm* too fucking good for *you*. What you really need is to be used like the dirty slut you are. You just spread your legs for that asshole, didn't you? And you played all proper and shit with me. Well, not anymore, *honeycakes*. I'm going to treat you just like he does—like a fuck toy. That's what you want, isn't it? Then you'll want to be with me. Isn't that how it works for tramps like you?"

"Shut the hell up, you bastard," Maggie seethed, ripping her arm out of the way as he fought to grab her wrist. "Don't you fucking touch me!"

Chet was on her before she could think of where to go to get away from him. One second she was wrestling her arm from his grip, and the next, he had blocked every inch of her body against the door so there was no room for escape. She clenched her teeth and forced her body to relax against him. Pliant.

"That's better. That wasn't so hard, was it?" Chet whispered against her ear as one of his hands slid down the front of her button-down plaid shirt and squeezed her breast. "As long as you cooperate, I'll take good care of you, honeycakes."

It took everything inside Maggie not to flinch away from him. Inside, her stomach swam with revulsion and she pushed aside the hot wash of anger at being violated as he shoved his hands under the hem of her shirt and pawed at her body. He kept talking to her, but Maggie blocked out his words as a faint buzzing pricked at her temples until she crawled into a deep, dark hole inside herself that she didn't know was there.

As soon as Chet seemed lost in his little fucked up fantasy, that's when Maggie didn't hesitate—she went for his balls, wrapping her hand around his junk and massaging gently.

He moaned into her ear. "That's it, honeycakes. I like what you're doing to me."

Maggie fondled and played as his face slanted down onto hers for a passionate kiss, and she almost gagged as his tongue laid like a dead fish inside her mouth. There wasn't room in her brain to think clearly—everything was on autopilot.

Then Maggie tightened her grip into a vice and ripped upward with all her might as if she were going to tear his balls off his body and throw them in the corner. Chet let out a blood-curdling scream and jerked back while he tried to push her off of him, but Maggie hung on like a pit bull with a hell of a grudge.

"You … fucking … cunt!" Chet screamed in a high-pitched wail.

Maggie was so bent on hanging on to his junk that she never even saw Chet's fist until he'd swung it across the side of her skull. The blow made her head explode as she staggered back, then everything started to fade away and the room turned to black.

## CHAPTER TWENTY-FIVE

# FLUX

"YOU WANT ANOTHER one? I don't think we're done drinking to your homecoming." Smokey's words slurred together as he held up the bottle of Jack Daniels and wiggled it between his fingers. "This party isn't over until we have to break out another two."

Flux laughed along with the crowd that had formed around the bar after church, just like they'd always done when he was an active member. It was like he'd never left.

Smokey poured another round and slid them across the bar. As Flux downed the shot and the whiskey burned into his gut, he glanced around the room and saw that after all these years, nothing had really changed—but that everything was so damn different for him.

Tank was fucking Charlotte on the pool table, going at her from behind like a rabbit on steroids, and Kristy, Lola, and Brandi surrounded Hubcap, as per usual. Everyone around Flux was going all out and having themselves a good time. The guys never stopped living their best lives, and as much as Flux wanted to join in on the party and forget his life for a little while, it wasn't that simple anymore. What once was the only thing he lived for, losing himself in debauchery and over-indulgence, now made him kind of fucking sad. Flux wanted more in his life than a steady stream of booze and weed and throwing chicks out of his bed.

*Fuck. I want Maggie.*

The thought solidified in his brain until everything became crystal clear with the kind of clarity he hadn't had in years. As much as Flux loved his brothers and wanted to party with them, one crucial part of his heart was missing—Duchess. He wondered what Maggie would make of the MC, but he hoped that someday he could show this part of his life to her and that she'd understand and accept it. A life that screamed at him to reclaim, and now that he'd found a new lease on life with Maggie by his side, the pull to his old life was stronger than ever.

Flux put his forehead on the bar and took a deep breath. He was a fucking goner for his Duchess. It was never more evident to him as he watched his brothers drink, fuck, and smoke the time away, while he played the goodie two shoes who couldn't wait to get back to his woman. *My woman. I like the fuckin' sound of that.* Flux had only felt that way about one other woman, and he'd done the right thing back then too. He'd claimed Alicia and married her, promising to never let her go, and then she was taken from him.

Flux would never let that happen to Maggie. He'd never make the mistake he'd made with Alicia, and he'd keep Maggie safe at all costs. Anything else, like ignoring his feelings because it was hard and fucking complicated and not the right damn time was all utter bullshit. When it was right, it was right, and he refused to let Maggie slip through his fingers because he was scared of what might happen to her if he let her into his life.

"Rosie's been waiting for you, bro," Smokey said as he tapped Flux on the shoulder.

Flux jerked his head up, rubbed his eyes, and glanced out the window at the streaks of red and gold painting the sky.

"I've gotta get back. See you in the morning in Kremmling."

"I thought you were staying the night," Smokey said.

"I changed my mind."

"But Rosie's so ripe, dude. Are you sure you—"

Flux cut him off with a grin that was so damn wide that it hurt his fucking facial muscles because they hadn't been used like that in a long time.

"You look like a fuckin' demented clown." Smokey howled.

"Whatever. See you tomorrow." Flux bumped fists with a few of the brothers, then walked out into the cool air. The sweet scent of wildflowers danced on the soft breeze and a flock of birds squawked overhead as he jumped on his bike and switched on the engine. In less than five minutes, he was on the main highway making his way to Maggie.

An hour later, when Flux pulled up next to Maggie's truck in the parking lot, he could barely function from the sudden nerves that shook through him—the kind of vibrations that ripped through him as if he tore across a rumble strip on his motorcycle. What the fuck did he say in this kind of situation? Fuck him, he was lost and idiotic.

He took his phone out of his pocket and quickly sent a text.

**Flux:** *I'm back, Duchess. Need u.*

The idea that he might get to see her soon sent a ball of excitement to the pit of his stomach like he was a damn seventh grader with a hard-on for the first time.

Flux rolled his shoulders and tried to get ahold of himself before he headed to all her usual haunts. Maggie wasn't in the stables or in the mess hall, and he knew she wasn't in the ring because she wasn't scheduled until later on the docket that night.

"You looking for Maggie?" Jack stopped Flux in his tracks halfway outside the stables.

"Yeah. Have you seen her?"

"She was here earlier helping one of the newbies, but I haven't seen her since."

Flux scrubbed his face with his fist, ignoring the bad gut feeling brewing in the back of his head. "Have you seen Chet lately?" *Fuck, I hope I'm wrong.* The asshole cowboy wasn't one to give up, and Maggie was vulnerable without Flux on the grounds. A flare of liquid rage burned in his belly funneling out through his arms and legs as he considered the possibilities of what she could be doing with him.

"No, I haven't seen him either. Sorry I couldn't be more helpful." Jack brought a rag to his face and wiped some of the face paint off his skin then meandered away toward the washroom.

There was only one area left to check and Flux had a sinking feeling that he was right on the money where his Duchess was on the property. *Let me be wrong.* He booked it toward the back rooms, his surroundings a blur.

By the time Flux was inside again, he cursed his fucking heart because it was beating so fast and he couldn't hear anything going down in the hallway. He tried to focus.

There. A small sound. Muffled shouts.

But it was too far away still, and Flux sped down the hallway until he took a sharp turn and came face to face with a conference room that was used for VIP clients.

Flux didn't hesitate. He brought his leg up and rammed his shitkicker into the doorknob, crushing the hunk of metal and breaking it off the door in two hits as he barreled into the room.

What he saw made his blood go cold.

"Fucking hell!" Chet yelled, shaking his head with his pants around his ankles and his dick hanging out. Splayed on the desk was Maggie on her stomach. "Get the fuck outta here, asshole." A slight quiver cut through the bravado in Chet's voice.

At first the situation before him didn't really sink in, and he stared at Maggie's tear-stained cheek as she looked at him from where her face was slammed against the desk. Her shirt and jeans were down around her ankles, and another guy held her hips as if he was about to ram home inside of her. Chet held Maggie's arms behind her back.

"Flux," she sobbed softly.

A white-hot, seething rage shot through him in a quick burst of sensation.

Then he saw red.

## FORGIVENESS

The whole universe condensed down to his hand, and in two quick strides Flux was in front of the first motherfucker, clocking him so hard the pussy landed flat on his back, out cold. Flux rounded out the beating with a few solid kicks to the asshole's ribcage.

Maggie struggled up from the desk, and Flux put himself in front of her within a split second and caught Chet's fist as it flew through the air.

"Fuck. She's got bruises from you. You're gonna pay for every fuckin' one of them," Flux rumbled low in his chest as he gripped Chet's fist and threw him off his feet. "Let's see you do the same shit to me that you did on Maggie. Fuckin' pussies like you always pick on the women."

Before Chet could reply, Flux locked an arm around the bastard's neck and dragged him back off balance, nailing him over and over again in the kidney with Flux's knee. The first blow knocked the air out of the wimp. After that it was all muffled screams, small pleas, and useless attempts to breathe. Flux didn't relent for a one second. He pounded the guy in the nose *again* for good measure and swung Chet around and pushed him toward the desk as Flux held the cowboy's arms behind his back.

"Give him something to remember you by, Duchess. You get a piece in this fight too."

Flux locked eyes with Maggie as her lower lip trembled and she licked at the dried blood, wincing. He wanted to keep beating the fucker until he was dead and buried. Instead, he settled for tightening his grip as Chet moaned in pain.

"If you pass out, I'll fuckin' wake you up. I'm not done with you yet," Flux growled in Chet's ear as Maggie stared at them both, a vacant look in her eyes.

Flux nodded and jerked his head toward the bedraggled bull rider. "Go on, Duchess."

Maggie hesitated for a second then kicked her leg forward and delivered a solid blow with her foot right between Chet's legs. He groaned and sunk to his feet, and Flux dragged his ass back up so Maggie could deliver a second blow.

Flux laughed dryly when Chet groaned again. "There's a rumor going around that you fuckin' suck in bed, asshole. Maybe my woman will make that true for you. It's kinda hard to perform without functioning balls, asswipe."

Maggie doubled up her fists and landed two good blows to the other man's stomach. Flux felt them shudder through his spine and he couldn't help but smile at his woman with a look of straight pride written across his smug face. She wiped a hand across her mouth and it came away with blood from a split lip. Another sharp stab of hatred made Flux twist Chet's arm until he was half-naked and on his knees before Maggie, who spit on his head.

"The only fuckin' thing keeping you from the goddamn grave is that I don't want my woman to be a party to your murder. But if you ever so much as speak or even look her way again, I'll make sure you meet the grim-fuckin'-reaper, pretty boy." Flux dropped the rider's arm, slammed his shoe into the back of his spine until Chet yelped and went flat to the floor. "You stay there like the fuckin' slug you are and think about how every damn minute of the day you should be thanking me for sparing your pitiful life."

Without another word, Flux scooped up Maggie into his arms burrowing his nose into her hair and whispering all the sweet nothings he could think of that might comfort her after what she'd been through.

"Is it okay that I'm doing this? You're not … sore or anything?" Flux asked, carrying her out into the hallway and making a beeline for her truck. But what he really wanted to ask was if he was only making things worse by touching her now. He hoped the shit she'd suffered at the hands of Chet and the other fucker hadn't bled through to Flux touching her.

But he had his answer when Maggie's teeth chattered against him and her fingers dug into his T-shirt, as if she never wanted to let him go again.

"Okay … shh … I'm taking you back to the motel, Duchess. I've got your back—always."

## CHAPTER TWENTY-SIX

# FLUX

BY THE TIME Flux had gotten a few sips of whiskey into Maggie and had her tucked into bed, some of his rage was now a simmer instead of a full rolling boil. When they'd arrived back at his motel room, she'd asked him to join her in the shower, and a huge amount of relief spread through him at the request. Maggie had turned the water on full blast and maximum burn-your-skin-off temperature, and Flux had washed every inch of her from top to bottom—twice at her insistence. When he'd wrapped the towel around her, all of her skin was baby pink except for her face, which was still pale and haunted.

Without saying a word, he'd given her one of his shirts and a pair of sweatpants he never wore to bed, tucking her in as if he knew how to do the caretaker bullshit. Every five seconds he kept asking her if she was okay and if she needed anything. He figured he was annoying the hell out of her, but he couldn't help it.

"You need to sleep, baby," he'd said in a low voice.

Maggie had nodded but kept her gaze pinned on the hunk of junk TV on the scratched-up dresser. There was some kind of musical on—an old one in black and white, but he didn't watch much of it because he couldn't take his eyes off her for a single second.

Flux stood up and shoved his hands in his pockets, fishing around for some coins and dollar bills. "I'll be right back," he said as he opened the door and looked at her. She didn't say a word or give him a glance, her eyes stayed fixed on a skinny dude whirling a pretty girl around a dance floor.

Flux stepped out into the cool air and made his way to the dented vending machine around the corner. He bought a hot chocolate and a small bag of M&Ms, and anything else that was chocolate and candy coated. He hurried back, not wanting to leave her alone for more than a few minutes. Flux closed the door and put the purchases on the nightstand next to her then went into the bathroom to wash his hands.

When he came back into the room, Maggie sat up in bed, surrounded by wrappers and clutching her Styrofoam cup. He glanced at her death grip and a ball of tension settled in the pit of his stomach. *Shit. I don't know how to make it better for her, and it's fuckin' killing me.*

"Flux?" Her voice was hoarse as she snuggled down into the pillows.

"Yeah, Duchess. Whaddaya need?" He peeled himself off of the wall right next to her bedside. "Is your drink cold? You want another one?"

"Will you come sit with me, please?" she whispered.

Fuck, he wasn't used to this small, vulnerable voice coming out of his sassy, shit-kicking Duchess; it nearly ripped him in half. Flux cleared his throat and took a seat on the edge of the bed on top of the covers. He didn't want to overwhelm her right now, and if she needed more than that, he hoped she'd ask for it.

When Maggie's arms opened for him, he scooted next to her without hesitation and curled around her body angling her head on his chest. They stayed like that for a long time, and every now and then, she'd sing a line or two with one of the actors on the screen. Flux ran his fingers through her hair over and over again mostly to convince himself that she was there—that she was safe. *No one's ever gonna touch you again, Duchess, or I'll fuckin' kill anyone who tries.*

Sighing and wincing, Maggie rearranged herself so she looked up at him from her nest in the pillows.

"Are you okay? Am I hurting you?" he asked, unable to keep the concern from his voice.

"No, it's okay." She ran her fingers down the front of his T-shirt. "I realized something today."

"Oh yeah?" Flux leaned his head on his hand, resting his elbow against the bed as he looked at the most beautiful woman he'd ever seen in his life. "Tell me."

"I love you, Flux. I've tried not to because I know it makes things all kinds of complicated between us, we agreed we'd be casual and—"

"Duchess," he cut her off and then a huge-ass grin spread across his face as he grabbed one of her hands. "I love you too. You're what I've been waiting for. You brought me back to life again. And I don't care if it breaks our fuckin' agreement. You wanna know something, darlin'? You had me from the second I saw you swaying your hips by the jukebox and you gave me a whole lotta sass. I didn't want to admit to myself how serious I could fall for you until it was too late."

"S-so, wait ..." Maggie stuttered, slightly brightening as her hand squeezed his back. "You mean?"

"I want you in my life, Duchess, and not as a fuck buddy. I want you to be mine, and nothing made that clearer than when I saw you in that fuckin' room." Pricks of anger burned through his veins.

"It's okay," she said softly.

"I think you're the sexiest, most beautiful, and most genuine woman I've met in a damn long time, Duchess." He locked his gaze on hers. "You make me want to be a better man."

Maggie's lips twitched as a flush crept up into her cheeks. Groaning softly, she hid her face in the pillow.

"It's so fuckin' adorable when you get bothered, Duchess. Every part of you is amazing and if I ever stop appreciating you, you have my full permission to deck me in the damn face and rip my fucking balls off, got it?"

"Noted," Maggie said, her face still buried in the pillow.

"Glad that's settled. Now for starters, you're gonna stay with me while we're in town."

"Kind of like moving in together?" she asked, this time bringing her head up, her brows drawn down low.

"Fuck, yeah. You staying two doors down from me is bullshit, but if you don't want—"

"No. It's perfect. Of course I will!"

Flux barely had time to breathe a sigh of relief before Maggie jumped on him and tackled him down on the mattress as she rained kisses all over his face, neck, and collarbone. Flux clasped both sides of her face between his hands and kissed the hell out of his woman as if it was the last kiss they might ever share together.

He was achingly aware how fleeting life was, and he wasn't about ready to waste a moment of it without Maggie along for the ride. *This time I won't fuck up. Things will be different.* As he continued to make out with Maggie and savor every second beneath her touch, he sent up a small thank you to Alicia, knowing she was smiling down on him with their daughter tucked in her arms.

The way Flux's life had turned around so fast in the past few weeks, he had every notion that his sweet Alicia had brought Maggie into his life. He was convinced that Alicia wanted to stop the destructive road he'd taken. Although guilt still riddled his body, and he had a ton of self-forgiveness to go, for the first time since his family was killed, he was back on the right path again.

"Thank you," he whispered into Maggie's hair as she kissed his neck and her lips moved over his jawline. "Thank you for tearing me away from the asshole I used to be and for helping me become a man worthy of you."

Flux felt her physically melt into him at the same time that his arms wrapped around her waist as their bodies fused together. The sweet sounds of whatever musical was on TV played in the background as they clung onto each other like magnet to steel.

"Do you believe in happily ever afters?" Maggie whispered. "I didn't used to at all. In fact, I thought my luck with men was pretty shitty and that I'd never fall in love. That's why I put everything into my career—it didn't need to love me back."

"What changed, darlin'? Me showing up at that bar and rockin' your world?" Flux laughed.

"It was the way you held me when we danced, it was so … tender. You treated me like something special and precious even though you didn't know me. I don't know … that just stuck with me." She craned her neck and kissed the base of his throat. "Even though you're rough around the edges, you've always treated me like a princess."

"You deserve it, Duchess."

"And you deserve to be happy, despite everything you've been through, Flux. I want to make you happy."

"What the fuck do you think you're doing right now? At this very second?" Flux cupped his hand under her jaw. His pulse hammered at the silky-soft feel of her tender skin under his rough fingers.

"It's one moment of many," Maggie whispered against his lips as she slid her hand under his shirt, caressing up his stomach toward his chest, and bringing his shirt up with her arms.

Flux growled and ground the hard bulge in his pants against Maggie, then took her mouth in a wild kiss.

## CHAPTER TWENTY-SEVEN

# FLUX

*The next night*

"YOU CALLED CHARLIE and made an appointment to tell him about that fucker and what type of shit's going on in his rodeo, right?" Flux double-checked as he threw on his favorite black T-shirt and tied a green bandanna around his head. "Unless I'm with you, I don't want you leaving the room until Charlie takes care of that psycho bastard, okay?"

"Okay, and Charlie's coming by later to talk about what happened and why I'm not competing tonight. I'll stay put. I never pictured you as a worrier." Maggie laughed. "You fret over me like a mother hen." Maggie threw off the covers and walked naked and barefoot over to him. She bent down and picked up his white T-shirt and slipped it on over her head.

"Fuck, you're the hottest woman I've ever seen in my life. If I didn't have a damn obligation—" He cut off the thought and cupped her ass with one hand while his free one twisted all that hair and yanked her head back. He kissed her hard and deep.

When Flux broke away, they were both breathing heavily, and he had a boner that was going to be annoying as fuck when it came time to grind down on the damn Satan's Pistons.

"Where're you going?"

"I told you I got some club business."

"What does that mean?"

"It means I can't tell you shit." He smiled and tweaked the tip of her nose then swatted her ass.

"Why not?"

Flux shrugged as he slipped a hunter's knife into the pocket of his cut. "It's just the way it is in the outlaw world."

Tears sprang up into her blue eyes as she stared at him. "Be careful, Flux. Come back to me in one piece. I don't want to lose you now that we just found each other."

He drew her to him and squeezed her tight as he rubbed his hands up and down her back. "Don't worry about me. There's no fuckin' way I'm not coming back. Double lock the door and stay safe. That's an order, Duchess." He kissed her gently then pulled away.

"Yes, sir," she teased, but her gaze still held concern.

"Go on back to bed and watch a movie. I'll be back before you know it. If Charlie gets here before I do, make sure it's him and he's alone before you open the door. If some shit goes down, call the fuckin' badges."

"I'll be fine, really."

"Do you know how to use a gun?" Maggie nodded. Flux crossed the room and rummaged through his duffel bag and pulled out a thirty-eight revolver.

Maggie's eyes widened. "Is that something you carry around with you all the time?"

"Yeah. I'm on my own a lot so I gotta have protection." He laid it down on top of the nightstand. "If you need to—use it."

"Okay," she whispered.

He hated to be away from Maggie for even a single second right now, but his club had a score to settle with the Pistons. For the better half of the morning, Flux and the rest of his brothers had met about thirty miles away from Kremmling to discuss the plans for later that night. They decided a beatdown was in order and deadly force would only be used if one of the Pistons took out a weapon.

Flux opened the door and looked at her before he headed out. "I'll be back as soon as possible. Call if you need anything, Duchess, or text if I don't answer."

Maggie nodded and shooed him off with a wave of her hands, but he hesitated in the open doorway, halfway in the world and halfway out of the reality he wanted to be his forever.

"Oh, and Duchess?"

"Yeah?"

"I love you."

Then he walked out into the darkness, closing the door behind him.

★ ★ ★

FLUX MET HIS Insurgent brothers outside the rodeo grounds, in a vacant dirt lot that was less than a block away. They did the meet and greet routine, and then Hawk went over the ground rules again. The club wanted to keep contact with the badges at a minimum, but if they had to use deadly force they would, but they'd have to hightail it out of there before any badges showed up.

Flux glanced around at the well-rounded group of brawlers, knuckle busters, and dirty fighters and chuckled. *Satan's Pistons are royally fucked.*

"You think the pussies are gonna show up?" Animal asked as he lit up a joint.

"They're too fucking stupid not to," Steel, the president of the Night Rebels, answered.

"After we're done kicking their asses, maybe we can see if we can pick up some rodeo chicks. Do you know any?" Smokey asked.

Flux nodded. "A few."

"We're heading back to Pinewood Springs. We don't need any fuckin' trouble with the damn badges. You can fuck a club girl or a hangaround when you get back," Hawk said as he glanced at his phone. "What time are these fuckers supposed to be here?"

"I left a note on one of their bikes telling them to meet us at ten. We got some time," Flux said.

"What if they thought it was a joke?" Wheelie said.

"The grapevine says they didn't. They've found out Flux is an Insurgents' nomad," Hawk answered.

"Too bad this shit didn't go down in southern Colorado. We'd ride into Arizona and blow their fuckin' clubhouse to hell and back. These assholes don't know shit about respect." Army kicked at the dirt on the ground. As a Night Rebel member, he and his fellow brothers had a special axe to grind with their rival.

A sudden silence fell over the group of outlaws as the familiar sound of motorcycles rumbled in the distance.

Animal threw the partially smoked joint to the ground and stubbed it out. "Looks like it's time to rock and roll."

"Everyone, take your positions," Hawk said. Several of the bikers disappeared into the shadows and took cover behind the large evergreen trees.

That morning, Flux had noticed several more bikes in the rodeo parking lot so he'd figured the Pistons sent for reinforcements. If the assholes thought they outnumbered the Insurgents and Night Rebels, they'd have a false sense of confidence and that was when mistakes—usually deadly ones in the outlaw world—happened.

"Do what we got to do, you hear me? First sign of a weapon and there's no holding back," Hawk said.

The men grunted and checked the insides of their cuts, waistbands, and boots—all signs that they were ready to throw down hard. Flux rolled his shoulders, cracked his neck, and jumped up and down a few times to loosen his joints. It'd been quite a while since he'd been in a halfway decent fight.

The pussy dustups with Chet-the-asshole didn't count for shit and didn't even begin to compare with a brawl between outlaw clubs. Besides, the pretty-boy cowboy had a jacked-up swing and Flux had easily taken him down. It'd been fucking child's play. As for a good old-fashioned fight, it must have been at least two years ago. Flux didn't usually make it a habit to throw out a signal to the world that he was in town. Since going nomad, he'd learned that the best way to play it was under the radar.

Now, with his club behind him, Flux didn't have to give a flying fuck. He could let shit get as crazy as he wanted to, which was a good deal given the fact that he had a ton of pent-up rage from the day before brewing in his guts. Flux spat on the ground and threw out a few practice punches.

The roar grew closer. Shit was about to go down in a big way—and Flux was more than ready for it. He knew there wouldn't be many words involved, that was a given. The biker felt a large hand land on his shoulder and he looked back at Hubcap.

"We're going before the word go." Hubcap squeezed Flux's shoulder laughing. "This is gonna be a fuckin' blast, dude. I haven't cracked some skulls in at least six months. I'm so fuckin' ready."

Hubcap threw his head back and let out a wolf howl, then a few of the other members echoed the noise as a hot line of excitement licked through Flux's veins. Tell the fuckers what the problem was then attack—that's how this was going down for damn sure.

A long line of motorcycles turned around the corner and Flux figured the Pistons were outnumbered by at least five men. *Fuck, it feels damn good to be back in the saddle.* The same hit of adrenaline that jolted through him during a bull fight rode him hard now.

By the time the assholes pulled into the dirt lot, grime spewing out everywhere, the tension and excitement were so damn thick that it'd take a shitload of hunting knives to cut through it. Demon dismounted and the other Pistons followed suit. They stood in a straight line, glowering at the Insurgents and Night Rebels.

"You're dealing in Insurgents' territory," Hawk said in an even voice.

"We're not doing shit." Demon took a step forward.

"Didn't figure you went in for rodeos." Hawk took a step toward the

Pistons' president.

"We like the pretty bitches in cowboy boots," Demon snarled and his club members snickered.

Steel stood next to Hawk. "We don't give a shit what the fuck you do with the bulls or the wimpy ass bull fighters."

"Steel. I shoulda figured you'd put your fuckin' nose in this." Demon raised his hand to his cut.

"I wouldn't do that," Steel gritted. "This can go down as a beatdown or blood bath—it's your choice."

Demon's hand froze in mid-air.

"What we give a fuck about is the meth you're dealing in our territory." Hawk took another step forward. "Disrespect, shitting on our turf, and being so fuckin' stupid adds up to you getting your asses kicked." Hawk jerked his head back.

All of a sudden Goldie, Diablo, Rock, Hubcap, Jerry, Army, Throttle, Wheelie, Sangre, and Smokey bum rushed the assholes where they stood. The fight was on!

Flux took whoever was closest, which happened to be a tall balding asshole with a mustache out of some kind of fucked up '70s porn. Maybe if he hit the jerk hard enough, he could knock him back to that decade. The Pistons' patch said his name was Torro. *I can't get away from fuckin' bulls.* Flux chuckled just as Baldie shoved himself off the bike and let it fall on the dirt. His expression was half-menacing and half-surprised that shit had gone down so quickly. But thinking stupid shit and laughing about it was exactly how dudes ended up dead in these kinds of clashes. Flux clenched his hands and rushed toward the bull. The second he was in range, Flux hurtled a fist backward and pounded the asshole in the face, countering with another quick side blow that should have left little birdies flying around Torro's head.

Instead, the bald asshole manned-the-fuck-up and rocked back on his heels, sneering and wiping the blood that was dripping down into the dirt from his nose. He took a series of good shots, but the fucker was clearly more resilient than Chet. Torro started laughing, a weird maniacal sound that burbled from the cuts in his mouth.

"You're a piece of work, motherfucker." Flux squared up again and waited for the jerk to take a cheap shot or two. He almost wanted to give the guy the chance to get in a few good ones, so Torro's ego didn't bruise when it was all over for him in the next two seconds.

The two bikers circled each other while the growls and noises of pain sounded out around Flux as his brothers kicked the Pistons' sorry asses. From his peripheral, he saw that shit was going down hard all around him. There was a loud noise, like someone rammed someone else into a bike and everything toppled to the dirt. Loud grunts and a slew of insults filled the night air. Oh, yeah, Flux was back in the game, and it hadn't changed at all. Unlike bullfighting, he didn't have to mind his damn p's and q's here. All that mattered was he hit hard, fast, and didn't wind up on the ground.

Flux stepped in to deliver another right hook, but Baldie went low instead of high and nailed him in the stomach with a blow that knocked the wind out of him. Letting out a quick, sharp gasp, Flux tried to recover before the fucker had any more badass intentions in his brain. Quick as hell, he self-corrected and grabbed his own fist that he had around Baldie, connecting it with his other one and bringing the weight of his body down onto the fucker's back. Dude buckled like a seventh grader in his first fight as Flux brought his knee up into his stomach.

A hit for a hit was only fair, dammit.

The guy made a sharp grunt, his hands shooting out. Before Flux could track it, Torro whipped Flux's legs out from under him with two sharp pulls of his hands. The air *whizzed* past his ears and he had half a second to compute that this was going to fucking hurt. Luckily, he wasn't going down alone. The other bastard had caught him enough by surprise that Flux hadn't had time to loosen his hands around Torro's neck, so when he took a dirt nap, so did the big sonofabitch.

They landed with a *thud* that jutted through Flux's spine, afraid he wouldn't be able to move right in the morning. But the second he got a small sip of air, Torro got his ass half off of Flux, bracing himself with one hand. Shit, time to motor. But there wasn't time. The other man grabbed Flux's undershirt and went for a beat down straight to his face.

"Ugh, fuckin' asshole," Flux grunted, blocking his face with his forearms and fists, catching an off punch with one hand. The asshole was tiring. Now, there was some good news.

Flux didn't waste time. He angled his hip off the ground, rolling Torro to the right and throwing his leg over him until they were in the exact same position, only Flux had the upper hand this time. His face still smarted something awful, but at least he could see, Torro's eye was starting to swell shut. A small laugh trickled out from behind Flux's busted lip, and he could sense it swelling as he threw another rough punch toward the guy's temple.

"You always talk during a brawl, asshole?"

"When it's fuckin' boring, yeah," Flux taunted him.

Torro came at him again, and Flux stepped back. *I'm ending this shit right now.* He stiffened his hand and when the asshole came close, Flux chopped him on the side of the neck. Torro groaned and bowled over, and Flux swung around and clipped him with his left foot. That did the trick, and Torro face planted in the dirt.

Without wasting a beat, Flux spun around and took in the rest of the scene. Shit was getting spotty and everyone was giving out; random guys were grappling on the ground while two-on-ones were happening all over the place. Jerry was caught in a headlock with two bastards going at his head.

Yeah, that shit wasn't going to fly.

As Flux rushed over to help Jerry out, he saw the blade of a knife gleaming in the moonlight. Demon whirled around.

"Hawk! Fucker's got a knife!" Flux yelled.

Then all hell broke loose.

## CHAPTER TWENTY-EIGHT

# FLUX

Knives. Chains. Kill switches. The bar had been shoved up in a big way.

Blood splattered everywhere.

Cries. Groans. Curses.

The sound of bones splintering, air escaping from lungs, and the *thud* of bodies hitting the ground. Then a metallic scent filled Flux's nostrils, and he knew the fist fight had turned into a carnage. The smell of blood was something Flux would never forget as long as he lived. Images of Alicia and Emily flashed through his mind as he warded off an attack by a Satan's Piston who was built like a goddamn brick-house.

"Fuck!" Tank's voice rose above the noise. The Insurgent had come out from behind the trees with the others to throw themselves into the fight.

Tank was on the ground and a burly motherfucker with a big ass knife in his hand straddled the Insurgent. Without thinking, Flux slipped his hand inside his cut and withdrew the hunting knife as he rushed over to help out Tank. Just as the asshole was ready to sink his blade into Tank's gut, Flux plunged his into the asshole's back. The guy cried out and it gave a split-second advantage to Tank who threw the Piston off him, and then began to kick the shit out of him.

Flux looked around at the carnage. A majority of his brothers were still standing, Diablo and Smokey half-dragged Rock to a safer spot from what looked like a gnarly jagged knife wound in the sergeant-at-arm's calf. *Fuck, that isn't something he can just sleep off.* Flux winced and surveyed the remaining bikers who were still duking it out something fierce.

Sirens in the distance sliced through the hatred. *Sonofabitch, what fuckin' narc called the badges?* Flux glanced over at Hawk, who'd just clobbered a Piston on the back of the neck with a kill switch. Hawk let out two loud whistles that told the members to disengage from whatever they were doing and get the fuck out. The sirens drew nearer. They were running out of time, and none of them wanted to deal with the legal bullshit.

"Fuckin' badges!" Flux yelled, in case some of his brothers hadn't heard the whistles in the heat of the moment. With his own adrenaline pumping, there were times when he could've easily missed the signal because he was so intent on beating a dude's face to a pulp.

He watched Steel and Goldie scramble toward one of the SUVs carrying Sangre in between them with both his arms on either shoulder as his legs dragged behind him. The rest of the members hustled to the SUVs, and Flux looked behind him and saw that more than a few Pistons weren't moving from the dirt. The ones who were still standing rushed to drag their injured on the back of their motorcycles.

"Come on, dude!" Tank yelled as he held open the back door of one of the SUVs. Several of the others had already hit the road, their tail lights disappearing into the night.

"I'm good. Just get the fuck outta here!" Flux shouted back.

The flash of red and blue lights above the hill reflected in the haziness.

"Go!" Flux yelled.

The black vehicle took off before Tank closed the door. He lifted his chin at Flux then the door slammed and the car hit the road. The screech of tires behind Flux told him that the Pistons were hauling ass away from the lot. It was time for him to follow suit. Flux swallowed, cracked his neck, and booked it on foot to the rodeo arena. Still sore and aching in places that were going to hurt like a-bitch-and-a-half in the shower the following morning, he ran until his lungs ached. When he arrived at the fairgrounds, he got lost in the rodeo crowd then ducked into a bathroom to clean himself off. A quick rinse on his face and arms, and a clean T-shirt and pair of jeans from his locker behind the ring, and no one would be the wiser, aside from a few scrapes, cuts, and a slight swelling of his bottom lip.

The bruises that would crop up by the following day would be hidden under his clothes, only Maggie would know about them. Flux made a small noise in his throat, enjoying the imagery of his girl kissing every inch of him, trying to make the pain go away before she slipped his hard dick between her full lips. Fuck, that would put a nice cap on the end of his day. He made a mental note to text her a request before he went back to the motel.

"Where you been?" Jack asked as Flux came out of the bathroom, freshly cleaned and dressed, and glanced at the crumpled clothes Flux held in his hands.

"Around. I still feel like shit from yesterday. I think it's food poisoning."

"Oh yeah? Where'd you eat?"

"Got some chili at the convenience store. Did they get someone to replace me out in the ring tonight?"

"Yeah. Chet's in bad shape. Some fuckers ambushed him when he was in town. They beat him up pretty bad."

"Too bad." Flux opened his locker and took out a paper bag and shoved his clothes inside it.

"Yeah. He'll be outta commission for the rest of the rodeo. Heard he's gonna go back to Arkansas." Jack shrugged. "No sense in stickin' around if you can't compete."

"When's he leaving?" Flux clenched his jaw.

"Probably soon. I don't know for sure. Charlie's talking to him now."

"Keep me informed. I like to know whose ass I'm protecting in the ring."

"Will do," Jack said then ambled away.

Flux went to the stalls in search of Pete to ask him to give Flux a ride to the motel. He couldn't wait to get back to Maggie and find out what Charlie's response was to everything he and Maggie had uncovered with Chet taking shit and Eddie doping the bulls. Flux rubbed his forehead. It was enough to give him a nasty headache—everything was so damn screwed up.

But none of that changed the importance of Maggie's competition the next night. Flux knew Maggie wouldn't put herself on the sidelines when she had so much riding on her performance, and her sponsors would want her out in full force during the big night. A quick check of his phone confirmed there weren't any missed messages from his woman. After the bullshit with Chet, and Flux having been out on club business, he hoped Maggie was resting instead of worrying about things. She needed to be back in form before riding Odysseus the following night.

The semi-rodeo finals competition was what Maggie had been training for her whole life, and Flux planned to take his woman out to celebrate her victory. If she won in barrel racing, she'd be heading to Las Vegas in December for the finals, and he'd be right by her side with the biggest grin on his face. In Las Vegas, the competition was for a giant cash prize and the prestige to take her pick of jobs from any rodeos in the country. The following night would determine if she'd compete in Vegas—the Super Bowl of rodeos, and Flux was damn honored to be in on the journey with her.

Flux took out his phone and shot a quick text her way wishing her luck in advance, sending his love, and slapping on a few sappy, stupid emojis. It wasn't really his thing, but he knew she'd appreciate the sentiment. As a quick side note, he typed out a shortened version of the fantasy going down in his head and sent that too.

Within seconds, his phone beeped in response and a text fired back on the screen's window.

***Maggie:*** *U got it, big guy. But if I'm 2 tired tonight, I'm making u do all the work. U'll be riding me. Think u can tame me into submission?*

Maggie included a fucking little "winky face" at the end. Flux snorted. *Hot little vixen.* He was thankful she was feeling more up to her regular self after what had happened with Chet. Despite all the teasing, that night Flux would be sure to take it as slow as Maggie needed in case it triggered something or if she had any reservations.

He frowned, his hand tightening on the phone. Another text sound beeped through and he checked his messages.

***Maggie:*** *I'm okay. Everything is okay.*

*How the hell did she know?* Flux blinked and shoved a hand through his hair. Damn, everything about their relationship had felt right from the beginning, so he guessed it only made sense that they'd read each other like an open book. Fuck, he was starting to sound like those sappy, made-for-TV movies.

***Flux:*** *Good, u still down for what I've got planned even with all the other shit going on?*

Another quick ding. Duchess must be hovering over her phone bored out of her mind without being at work. He imagined a million and one ways to relieve her of that.

***Maggie:*** *Absolutely. I need you now more than ever, big guy.*
***Flux:*** *Oh yeah, darlin'. I'll be there soon.*

Without a doubt, he would have a blast bringing his Duchess to her knees. He grinned to himself as he took his swaggering, sore ass to the bull pens to find Pete. Now that he was back, he didn't want to waste another damn minute away from her.

★ ★ ★

THE NEXT NIGHT, Flux watched from the sidelines as Maggie threw herself into a tough turn that would've given anyone else a hard time, but his woman took on the challenge like it was nothing. He couldn't take his eyes off her: long blonde hair caught in the wind, lips compressed in concentration, thighs tight on her horse.

The course was almost done and Maggie was hands down annihilating any of her competitors. All she had to worry about from here on out was dodging the last set of barrels and making it to the end of the course to the sound of the buzzer for her final time. Strings of saliva hung from Odysseus's lips as his hooves dug into the dirt of the ring. From where he stood, Flux heard the horse's snorts and pants of exertion, and then Maggie came to a hard stop, reining back at the end of the finish line to a roar of applause.

Flux didn't waste a second; he was over the rail and charging toward her before she could even dismount. Maggie slid into his arms with a huge smile plastered on her flushed face, eyes glossy from unshed tears. Her arms hooked around Flux and he didn't hesitate to swing her off her feet and claim her lips with a kiss that even left his stomach with fucking butterflies.

"You nailed it, Duchess. I'm so damn proud of you. Of course, I never doubted you for a fuckin' second," Flux rasped in her ear as he held her close. He could feel every curve of her luscious, warm little body. "We're celebrating tonight."

"Big guy, I wouldn't miss it for the world." Maggie beamed back at him as the rodeo announcer called her up to the center of the ring where he would hand her a check and a trophy.

Flux broke away so she could collect her prizes, but Maggie nabbed his hand and dragged him with her out in front of all those damn people. When he hesitated, she laughed at him.

"Come on, I want you there with me. We're on this journey together, aren't we?" She kissed him lightly, a peck that spoke volumes, before she continued to walk toward the presenter.

The rest of the presentation was an all-out blur for Flux: clapping, shouting, and pats on the back. A couple of times he held back a wince when Maggie clung to him too hard, hurting one of his covered bruises, but nothing mattered because he was so damn proud of his Duchess. Flux wanted everyone to know that Maggie was *his* woman and that she was a class A champion in anything and everything in her life.

For an instant, Flux remembered what it felt like to be part of a unit with a partner—someone who would fight for him just as he would fight for her too. Though he couldn't be positive of the future, he knew his world was so much better with Duchess in it. And he was a damn lucky sonofabitch for it.

## CHAPTER TWENTY-NINE

# MAGGIE

Never in her wildest dreams did Maggie think she'd be this close to the finals with the life she'd longed for at her fingertips. Not only was she at the pinnacle of her career, Flux was supportive in every sense of the word. When she'd received praise and a giant check, he never stopped looking at her as if nothing else mattered to him. A warm glow of love and peace spread through her. Knowing Flux was fully behind her made her victory that night sweeter than it ever could've been by herself.

Flashes of light blinded her momentarily as she held up the big check for the photographers, who'd blast the picture across the morning papers the following morning.

*This is real. This is real.*

She kept repeating the words to herself as she petted Odysseus's nose and he gently nudged her shoulder with his snout. "You did so great out there tonight," she murmured into his ear. During her run, there'd been a spot about halfway through where she'd thought he wouldn't make it, but she relied on their connection and it got them through together.

The majority of fans had vacated the stands for the night, but a few reporters remained and asked her questions even though the bright houselights that swathed the arena switched off one by one. As the questions buzzed around her, her mind was on the next few months as she prepared for the biggest competition in the rodeo—the National Finals Rodeo. Shivers tingled down her spine just thinking about it.

"Guys, I think that's enough for the night. If you have any other questions, please see our PR person, Shania, at the front desk. She's waiting to answer any and all questions you may still have while we let our winner go and relax for the night. She deserves it, wouldn't you say?" Barb, the rodeo manager, shooed the rest of the press away, looking over her shoulder at Maggie with a wink.

"Fuck, I thought they'd never leave you in peace. Good thing Barb butted in because I was gonna say something but it wouldn't have been as nice," Flux breathed out as his arms went around her waist and he rested his chin in the crook of her neck. "How do you handle all that bullshit?"

"How do you handle facing a 2,000-pound bull?" Maggie retorted, wrapping her free hand over the top of his and squeezing. "Come on, let's get Odysseus back to the stables. My boy deserves to be pampered after his performance tonight."

They walked in silence, holding hands, as contentment rolled through her slightly tense muscles. Every few minutes she sensed her body becoming less and less keyed up from the race. By the time she walked Odysseus into his stall, she tried to close her mouth on a yawn.

"You want me to take care of Odysseus and give you a rest?" Flux ran his hand down her horse's side. "Go sit down in the corner and I'll get this, okay?"

"Are you actually asking me, or are you telling me?" Maggie put her hands on her hips. "I'm not a china doll who needs to be coddled, you know, I'm fully capable—"

"I know that, but just because you can doesn't mean you should have to, Duchess." Flux smiled gently, his face suffused with an emotion she'd never seen before on him. Something way too tender to really recognize because she was afraid as soon as she gave it a name, it would be gone. "Let me take care of you. Sit down."

Maggie shook her head and stretched, no point in lying to herself that it wasn't a nice change of pace for someone else to go through her horse's nightly ritual while she watched them. This time when she yawned, she let it out.

"There you go, Duchess. Doesn't that feel better?" Flux teased as he unsaddled Odysseus. "Just relax."

Captivated, she watched him with her horse. Flux was so gentle and thoughtful, and with every small movement, he kept a friendly hand somewhere on her horse's body, exactly as she would've done it herself. He didn't say a word as he worked, and she was mesmerized by his movements: putting all the tack back in the tack room, brushing out Odysseus with a curry comb, soaking the horse's back and neck with a warm sponge to get off any gunk or grime.

Maggie couldn't imagine this biker doing anything unkind to anyone. Though her memory of Flux beating up Chet was still fresh, *that* man and *this* tender, gentle one seemed like two halves of the same coin—only she knew that Flux would never turn the other side on her so long as he lived and breathed. He was protective, sweet, kind, and gruff in his own way, and all of that revolved back to his sense of loyalty and his willingness to right any wrong.

Maggie was convinced Flux didn't have an actual malicious bone in his body unless he was teasing her with his lips, tongue, and teeth. Only then could he be a downright tyrant—one she readily welcomed into her bed. A flash of the night before flickered through her consciousness. She bit her lip as she remembered his calloused hands pushing up her dress and coasting up her outer thighs before he yanked her off her feet and slammed her down on the small table in their motel room.

Flux's eyes had blazed with all kinds of unspoken naughty thoughts, and the grin he threw her spoke volumes about what he'd planned for her body. She'd shuddered then, as her hands automatically reached for him, but he'd grabbed her wrists, opening her palms until he put both hands on the back of her head.

"You remember what we did our first time together, Duchess?"

Maggie had nodded, wordless in response to the hunger flickering in his gaze. His intentions were predatory as his fingers continued to roam her flesh and dragged her dress higher until he'd exposed her panties. Without asking, his fingers roamed to her inner thighs putting enough pressure that she knew exactly what he wanted from her without having to say a single word.

Maggie opened her legs, revealing herself to him as her lips tipped up into a knowing smile. Flux groaned and slid his hands through her hair, holding the ends at an angle as he took her mouth and she'd wiggled to get him closer.

"What're you thinking about, Duchess? You've got fuckin' stars in those beautiful eyes." Flux's light drawl came from right next to her in the stall, and she jerked away from the wall. He chuckled. "You look downright guilty."

Brought back to reality, Maggie wiped her palms on her jeans. "I'm not thinking about anything," she said, but that damn telltale blush gave her away as she pushed her hair back with one hand and looked down toward the hay. "Are you ready to go back to the motel?"

"Well, you would've noticed I've been done for about five minutes, but you were a little preoccupied. So tell me what was on your mind." With each word Flux spoke, he stepped closer and closer until his body drew her back into the boards of the stall with a soft *thud*. Her gaze startled up from the hay and into his way-too-pleased face.

"Tell me, darlin'" he whispered against her ear, tracing his finger down the "v" of her flannel shirt then over the swell of her breasts. Her nipples hardened and poked against her bra while a flood of goosebumps prickled along her flesh. "Tell me or I'll have to guess, and whatever I guess might just embarrass you more." His penetrating gaze held her.

Maggie bit the inside of her mouth and trembled when his hand scooped down under her bra to tweak her sensitive nipple. Heat pooled between her legs, and she caught her breath as both hands glided down to his butt. She squeezed him through his jeans, loving the way his muscles tightened against the touch.

"Now how's that playing fair?" Flux said in a low voice as he toyed with her other nipple and his mouth lingered along her neck, warm air teasing where he had left a sensitive line from his tongue.

"I was ..." Maggie started before he took her breath away with his teeth nibbling along her cleavage. "I was thinking about last night."

She let out a sigh of relief now that the truth was out. As much as she hated following his commands, she loved how he could coax almost anything out of her. It was like a secret game between them: his power plays for her willing submission. Maggie arched toward him at the same time that Flux pressed his hips into her belly, and there was no doubt how aroused he was in their current situation.

Maggie licked her lips and moved one of her hands to the front of him, cupping him through his jeans before gripping him tightly. A hiss exploded from between his teeth. Oh, yes, she'd been taking notes, and Flux liked a certain touch.

Odysseus stomped his hoof with a small snort, and they both parted from each other and looked at the horse at the same time. *Shit, I'd forgotten my boy was even here. Flux makes me all kinds of mixed up.*

Maggie cleared her throat. "I need to give my boy a treat." A bolt of regret tightened her chest as Flux removed his hand from her breasts and stepped away from her body. She walked over to Odysseus and took a tote bag down from the shelf, then rummaged through it until she found a bag with apple and carrot slices. Maggie ran her fingers through the horse's mane then bent down and dropped the treats into a bucket.

Flux's hands rubbed over her ass and she straightened up and leaned back into him; his erection was thick and hard against her.

"Let's get back to the motel, Duchess. I'm gonna fuck you all night long."

It wasn't a question. Certainly not a demand. In his low, brisk voice that rolled like gravel, Flux had told her both a fact and a promise.

## CHAPTER THIRTY

# MAGGIE

*Las Vegas, Nevada*
*Four months later*

"WE CAN DO this, baby boy, okay? Just stick with me out there and no surprises, just like we practiced it," Maggie whispered in Odysseus's ear as it twitched in an affirmative reaction before his head nudged her shoulder. "We're going to be amazing out there."

She nuzzled him back and took a small sugar cube out of her pocket, feeding it to him as he made a pleased noise and lapped at her open palm.

"There'll be more of that later, after we win." Maggie took a deep breath into her abdomen and shifted her focus from her horse and the ride—to the course that was mapped out in her brain like the back of her hand.

It would be close. She'd been monitoring the scoreboards all night and she was the last one in the ring. Crappy luck, but she told herself not to worry too much about it. Whether going last or in the middle, none of the numbers defined her performance. It was all up to Maggie and her trusty steed. She applied a quick coat of lip balm, her pre-racing ritual, and shoved the tube in her jeans pocket before mounting up on Odysseus.

*This is it.* What she'd been waiting for her whole life was here in a blink of an eye. Maggie swallowed through her tight throat and closed her eyes, envisioning them both at the finish line as her name blared across the loud speaker in front of the whole rodeo. She glanced at the stands and smiled at her parents and three brothers. On the sidelines, a flash of Flux's proud facial expression made a warm, gushy feeling explode in the center of her chest.

A rap on the stall door made her jump and she focused her attention on Odysseus. It was the two-minute signal. Without wasting time, she navigated her horse out of the stall and closer to the ring then into his own holding shoot as the roar of the crowd soaked into her skin. This was the life she'd worked for, she'd begged for, and had given everything to experience. It was all paying off, big and bold, and she wished she knew with certainty how she'd gotten so lucky.

"... Odysseus!"

Maggie heard the tail end of the announcement, and then everything was a blur of speed, light, sound, and momentum. She kicked her baby boy into high gear and relished the feeling of the wind in her hair. Odysseus's quick cantor made her thighs ache as she gripped him hard so as to remain in the saddle. Her heartbeat pounded in her ear drums as adrenaline pumped through her veins.

One barrel. Two barrels. Three barrels.

They were charging toward them, her arm muscles tight with strain, her thighs burning, and sweat licking down her back. The cheers and shouts of the crowd barely registered, and everything else faded away but the task that was set in front of them. It all narrowed down to her slightest movements while they plunged through the course, and she fought to keep them both calm, connected, and shifting through the route without losing their footing.

Within seconds, it was over. Maggie pulled Odysseus up to a halt at the front of the run; they were both breathing heavily, and she wiped the sheen of sweat off her forehead. Her stomach flipped and she rode the adrenaline high and hard. There was no way to know how she'd placed until they figured out the qualifiers, and that normally took about three minutes after the last ride. Instead of jumping off and escorting her horse into the back area, Maggie kept herself saddled and steadily stroked Odysseus's flank with her hand.

He neighed and pawed the ground with his hooves, pacing from one side to the other, still slightly agitated from their quick run that had felt damn incredible. It was better than Maggie could've ever hoped in her wildest dreams. She blinked, pushing back the burning sting of tears. So much exhilaration for such a short life-defining moment. All around her, people took videos on their phones, cheered, and genuinely acted like fans while she absorbed the moment as best she could while trying not to tally the results in her head.

"Our top three have been tallied and their timed scores reviewed," the announcer's voice rang out through the stadium. "The National Finals Rodeo Champion in barrel racing with a score of fourteen-point-ten seconds is Maggie Haves."

The crowd roared.

"Ms. Haves, please come to the center of the ring with Odysseus to collect your winnings."

For a second, Maggie thought she might've blacked out because everything went a little hazy around the edges.

"Ms. Haves, please come to the center," the announcer said again.

Maggie clutched Odysseus's reins and negotiated their way to the center of the ring on autopilot. When she dropped down out of the saddle, there were at least a dozen people clamoring to get her photo, and an older man with a weathered face pushed back his white Stetson and handed her a gold-colored trophy and a check for more money than she'd ever earned along with a folder filled with sponsors who wanted to work with her.

Maggie blinked, lost in the roar of what was once unbelievable but now was her reality. A huge grin spread across her face, and the first thing she did was glance around the sidelines for Flux. When their eyes locked from across the stands, she couldn't hold back her tears anymore. What once had seemed elusive in her life—falling in love, was now realized, and coupled with winning the finals, Maggie felt that she'd finally grabbed the brass ring. She clutched the trophy to her chest and rattled off a bunch of answers to the bloggers and reporters who were eager to get a sound bite from the barrel racing champion.

"You fuckin' did it, baby!" Flux's voice resonated throughout the stadium. Almost as if he was—

Maggie jolted and jumped as strong arms wrapped around her from behind. Flux swung her around in a tight circle and she squealed before he put her back down again. He wouldn't let go of her hand and forced her to spin around and face him. Then he snagged her around the waist and drew her to him for a passionate, never-ending kiss that made everything around them fall away to nothing.

When Flux pulled back, they were both panting and he wore one of the biggest smiles she'd ever seen on him. He squeezed her waist, nuzzling into her neck with a soft sigh.

"That's my woman. I just fuckin' knew you'd win this, darlin'," he whispered, his voice raw with a mix of emotions. He stared down at her and wiped a tear from her cheek with the pad of his thumb. "Next up, world domination?"

Maggie laughed and shrugged, unsure what mountains were left to climb anymore. This had been it. Afterward? Literally anything was fair game. No limits. She could live the life she had always dreamed, *outside* of the rodeo. Preparing for this single moment had taken so much out of her life and given so much back to her ambition, but as the dawning of the title fell into place inside her heart, maybe prioritizing things other than her career might not be too bad. It may even be fun.

With a quick kiss to her man's cheek, Maggie turned to smile again for the cameras knowing that the hot kiss they'd shared would be plastered across the internet in a matter of minutes, but she didn't give a rat's ass about it, another first for the career-conscious Maggie.

"Maggie," her mother cried out as she rushed toward her, arms outstretched.

She fell into her mother's embrace then her father was there right beside her, his arms wrapped around her as her three brothers stood to the side grinning at her from ear to ear.

"We're so proud of you," her father said as he pulled her back into another hug.

"You were great," Tyler said.

"Thanks." She smiled at her younger brother.

Her mother glanced at Flux, and Maggie reached for his hand and tugged him to her. "I want you to meet Flux," she said, tightening her hold on his fingers. She glanced up at him. "Flux these are my parents, and these three guys are my brothers—Tyler, Chris, and Jess."

Flux held out his hand and shook the hands of her father and brothers and tipped his head to her mother while saying, "Pleased to meet you."

Maggie ignored her mother's inquisitive look—there would be time enough to answer all her questions when Maggie returned home in a few days.

"Did you want to go out and celebrate tonight?" her mother asked.

Maggie felt Flux stiffen next to her. "Not really, Mom—I'm totally beat."

"Of course you are, sweetheart," her dad said. He looked over his shoulder at the crowd of photographers and reporters. "They're all chomping at the bit to talk to you. If you need anything, let us know. We'll talk to you tomorrow." He threw a quick glance at Flux then put his arm around Maggie's mom. "We should get going, Nellie."

Maggie watched as her family walked away then glanced up at Flux and winked. She then took a deep breath and faced the reporters.

As the rest of the rodeo died down and the crowds dispersed, Maggie inhaled deeply, loving the familiar smells she'd known most of her life: sweet hay, dirt, sweat, manure, and buttered popcorn. She doubted she could ever give them up entirely. The win that night opened the door to her future, and anything was possible; it was the most freeing feeling she'd ever had in her life.

Still in the center of the ring answering questions and smiling for the cameras, Maggie thought it would never end. She'd been at it for nearly forty-five minutes and her head was ready to explode.

"We should get Odysseus back to the stalls for cleaning." Maggie gently nudged Flux and he immediately got the hint that she was ready to get away from the chaos that came with her big win.

"No problem—leave it to me, Duchess," he whispered against her ear before turning to the reporters and photographers. "Interviews and photos are done. Maggie's beat and so is her horse. Thanks for showing up."

"Just one more question." A balding man pushed forward, a microphone in his hand.

"You don't hear so good, do you? I said we're fuckin' done here." Flux glared at the man whose face fell, and Maggie suppressed a laugh as love for her man gushed through her.

Flux put a hand on the small of her back, and the tension from the race and the aftermath slowly leaked away. In silence, Maggie allowed him to lead both her and Odysseus to the stables behind the rodeo, where she'd spend the next hour and a half pampering and spoiling the hell out of her horse.

"I've never seen anything like tonight. Fuck, this was really the big leagues. I'm glad my ass wasn't in the ring fighting those damn bulls." Flux chuckled.

"At least they weren't pumped up. The Nationals are real strict with that kind of crap. They test all the animals and the competitors. A lot of barrel racers flush steroids into their horses. I can't imagine doing that." She stopped and gave Odysseus a quick peck on the side of his face.

"That shit won't get any of those assholes anywhere. They won't be able get the big win if they happen to make it here from cheating."

Maggie nodded. "You're right. I was just disappointed in Charlie's decision. I kind of figured he wouldn't do shit about Eddie because they're friends from way back. Charlie just told him to stop it—like Eddie's going to really do that."

"He won't be doing it for a while in Colorado at least."

"Why do you say that?" The faint lines across Maggie's forehead deepened in confusion.

"Just a hunch. Charlie shoulda thrown that fuckin' bull rider out on his ass," Flux said, anger lacing his voice.

"I knew he wouldn't. Chet's become the golden boy on the amateur circuit, and if he'd stop using shit to enhance his endurance, he'd probably be a real contender for the Nationals. There's big money in the rodeo world. But at least Charlie gave him a four-month suspension, which I know didn't sit too well with Chet."

"You're done with the amateur shit now, so you don't have to see any of those SOBs, including Charlie."

Maggie laughed. "Charlie's not bad—he's just a businessman who can be really greedy. I've known him since I started on the circuit, but I'm glad that I've moved to the professional level—it's so much more challenging."

"You worked fuckin' hard to get where you are, Duchess. Changing the subject, I wanna take you out to dinner after you finish with Odysseus. We're in a city that never fuckin' shuts down, so I made reservations at some fancy-ass restaurant—cloth napkins and all that bullshit. For a second there, I thought your family was gonna blow my plans to hell."

Maggie paused as she tied Odysseus's harness to the tethers on either side of the box stall to wash him with soap and water. She tilted her head to one side, enjoying the image that popped into her brain.

"Dress pants and button-down shirt, big guy, or it's no deal. Do still want to take me?"

"Are you kidding? Wild horses couldn't fuckin' drag me away." Flux smirked and grabbed her ass as he brushed his lips across hers. "With the expectation that you get slutted up for me too."

"Nope, just a brown burlap sack for you." Maggie giggled and covered her mouth, looking up and then down, suddenly feeling shy. "It's all coming together, isn't it?"

The soft words made Flux take a few steps closer to her as he put her head against his chest and cradled the back of her neck with his palm. His other arm rested tightly along her waist, encircling her protectively.

"A lot of it is, yeah. Shit, I still can't believe this happened. I never thought I'd fall in love again. I just figured I'd spend the rest of my life like some goddamn zombie." Flux kissed the top of her head. "But it's real, and you Duchess ... you're everything."

Maggie's legs went to mush as she melted into him, and his strong arm held her up. No one had ever said anything so romantic to her, and the fact that the words came from a brash, tough-as-nails, tattooed biker whom she was proud to call her man, made his sentiment even more special.

"Right back at you, big guy. I can't begin to imagine a life without you in it."

Flux grunted and squeezed her even tighter and she closed her eyes, listening to the pounding rhythm of his heartbeat against her ear.

"Are you scared too?" she asked softly, playing with the fabric of his T-shirt at the back of his pants. "Of all this love stuff?"

"Duchess, I've never been so terrified in my whole fuckin' life. But it's worth it. *You're* worth it."

## CHAPTER THIRTY-ONE

# FLUX

THE GUY IN the overpriced penguin suit brought out the restaurant's twentieth bottle of red wine and held it out for Flux to examine the pretty label—as if he knew what the fuck he was doing in a fancy joint like this one. Still, he looked over at Maggie with a half-smile, and nodded toward the wine dude.

"It's cool."

The waiter poured a small amount in Flux's glass and he threw it back like it was a shot of whiskey. The stuff still burned, so it was really all the same to him, but Maggie glowed across the table from him as she sipped from her glass.

"More, sir?"

Flux inclined his glass out with a muttered thanks, unable to take his eyes off his woman. Fuck, she was every inch of beauty, sexiness, and sass. The mystery was how the hell he'd gotten so lucky to have Maggie in his life. He took a slower sip of wine then put the glass on the table. Maggie's eyes connected with his and she smiled as a light flush swept across her face.

"Would you like to order, sir?" the young man asked.

"Filet mignon—princess cut, medium rare—for the lady. A porterhouse—rare—for me. Bring me a loaded baked potato, a salad with Italian dressing for my woman, and those fried up mushrooms for both of us."

The waiter tipped his head, then walked away, and Flux sat back in the high-backed red leather chair to admire his woman.

"What?" Maggie asked. The corners of her mouth lifted up into a smile as she wrapped a strand of blonde hair around her finger. "You've been drooling over me since we got here."

"Can you blame me?" Flux fiddled with the pile of cutlery in front and to the side of his plate. "I'm not made for this kind of thing, but you? You shine like a fucking diamond, and it's an intoxicating sight, Duchess." He steepled his fingertips together with a wry grin.

"You're breaking out the big words tonight, huh?" Maggie teased, shifting in her chair before taking a big gulp of wine.

Flux couldn't help the loud guffaw that popped out of his mouth. He'd picked the best steakhouse in town for their celebration, and Maggie looked every inch his queen in her slinky, tight black dress and fuck-me heels. He didn't know anything more complicated than that about women's clothing, but she looked damn hot.

"Your food is on its way," the waiter chimed in as he wiped a single bread crumb off the tablecloth. "Please enjoy, compliments of the chef."

Another penguin-suited guy set down a tiny plate with a mini spoon in the center of the table. Flux jerked his head back and stared. *What the fuck is this?* It resembled gruel and had a bunch of herbs piled on top of it. He blinked and watched his woman dig into the small portion, tipping it back so it slid down her throat like a shot of booze.

"Mmm," she moaned. "That's delicious. Are there cooked scallions in it?"

"You have a refined palette." The food nerd grinned in approval.

*She actually likes this shit. If that asshole keeps bonding with her over the food, I'm gonna stuff this shit down his fuckin' throat.* Flux sat straighter in the chair, his muscles stiffening. Why the hell did he think stuffy and pompous was the way to go that night? A muscle worked in his jaw as his narrowed eyes fixed on the asshole who was still talking about the damn slop on the miniature plate. Hell, Duchess and he should be drinking a beer in a bar, halfway to taking off each other's clothes in the bathroom. Instead, he was keeping his anger in check as the damn waiter yakked like a fuckin' pussy about recipes. Flux leaned forward and Maggie glanced at him and her eyes caught the reflection of the chandelier and sparkled. *Damn, she's beautiful. I'm glad as fuck that I took her to this fancy-ass place.*

The scent of her spicy perfume wafted around him, and he hooked his finger under her chin and leaned over and pressed his lips against hers. From the corner of his eyes, Flux saw the waiter step away and disappear from view and satisfaction mixed with desire coursed through him. Maggie tasted like wine and basil, and he wove his fingers into her hair and deepened the kiss. A small moan spilled from her lips and it took all his willpower to pull away when the waiter returned with their food. Winking at her, Flux settled back in his seat, his gaze never leaving hers.

As he dug into his dinner, he was acutely aware of Maggie staring at him.

"What? Do I have sauce on my chin, Duchess?"

"No, nothing like that." Maggie wiped the corners of her mouth with a napkin.

"Then what?" Flux took a gulp of red wine.

She reached over and brushed her fingers across his hand. "It's just that no man has ever treated me this way. I'm pretty sure you'd rather be sloshing down beer, but you're here for *me*. You're a generous and wonderful man. Thank you, Flux."

Flux glanced away as he shifted in the chair. In his world, he gave out the compliments to women, not the other way around unless it had to do with his sexual performance. He cleared his throat and looked back at her. "So, you're assuming I'm paying the check?" He deadpanned with a feigned wince. "As I remember it, you're the one with the giant rodeo winnings."

Softness spread over Maggie's face and she placed her hand over his and squeezed it lightly. "I love you." Picking up the wine glass, she took a sip, her gaze still locked on his.

"Me too, Duchess. I'm so damn proud of you." Flux swallowed through the tightness in his throat and undid one of the top buttons of his shirt. "You're really something. I knew you'd kick all the other competitors' fuckin' asses, but what really blows me the hell away is your tenacity. You're amazing, woman."

"You're not too shabby yourself, big guy."

"Now, I didn't say what I did to get you to tell me how great I am."

"I know, but it doesn't mean you aren't." Maggie popped a piece of steak in her mouth and chewed.

But something was bothering him. Something that had hit a nerve and he couldn't iron it out in his head. Now wasn't the time though, it was too perfect to ruin everything. This was Duchess's night, and he'd be an asshole for spoiling it. So they got through some chocolate dessert thing he couldn't pronounce, another bottle of wine, and then they were in a taxi—back to their lavish hotel suite on the Strip.

Flux slid the to-go box into the mini fridge and stood up, looking out at the sight laid out in front of him. Maggie leaned against the balcony railing, and the glaring lights of Vegas backdropped her curves as if she were a forbidden angel hellbent on sin. Without making a sound, he snuck up behind her and fit his front to her luscious ass and wrapped his arms around her waist. She leaned back into him with a contented sigh and a little wiggle that instantly woke up his dick.

"Duchess, I've been thinking about things ..." Flux had to stop a beat as he cleared his throat, unsure how Maggie would react to what he was going to say. "I need you to know something."

He could feel her tense against him as she turned in his arms and looked up into his face. Concern whispered across her brow.

"What is it?" she asked in a barely audible voice.

Flux groped with the words and Maggie stayed still in his arms watching him. *Fuck it!* He quirked his lips and let it fly out.

"I've been thinking long and hard since I spent some time with my brothers. I've come to the realization that I don't wanna be a nomad anymore." Flux scrubbed his fist against his face. "I wanna be back home again in the MC where I belong. For so long I've been riding and dodging the fuckin' memories, but I'm done with the solitary life." He ran his hands up and down her back. "You made me see that traveling through life alone isn't the way I wanna go. It's not like the memories and the guilt won't be there anymore, because I know they'll always be a part of me. But ... I can deal with them better, now that I have you in my life. Duchess, you bring out parts of me that I thought died a long time ago. I miss the lifestyle I fell in love with a long time ago, and I'm itching to be active again with the Insurgents. And it's all because I fell in love with a sassy, beautiful, sexy barrel racer. Life is fuckin' wonderful sometimes." He dipped his head down and captured her lips.

Maggie looped her arms around his neck and pressed closer to him. After several heartbeats, she pulled away. "And?" Maggie's voice hitched.

Flux thought his chest would crack in half watching her blink away the tears pooling in her eyes. He shrugged and shook his head.

"And I don't know where that leaves us, Duchess. I wanna go back to Pinewood Springs and the Insurgents. That means being a full-time patched member again, but you've got a whole future staring you in the damn face. What the hell kind of man would I be to ask you to give that up? I wouldn't ... I couldn't. I've got a shitload of flaws, but I'm not that fucking selfish. I was once, with Alicia, but ..." Flux's voice trailed off and the day he got patched in flashed through his mind replete with Alicia's proud, smiling face. He jerked his head back and the lights of the Strip sparkled in front of him. He stared into Maggie's blue orbs. "I won't be that selfish again." He gipped her shoulders hard. *Fuck, I don't wanna loose her.*

Flux tried to pull away but Maggie held on to him something fierce. She blinked a few times and licked her lips. *Damn.* He couldn't even look at her as his stomach tightened into knots. He looked out into the distance and watched the procession of headlights on the Strip as tail lights snaked their way down the boulevard—cars bumper to bumper.

"I'm not surprised. You never were a cowboy." Maggie snorted softly. "Falling in love with you was definitely not in my grand plan ... but—"

"But what?" Flux scanned her face. "I've been roaming the country ever since I buried Alicia and Emily. Guilt and bitterness and rage were my constant companions along with mind-numbing grief. I wanted to keep the pain alive as a reminder that I fucked up and failed my family." He put two fingers against Maggie's lips to silence her. He had to tell her how he felt, how *she* made him live again. "I also wanted the pain because I was so fuckin' scared of forgetting how they sounded, how they looked, how they smelled. I didn't want to let go. I hated myself for being alive when they were dead."

Maggie peppered light kisses along his jaw, murmuring, "I'm so sorry."

"Don't be, Duchess, because you made me realize that Alicia would never want me to be the walking dead. I found you in a crummy bar in a desert city in a dusty rodeo. I still can't believe it, and now I can't have you. You've got to live the life you were meant to. The damn rodeo flows through your veins. I've got to let you go, Duchess."

"Do you want to let me go?" Maggie whispered.

"Fuck no, but ..." Flux tried to untangle himself from her grip, but she still wouldn't let go or back off, holding on even harder while he watched his words process across her face.

"Then don't," she said as if it were the easiest thing in the world. "I don't want to lose you." She pressed her lips together and shook her head. "Stop making decisions for me. I know what's good for me and what I want is—*you*."

Flux blinked. *What the hell's she talking about?* "I'm gonna be straight with you, darlin'. The long-distance thing isn't on the table. There's no fuckin' way we'd ever be satisfied with that FaceTime bullshit, and I can't ask you to give up the career you've worked so hard for. You just nailed it, and there are tons more competitions ahead of you. You deserve the life you always wanted."

"And who's to say what's best for me, Flux? Who gave you that power?"

Her anger flared across her skin as she dropped his remaining arm and turned back toward the Strip, arms around her waist hugging herself. Flux ran his hand through his hair. *Fuck, none of this is going right.* He should've kept his damn mouth shut and they would've figured it out later or some shit. Anything but what was going down in front of his face.

Flux groped for something else to say, but Maggie whirled around to face him again.

"Ask me," she said.

"What?" He swallowed as he took a step backward.

"Ask me to be with you, Flux."

That was the moment where time stood still for him. His tongue was thick in his mouth as he went hot and cold all at the same time. He stuffed his hands in his pants pockets and started pacing the small concrete balcony.

"You're fucking nuts, Duchess. I'm not gonna ask you to give up barrel racing for me. You'll regret it and end up hating me a few years down the road."

"I won't regret it, and I could never hate you," she replied so softly that he almost couldn't hear her over the pounding of his own footsteps.

"Being in a long-term relationship isn't all sunshine. You got good and bad times and having a load of regret isn't gonna get you through the tough times. Being with a biker is a hard as fuck life, and you gotta accept him and his brothers or it'll never work." He stopped and stared at her.

"I won't regret anything because I can still compete, but on my terms. I can pick and choose the rodeos I want to participate in. I won't be ruled by my career anymore." Maggie reached out and grasped Flux's hands. "I already grabbed the brass ring tonight. Winning in the Nationals was something I worked for since I was a kid, and everything that comes after it now is just the icing on the cake. Even though I'm a competitor, I never wanted that to be my whole life. I've always dreamed of falling in love with the right man and living a happy life with him. So, why the fuck would I walk away from *you*?"

A rush of adrenaline shot through Flux followed by a warmth he hadn't experienced in a long time. There was no fucking way he wanted Maggie out of his life, yet nothing else mattered but her happiness. Hearing Maggie say that she wanted to be with him made the high he was feeling so much better than any premium weed he'd ever had. Maggie soothed his flames to a steady heat, calming the consuming inferno that had raged within him for years. Being in love with her quelled the anger, the guilt, and the pain. She was his lover, his addiction, his woman, and now she wanted to share her life with him. *Fuck.*

Flux inhaled sharply then yanked Maggie to him, cocooning her in his arms while breathing in the citrusy scent of her hair. "You fuckin' make me happy, woman. We'll build our life together. Maybe have a couple of kids." Emily's sweet smile flitted across his mind and his heart squeezed.

As if sensing his pain, Maggie tilted her head back and kissed the base of his throat. "I'd love to have a family with you. You're one special man, Flux. Being in love with you beats out any adrenaline rush I've ever had in the ring. You're all I want and need, and I love that we'll be building a new life together."

"Me too, Duchess." Flux bent his head down and crushed his mouth on hers and they stood on the balcony fused together, kissing, as the warm desert breeze caressed them. After several minutes, he broke away and stroked her cheek with his fingers. "No matter what, I'll always have your back. When you go on the road to compete, my ass is with you. There's no fuckin' way I'm letting you go without me."

Maggie swept her lips across his. "I wouldn't have it any other way, big guy."

Peace settled over his shoulders, and an abrupt and warm sensation in the pit of his stomach made him reel for a second then he pressed her tighter against his chest. Maggie looked up at him through her long lashes and a burning desire rushed through him. He lowered his mouth and kissed her as if he was trying to push his soul and his promise of forever into her body.

## CHAPTER THIRTY-TWO

# MAGGIE

As much as Maggie could tell Flux wanted to take her back to bed with him, his arms straining to not throw her over his shoulder caveman style, she wanted something a little more. Just because the evening had been classy didn't mean that she couldn't whip out a few tricks and get really naughty.

"Take off my dress," Maggie whimpered against his lips, her nipples growing hard as her fingers danced over the buttons in his shirt, fighting to get them off. "I need you inside me. *Please.*"

Maggie knew the "please" pushed all of Flux's feral buttons. He growled deep in his throat; a possessive noise that ripped arousal through her flesh from her scalp to her toes as a shudder danced up her spine. Maybe she hadn't fully comprehended what she was asking for when his hands dove for the risqué plunge between her chest and he tore the fabric in half with a considerable noise that made goosebumps skitter across every inch of her skin.

"Oh shit." She gulped and stared down at her nearly naked body. "That was fucking hot."

"You liked that, huh?" Flux asked as his lips already meandered down the column of her neck at the same time his hands roamed her body, undoing the clasp of her bra and dropping it to the floor. "Put your hands on the railing and face away from me."

Without hesitation, Maggie's fingers curled around the cool bar of steel. Every sense was on high alert as she listened to Flux shed his clothing, her silent plea for his touch in the tension spread between them.

"Don't fuckin' move, Duchess."

Maggie stood as she was without uttering a word. By the time Flux came back to her, his hands carved themselves into her hipbones and dragged her ass back until she fit snuggly against his naked erection. A small moan escaped as she bit her lower lip. Damn, Maggie wanted him inside so badly, but instead, he teased her as he worked his thick cock against her cheeks and lower back, occasionally sliding in between her legs. So close, yet so far.

"Flux," she moaned.

He rubbed against every sensitive part until she was lightheaded and no longer knew up from down anymore. Maggie couldn't help grinding her ass back into him, even as he struggled to hold her still so he could keep up the torment. At one point, Flux *tsked* against the lip of her ear, but no sooner had he made the small reprieving noise, he slid her panties to one side and rubbed the head of his dick against her silken folds. She jolted forward with a gasp then wiggled backward for more of him.

"That's it," Flux coaxed, biting her neck. "You know exactly what you want for the rest of your life, don't you?"

"Yes," she groaned, as he angled the tip his cock into her opening, teasing her with only the briefest sensation of fullness. "More, Flux. More."

"You're so fuckin' eager—I love it. Now say it, Duchess."

"Say what?" she whined, helpless and on autopilot as he took small, short strokes inside her, refusing to ram home while he kept all the control.

"Tell me what you want for the rest of your life."

"I want you, Flux. I want you for the rest of my life," she cried out as his free hand plucked one of her nipples, pinching the sensitive tip before rolling it between his fingers. "Oh shit … I want nothing but you. Always you."

"Perfect," he whispered, leaving a light kiss on the back of her neck. "I think you're ready for me, Duchess."

Maggie moaned in frustration, her fingers white at the knuckles where she gripped the railing while his cock moved within her, almost touching her right where she needed him most. All the hairs on the nape of her neck raised, and a series of small whimpers escaped from her mouth.

Flux tweaked her nipples and massaged her breasts, and she was just about ready to plead with him to fuck the shit out of her when he thrust forward so hard that he trapped her body against the railing. He pulled out and before she could protest, rammed back inside her with a grunt that echoed through her and left her weak-kneed and breathless.

"You're mine, Maggie," Flux rasped as he squeezed her breasts. "Your tits"—he smacked her behind—"your tits, and your pussy are all mine. I'm claiming you as my woman, and I'll never fuckin' betray or hurt you. You've got my goddamn heart, Duchess."

At that moment, Flux filled up and claimed every single part of her world, her mind, and her body, and she knew none of it would ever be the same now that he'd worked his way inside her heart. She was his and he was hers and nothing in life could ever change that.

"You're mine too, Flux—always."

"Fuck, yeah," he rasped.

Flux didn't waste any time. No sooner was he as deep as he could go when he drew himself almost all the way out and drove back in again, a seductive pounding that left her feeling nothing but used and wanted. While the lights of Vegas painted their bodies in various colors, Maggie echoed his movements as much as possible while he continued to pin her half-naked body against the balcony railing.

"God, don't ever stop," she panted.

Her breasts bounced with every thrust, his mouth, his tongue, and his hands exploring every sensitive dip and bend of her body that was reachable without removing himself again. They joined in every way possible, Flux taking control as she allowed him to have all the things they'd both been longing for but were too afraid to take for themselves. Now, everything had fallen into place and it was fucking glorious.

"You'll never stop being mine, Duchess. Don't forget that. Even when I'm not inside you, you're *mine*."

"Oh, Flux," Maggie breathed out as her orgasm tightened through her middle and spiraled out into her veins.

Unable to take it, she tore her hands away from the metal and grabbed his where he was rubbing his thumb over her clit. Without skipping a beat, she moved his finger into quicker, smaller circles with a high-pitched noise at the back of her throat that was all animal and all pleasure. She sensed her inner walls tightening around him, and fluttered and flexed as he bit into her shoulder and drove deeper and harder.

"Come for me, darlin'."

That did it. Maggie came as the world tore itself to shreds and her knees went weak, and Flux's arm, tight around her waist, was the only thing keeping her standing upright. Pleasure stole away everything but the reality of their connection. Her focus caught on his short, sharp breaths against her shoulder, his hand on her clit, his hips hitting her ass, and his cock pulsing inside her pussy.

"I'm not ... far ..." Flux circled his hips and she went on her tiptoes with a cry of shock and surprise, his depth changing the angle and making her toes curl. "I want another one before I'm done."

Maggie's whimpers were her response. Each time, his hips touched some secret part of her until she was a trembling mess from the inside out. Flux laughed, low as he licked a line down her spine. Nearly undone, all she could do was shudder and thrust herself backward for more of him while the lust climbed her like a trellis.

"I'm ready," Maggie panted, arching and struggling to keep upright as she widened her legs and he bent her further forward at the waist.

"Good." Flux laughed again, a noise so filled with masculine satisfaction she thought she might lose it purely from that sound alone.

His hand shook where he held her hip, his thrusts growing more frantic. No sooner had her throat tightened from the ecstasy tensing its grip on her body when he spilled himself deep inside her. His fingers spasmed along her clit and she cried out, shocked by the extra stimulation that jolted through her as her eyes slammed closed and her hand clamped tight over his on her pussy.

"Shit, that was ..." Flux fought for breath and she nodded, floating on a cloud of euphoria that made everything more than a little bit foggy.

Maggie half-expected a standing ovation from one of their neighbors, and the idea made her grin grow wider as Flux's arms brought her back in close to his front. The warmth of his skin soaked into her behind until her breathing slowed as she lost herself in the safety and serenity of his embrace.

She rested her head against his chest, glad as hell that she'd kicked everyone else to the curb so that Flux could have the room to find her when she most needed him. Although they were both discovering new lives and finding themselves, nothing would be too hard so long as they were together.

"Let's get inside, Duchess. There's a huge ass sunken tub with your name on it."

"Sounds like we can come up with some ideas for that. Are you going to soap me up and wash me?"

A guttural sound rumbled in the back of Flux's throat. "Don't tempt me with a good time. It'll give me an opportunity to get reacquainted with every square inch of you. A sight I'll never get sick of, that's for fucking sure."

"Mmm," Maggie smiled and nuzzled back into his chest. "You treat me like a queen, you know that?"

"You deserve every second and more, woman. You're the reason real men are born, bred, and raised, and I intend to be everything you need me to be, is that clear?"

"As crystal." Maggie looked down as another annoying blush flooded into her cheeks at his words. "Who'd ever think a big, bad biker would be waxing poetic?"

"What? You think I've lost all my edge because I'm so infatuated with you, Duchess?"

"Something like that," she teased. He scooped her up into his arms, holding her as if she weighed nothing at all. "What're you doing?"

"Going for round two, and then the bath. Clearly I wasn't rough enough the first time to satisfy your cravings, and this big, bad biker wants you to be so satisfied that you can't remember your damn name in the morning. I'm more than up for putting in the fuckin' work."

And that was the beauty of their relationship, wasn't it? In the end, it wasn't work nor would it ever be anything like it. Maggie flung her head back and laughed as Flux slipped them through the balcony doors into the chill, crisp air of their hotel room.

She had a feeling nothing about her life would ever be planned again, and she was more than down for the ride.

Make sure you sign up for my newsletter so you can keep up with my new releases, special sales, free short stories, and other treats only available to newsletter readers. When you sign up, you will receive a FREE hot and steamy novella. Sign up at: http://eepurl.com/bACCL1

## Notes from Chiah

As always, I have a team behind me making sure I shine and continue on my writing journey. It is their support, encouragement, and dedication that pushes me further in my writing journey. And then, it is my wonderful readers who have supported me, laughed, cried, and understood how these outlaw men live and love in their dark and gritty world. Without you—the readers—an author's words are just letters on a page. The emotions you take away from the words breathe life into the story.

**Thank you** to my amazing Personal Assistant Natalie Weston. I don't know what I'd do without you. Your patience, calmness, and insights are always appreciated. Thank you for stepping in when I'm holed up tapping away on the computer, oblivious to the world. You make my writing journey that much smoother. Thank you for ALWAYS being there for me! I'm so lucky on my team!

**Thank you** to my editor Lisa Cullian, for all your insightful edits and making my story a better one. You definitely made this book shine. As always, a HUGE thank you for your patience and flexibility with accepting my book in pieces. I never could have hit the Publish button without you. You're the best!

**Thank you** to my wonderful beta readers Natalie Weston, Sue Anne Binder, Darlene Perry, and Maryann Reed. You rock! Your enthusiasm and suggestions for Forgiveness: Nomad Biker Romance Series were spot on and helped me to put out a stronger, cleaner novel.

**Thank you** to the bloggers for your support in reading my book, sharing it, reviewing it, and getting my name out there. I so appreciate all your efforts. You all are so invaluable. I hope you know that. Without you, the indie author would be lost.

**Thank you** ARC readers you have helped make all my books so much stronger. I appreciate the effort and time you put in to reading, reviewing, and getting the word out about the books. I don't know what I'd do without you. I feel so lucky to have you behind me.

**Thank you** to my Street Team. Thanks for your input, your support, and your hard work. I appreciate you more than you know. A HUGE hug to all of you!

**Thank you** to Carrie from Cheeky Covers. You are amazing! I can always count on you. You are the calm to my storm. You totally rock, and I love your artistic vision.

**Thank you** to my proofers who worked hard to get my novel back to me so I could hit the publish button on time. There are no words to describe how touched and grateful I am for your dedication and support. Also much thanks for your insight re: plot and characterization. I definitely took heed, and it made my story flow that much better.

**Thank you** to Ena and Amanda with Enticing Journeys Promotions who have helped garner attention for and visibility to my books. Couldn't do it without you!

**Thank you** to my awesome formatter, Paul Salvette at Beebee Books. You make my books look stellar. I appreciate how professional you are and how quickly you return my books to me. A huge thank you for doing rush orders and always returning a formatted book of which I am proud. Kudos!

**Thank you** to the readers who continue to support me and read my books. Without you, none of this would be possible. I appreciate your comments and reviews on my books, and I'm dedicated to giving you the best story that I can. I'm always thrilled when you enjoy a book as much as I have in writing it. You definitely make the hours of typing on the computer and the frustrations that come with the territory of writing books so worth it.

And a special thanks to every reader who has been with me since "Hawk's Property." Your support, loyalty, and dedication to my stories touch me in so many ways. You enable me to tell my stories, and I am forever grateful to you.

You all make it possible for writers to write because without you reading the books, we wouldn't exist. Thank you, thank you! ♥

## Forgiveness: Nomad Biker Romance Series (Book 1)

Dear Readers,

Thank you for reading my book. This book is the first one in my new series—Nomad Biker Romance. The book and series deal with those bikers who live a solitary life on the road, feeling the freedom of no boundaries. Each of the bikers in the series are loosely attached to MCs, but for various reasons, they've chosen to break away from the daily MC life and trade it in for a solo life on the road.

In the first book of the series, Flux was once an active Insurgents MC member who broke away after an unspeakable tragedy happened in his life. Not able to leave the club or the biker life altogether, he traded in his Insurgents' patch for a Nomad one, and he hit the open road on his Harley-Davidson. I hope you enjoyed the first book in my new series as much as I enjoyed writing Flux and Maggie's story. This gritty and rough way of life is never easy, but being on the open road has its own kind of rewards. I hope you will look for the upcoming books in the series. Romance makes life so much more colorful, and a rough, sexy bad boy makes life a whole lot more interesting.

If you enjoyed the book, please consider leaving a review on Amazon. I read all of them and appreciate the time taken out of busy schedules to do that.

I love hearing from my fans, so if you have any comments or questions, please email me at chiahwilder@gmail.com or visit my facebook page.

To receive a **free copy of my novella**, *Summer Heat*, and to hear of **new releases, special sales, free short stories**, and **ARC opportunities**, please sign up for my **Newsletter** at http://eepurl.com/bACCL1.

Happy Reading,

*Chiah*

## Retribution: Nomad Biker Romance
### Coming April 2019

**Nomad biker: a solitary life, riding from place to place.**

**Cobra once wore the Steel Devils MC patch and his territory was Montana. Now his bottom rocker reads Nomad.**

Cobra used to be the Enforcer in the Steel Devils MC, and his reputation for ruthlessness was well earned. After doing a stint in the penitentiary, he opted out of the MC life, and hit the open road. Still a biker and an outlaw, he goes where the road takes him. He hooks up with women for a while then when the restlessness sets in, he kisses them goodbye and is gone in a blink of an eye.

He doesn't want anything or anyone crimping his style. He came from a background that taught him to trust no one, and that loving anyone causes pain.

Yeah ... he's good on his own.

Then Dakota crashes into his life and turns it upside down.

The girl's trouble.

She's got a ton of baggage.

And she's driving him crazy with desire.

Dakota has demons inside her that no one can chase away. The last thing she wants is a man in her life. Men only want to use and abuse women, and she's had her fill of them.

But then she meets Cobra, and even though her logic tells her he's a dangerous and ruthless outlaw, her body wants him in the worst way.

As she gets to know him, a side of him comes out that Dakota doubts anyone has seen.

And just when she puts her guard down and trusts him, her world comes crashing down on her.

Can Cobra soothe the demons inside Dakota, and can she teach Cobra to let someone into his solitary life?

**The Nomad Biker series are standalone romance novels. This is Cobra's story. This book contains violence, abuse, strong language, and steamy/graphic sexual scenes. HEA. No cliffhangers. The book is intended for readers over the age of 18.**

# Animal's Reformation: Insurgents MC
## Coming May 2019

**A member of the Insurgents MC, Animal is a rough, free-loving biker.** Hanging with his brothers, riding his customized Harley, and partying with the ladies are his idea of the ideal life.

Years ago, he made a stupid mistake with a woman he barely knew, but he pays the child support every month and sends cards and presents to his out-of-state daughter on her birthday and on holidays.

He doesn't want a steady woman, and he certainly isn't ready to settle down and have a family. Life is just too good now, and there are always so many women who want to come and play with this rugged biker.

Then one afternoon, the mother of his child struts into the clubhouse with his daughter in tow and tells him she's done. She walks away, leaving Animal and Lucy staring at each other.

What's he supposed to do? He knows about bikes and hard partying, not seven-year-old girls.

He has to change his ways, and his new hot next-door neighbor isn't helping to keep his libido in check. The way her long dark hair swings just above her sweet behind has him thinking all kinds of nasty thoughts, but she doesn't give him the time of day.

What's up with that?

**Olivia Mooney is very aware of her neighbor's good looks and his**

**finely chiseled body, but she doesn't want to get involved.** He doesn't realize it, but she's his daughter's tutor at school, and she can't get involved. She spends her nights thinking about him and chatting with an intriguing man on an after dark dating site.

Then a series of murders occur in the surrounding counties, and it looks like they are creeping closer to Pinewood Springs. At first the cops are stumped, but over time a pattern begins to emerge: the women all used an after dark dating site.

As fear and danger slink closer, Olivia is thrown into the arms of the sexy biker, forever changing their lives.

**The Night Rebels MC series are standalone romance novels. This is Army's. This book contains violence, abuse, strong language, and steamy/graphic sexual scenes. It describes the life and actions of an outlaw motorcycle club. HEA. No cliffhangers. The book is intended for readers over the age of 18.**

# Other Books by Chiah Wilder

## Insurgent MC Series:

Hawk's Property
Jax's Dilemma
Chas's Fervor
Axe's Fall
Banger's Ride
Jerry's Passion
Throttle's Seduction
Rock's Redemption
An Insurgent's Wedding
Outlaw Xmas
Wheelie's Challenge
Christmas Wish
Insurgents MC Romance Series: Insurgents Motorcycle Club Box Set (Books 1 – 4)
Insurgents MC Romance Series: Insurgents Motorcycle Club Box Set (Books 5 – 8)

## Night Rebels MC Series:

STEEL
MUERTO
DIABLO
GOLDIE
PACO
SANGRE
ARMY

## Steamy Contemporary Romance:

My Sexy Boss

Find all my books at: amazon.com/author/chiahwilder

I love hearing from my readers. You can email me at chiahwilder@gmail.com.

Sign up for my newsletter to receive a FREE Novella, updates on new books, special sales, free short stories, and ARC opportunities at http://eepurl.com/bACCL1.

Visit me on facebook at facebook.com/AuthorChiahWilder

Lightning Source UK Ltd.
Milton Keynes UK
UKHW021848070321
379944UK00011B/176